THE CRIMSONS AND THE VIOLETS

Anna Reuben

PROLOGUE

The Violet man was enjoying the first moment of peace and solitude in his day. He had been out on the fields since dawn, overseeing the farmhands, and this was the first moment he'd had to himself. A leg of lamb was in the oven, already beginning to fill the house with its comforting, homely smell. He was now washing the vegetables and setting them aside to be chopped and sliced. The evening sound of crickets was all he could hear, as well as the call of a wood pigeon from somewhere nearby. A breeze swept the crops in the fields beyond their house and the man sighed with a sense of satisfaction, feeling he had much to be grateful for.

Then someone appeared in the doorway and the moment was over.

"Hux," called the voice. It was Calex, his ward, a Crimson boy of eleven. "Is dinner ready yet? I'm starving."

"Now, now," chuckled Hux. "You may be a growing lad but you're certainly not starving. Why don't you go back and play outside while I'm cooking."

"The others won't let me join in," Calex sighed. "They took my ball…"

"Calex" Hux interrupted as he began to slice the tomatoes. "It's not your ball, it's everyone's ball and... ouch!"

He dropped the knife he was holding, as Violet liquid began to emerge from the wound that had appeared.

"Hux!" cried the boy. "You've hurt yourself."
Hux clasped his other hand over the cut to prevent the blood from dripping onto the table and floor. His face showed no signs of disgust at the sight, only a look of slight discomfort.

"Calex, come here," he said softly. The boy had not yet been on the island for six months and his guardian decided this was a chance to teach him something about his people.

The boy came towards him. "Hux, are you okay?" he asked. "I'm sorry for distracting you."

"I'm fine," Hux said. "You see that plant on the windowsill, the one in that big pot? Bring it over here, will you? Careful now, don't drop it."

The boy did as he was asked, a little confused.

"Now, watch this," said Hux as he brought his injured hand over the soil.

As the first drops of blood reached it, the plant, which was nothing but a shoot, sprung to life. Its stalk grew longer and started breaking off into several smaller shoots, pushing out leaves and forming buds at their tips. That which normally took place over weeks was happening in a matter of seconds. The boy's eyes opened wide with fascination.

"Hold it in place, Calex," Hux said, charmed by the boy's excitement at the scene. Calex put his hands around the plant, feeling its metamorphosis taking place between his fingers. Its accelerated growth was accompanied by a creaking sound. The boy started to giggle as he tried to contain it between his hands. Finally, the twenty or so buds blossomed into yellow heart-shaped forms which then expanded and turned a ripe red. The plump pieces of fruit held tiny seeds on their surfaces. At last, all was still and before them was a fully-grown strawberry plant. The boy carefully let the now-heavy contents of his hands rest on the table.

"Can I have a go on another plant?" asked the boy, excitedly. "Just my fingertip." He gestured with the knife.

"No, no, Calex." Hux snatched the knife from him and put it aside. "It won't work for you. That's the difference between you and me, you see. I'm Violet blooded and you're Crimson." Hux was now bandaging his hand and didn't spot the sadness on Calex's face. When he finally turned to face him, the boy's eyes had filled with tears.

"I suppose that's why the other kids took my ball. It's their way of telling me I… I just don't fit in." Calex stopped talking. He didn't want to start crying yet again in front of Hux.

"Don't think like that." Hux put an arm around Calex, eager to reassure him. He hadn't wanted his lesson to upset the boy.

"Our blood is the only real difference between us. Apart from that we are the same and you are very, very welcome here. You're one of us now, you know that, don't you?"

Calex nodded and sniffed hard. A flood of tears had been stopped in the nick of time.

Hux brought Calex's attention back to the strawberry plant. "Well, why don't you try one."

"Is it safe?" the boy asked cautiously.

"Of course, my boy. They're just strawberries."

Calex plucked one from its stalk without having to

choose - they all looked equally delicious. He bit into it and savoured it. It was the fruitiest, sweetest, most perfect strawberry he had ever tasted, so divine that he let his eyes close in delight. The uncomfortable feelings that had plagued Calex moments ago had disappeared.

"Well, that's dessert for us all sorted," said Hux, and he headed to the pantry to see if they had any cream.

Chapter
ONE

*C*alex was dreaming of his childhood on the island of Kinsen as he did many a night. It was here and only here that he found himself in the presence of his mother, father and two brothers, in their spacious country home with its soap-making workshop. Calex remembered the perfumes as clearly as the images: bergamot, lavender and cinnamon on his parents' fingertips. In his dreams, his childhood home was bathed in a warm orange light. This glow was born of nostalgia and was an addition to the memories stored in his imagination. Calex always saw his father in his overall and gloves, splattered with colouring oils. That was Calex's future, back then: to take over the family business. His father planned on taking him out of school and making him his apprentice. The young boy was not keen on the idea, insisting that he loved school. In any case, the issue had no importance now and all that was left were a series of memories. The dreams kept these memories alive, for what was there now to remind him of this past: hundreds of kilometres across the Barromedian Sea, on the volcanic island of Quilemoyena? Sometimes it was hard for Calex to believe that the recollections were real, simply because they seemed to have no connection to his life today. Calex had lived within the shores of Quilemoyena for so long that it had lost all of its exotic novelty. The island was approximately circle-shaped with a diameter of around one hundred kilometres. Quilemoyena City was situated right in the centre and was an impressively bustling and busy metropolis occupied by Crimson folk.

The boarding house in which he resided was in the west of Quilemoyena City, reputed by one and all as the dodgy side of town. Despite all its flaws, the building faced east and so it benefited from the sun in the mornings. Light poured through the window in a perfect square-shaped beam, illuminating the specks of dust in the air. It fell hot on Calex's sleeping face but that is not what stirred him. Instead, he awoke to the sound of incessant banging on the door. Alarmed and still half asleep, he jumped into his trousers and rushed to open it. Standing in front of him was his landlady, out of breath after having gone up six flights of stairs, and she did not look happy.

"Calex Maro," she announced, hands on hips. "So, I've finally managed to get hold of you."

What did she say? He heard his name followed by a string of nonsense. It was only after a second that he realised she was not speaking in his native tongue. He rubbed his eyes, trying to wake himself up. "Good morning to you too," he slurred in a mock-friendly tone.

"This month's rent." The landlady dived straight in without a prelude. "Due yesterday."

Calex hesitated. He barely had enough cash on him for breakfast.

"I'm sorry," he said. "I can't pay you right now but I promise…"

"I don't know how long this can go on," she interrupted. "There's only so much I can put up with. This is the third time the rent has been late since you've been here, Maro." Nobody ever called him by his surname and it made him feel uncomfortable. He was eager to calm her down.

"I promise you I'll get you the money by the end of the week. I'll have fifty demarit by…"

"Listen here," she interrupted again, pointing a sausage-like finger at him. "There are plenty of other people who'd pay a whole lot more for a room like this."

Of course, he thought, if they could stand the stench of manure and waste from the dirty streets, as well as the raucous noise that would burst their eardrums. Calex was not entirely sure about her use of the word 'room' either; 'cubbyhole' would surely have been a more accurate description. His landlady's lecture droned on as he stood nodding and simultaneously apologising.

"Tomorrow it is then," he declared when she finally ran out of steam, hoping to close the conversation at last. "It won't happen again, Miss Kiberon." A burst of shrill laughter echoed through the stairwell as she wobbled downstairs, grumbling as she went. Calex shut his door and walked to the window, yawning wholeheartedly.

His room was a small, bare box. Greenish damp had begun to grow up the walls, some plaster having fallen out of their many cracks. Tiny crawling insects had invited themselves to establish a colony in the doorframe. Calex was aware that he was sharing his room with many uninvited guests. Yet he knew that the problems of his accommodation were minor compared to those of some city dwellers, whose lamentable woes were a common topic for late-night banter over a mug of ale. Many older buildings were made of wood which posed a huge risk of fire. One misplaced candle could result in disaster, sending all the residents in a building frantically fleeing in the middle of the night, awoken by the smell of smoke. The low-rent apartment blocks by the river were under serious threat when it flooded. Some of them, with floors haphazardly piled on top of one another for easy profit, would simply collapse with no warning. The shocking greediness of landlords resulted in sudden homelessness, and even death. When Calex heard the sorry stories that circulated around the city, he knew he should be grateful for what he had. Miss Kiberon's building was relatively new, sturdy and built of stone. When he went to bed at night he did not fear that he would wake up in a pile of rubble.

Besides, the view was impressive. The boarding house was near to the immense stone wall that surrounded Quilemoyena City, and therefore away from its hectic heart. From this hole in the sandy wall, Calex could see the metropolis becoming denser and denser into the distance, steadily inclining up to the base of the gently smoking volcano at the very centre. The civilisation had been built around it, and indeed because of it. On days when the wind blew west, Calex would often get whiffs of rotten eggs. The smell had bothered him when he had first arrived on the island, but now he barely noticed it, even on the windiest of days.

Calex became aware that it was time to set out on his hour-long trek to the farm where he worked. He had two shirts – a navy blue one and a dark yellow one. Sniffing both, he decided that the latter would be his best bet. He slipped it on to accompany his brown, knee-length trousers, wrapped his leather belt around his waist and finally put on his shoes. He tried the un-promising-looking water and bread that sat on the table. They were both warm and disgusting. Knowing it would do him good, Calex perfunctorily drained the jug of water. The bread, though, was as hard as a mud brick. Before he left, he tossed it out of the window to join the other debris down there.

Miss Kiberon let fifteen rooms in total and she had much of the ground floor for herself. With her own office, bedroom, kitchen and bathroom, her living quarters were extravagant compared to those of her tenants. There were also two rooms downstairs that were of interest to Calex: the washroom and the dining room.

Dinner was included in Calex's rent and every evening he ate with the other tenants. Miss Kiberon's cooking was far from gourmet, but it was always piping hot and hearty. A ladleful of vegetable stew was usually what landed in his bowl, along with a hunk of bread to wipe up the gravy. Occasionally, Calex would find a couple of pieces of chicken or pork, though admittedly this did not happen very often. He would take a seat at the long table and sometimes make conversation with the others. More often than not, however, they all sat in silence, chewing and slurping, before retiring to bed.

The tenants' shared washroom was a permanently damp and smelly place. As there was no water supply to the building via the aqueduct, unlike many of the mansions in the east of the city, Miss Kiberon filled buckets at the nearest public fountain several times a day. The toilets, offering little in the way of privacy, were at least connected to Quilemoyena's sewage system.

Coming to the bottom of the stairs, Calex passed the bathroom and headed to the door. The bad-tempered landlady caught his eye as he walked past her office. He quickly averted his glance, leaving her to interrogate his neighbours as he stepped out into the baking sun. It was going to be another swelteringly hot day.

Across the street, a man was selling triangular pastry parcels filled with lamb and vegetables from his cart. He appeared there once or twice a week.

"Good morning," Calex greeted him. "Just one please."

The vendor wrapped one of the still-warm parcels in a piece of paper, spooned on a yogurty sauce and handed it to his young customer. "Three demarit," he said bluntly.

"I've only got two fifty," Calex said with a shrug.

The vendor rolled his eyes and held out his hand to collect the money. "I come here all the time," Calex tried as an excuse, taking a deep bite into his breakfast.

Before long, he had passed through the city gates, where Violet merchants with ox-driven carts were queuing up to enter. These Violets were delivering goods from the countryside into the city: mainly food products like cereals, meat and vegetables. Now that he was outside the city walls, the Crimson faces of passers-by were replaced by Violet ones. Calex was Crimson, and so red-blooded, as was Miss Kiberon and everybody who lived within the city walls. The countryside was the realm of Violets: the blue-blooded. The racial difference was evident at first glance.

Calex's ears were relieved to be left in peace as the sounds of the city faded away behind him. The scrambled aural concoction of crowds, wooden vehicles and everyday urban life was soon replaced by the calm sounds of nature: the breeze and the birdsong. Calex smiled as the gentle wind brushed over him and he soon felt more relaxed. His lungs filled up with the freshness of the countryside. It was a wonderful feeling despite the overwhelming summer heat which was still present and already causing his shirt to stick to his back. Every morning seemed to be a little less tolerable than the previous one as summer crept on, one uncomfortable day at a time. Calex could not remember last year's summer, nor the summer before, being so hot. The hazy pale blue sky was scattered with a few clouds, and many residents of Quilemoyena City would glance at them hopefully that morning, thirstily wondering if they could possibly contain any rain.

Chapter
TWO

Not everyone was hoping for rain however. At his farm in the little hamlet of Tinklegrove, the Violet Hux Windberry considered this dry heat a blessing. He would be able to harvest the wheat a couple of weeks earlier than expected. His workers were clearing out the barn, preparing space to store the crop after reaping. The tools were also being prepared: damaged ones fixed and blades sharpened. Hux Windberry surveyed the crop from the cool shelter of his house. He was not without a sense of pride. His fields had produced a typically excellent yield, the wheat heads standing high and golden. This was partly due, of course, to the exceptional fertility of Quilemoyena's soil. Every seed planted in that volcanic earth sprung to life. This season Hux had been particularly lucky with the weather: his fields had been blessed with just the right amount of sunshine and rain. The dryness and heat was exactly what the crop needed at the end of its growth cycle yet it was somewhat of a mixed blessing. The workers were stopping every five minutes to take a break and the cart-pulling oxen refused to co-operate because they were too hot.

There seemed to be more farmhands crowded around the well, splashing water onto their Violet brows, than there were out on the fields.

The cause for Hux's anxiety was twofold as the prospect of rain loomed over his mind like a menacing black cloud. He wanted to finish the harvesting as soon as possible for fear of the rain. The great disadvantage of growing wheat was their thin, feeble stalks that easily gave way under rain, wind and the feet of intruding animals. Water was welcome while the wheat was growing but now it would merely weigh down his crop and prevent it from being cut. There was also the risk of wet wheat going mouldy, which Hux was equally eager to avoid. His fretful hope was to get all the wheat inside the barn before the next rainfall. As it had not rained for more than a week, a thunderstorm felt inevitable to the farmer, despite the reassurance of the flawless blue of the sky.

Hux took a deep, worry-ridden breath as he saw his strong farmhands walk into view. They looked exhausted as they wielded their scythes, struggling in the sun. It was not yet eight o'clock in the morning and the heat could only get worse. Hux brushed back his long silver locks from his ageing but still-handsome face. He was getting on for sixty now and anxiety exaggerated the wrinkles on his forehead and around his eyes. Hux wondered if he should go and help his farmhands in the fields, despite the growing problem of a bad back. There was business to attend to here first and he would make his decision later.

At the hearth, Hux set down the heart of one of his lambs as an offering to the goddess of the sky, as well as libations of wine. He knelt and began to pray in a quiet voice:

"Almighty Yena, great sky goddess, who watches over

our beloved island, please hear my prayer. Keep the rain away from my fields during the harvest. Send a swift wind to ease the labour of my farmhands and send clouds to guard us from the scorching sun. Oh Yena, goddess of the sky that covers our sacred..."

The creak of the door broke his concentration. Hux turned to see who it was, hoping that the reason for his disturbance had at least some importance. In the doorway stood a young Crimson man who he knew very well indeed.

"Calex, my boy!" Hux exclaimed, getting up to his feet.

"Good morning, Hux," Calex said with a hint of apprehension. "I went straight to the barn as usual but the others said you wanted to speak to me."

"Yes, that's right." The heart to heart he planned to have with Calex had been on his mind all morning, and indeed for some time before that. The issue he needed to tackle gave him the greatest reason of all to feel stressed. Hux gestured for Calex to enter the room and they both took a seat on the wicker chairs facing each other over a small, round table of oak wood. There was a pot of tea waiting for them and Hux leaned towards it. "You'll have some tea, won't you, Calex?"

"Now when did I ever say no to a cup of tea?"

"Help yourself to the carrowbean rolls, my boy," said Hux, pouring from the teapot. Despite already having had breakfast, Calex took a roll. They were filled with the paste of carrowbeans, a plant that grew exclusively on the island of Quilemoyena. The beans were easy to grow but totally unpalatable before being boiled, mashed and sweetened with honey. The paste had a very specific taste that was quite unlike anything else and could be used in the making of several sugary delicacies. These carrowbean rolls on Hux's table were spheres of bread with paste in the middle, freshly made

14

that morning in Tinklegrove's local bakery.

"I really hope it doesn't rain," Calex said, munching keenly. He knew very well that rain was a farmer's greatest worry come harvest time. He too had the same feeling that after days on end of sunshine, the clouds would have to burst eventually. But Hux's thoughts were elsewhere now and the farmer mumbled a quiet "yes".

"These are delicious," Calex said, waving the remainder of the carrowbean roll.

Hux's eyes came to rest on Calex, a sad little smile appearing on his face.

Calex stopped eating and frowned. "What is it?" he asked. "Why are you looking at me like that?"

"My dear boy," he sighed. "You really do seem to get taller every day."

"Come on, Hux. Don't get all sentimental."

But Hux could not help but notice. Calex was so different now from the little sprite he had been when they had met. The eleven-year-old Calex was a scrawny and frail boy who had never known work in the great outdoors. Hux had given him an opportunity to learn, and had been a guardian and friend when he needed one. In return, Calex had worked hard to ensure that Hux knew he was grateful. Anyone could see that some six years of farm labour had done him good. What did remain from the day they had first met were the thick, dark curls that spilled around his face and his gentle, emerald eyes. Hux looked at Calex these days and felt proud. Nevertheless, he knew what he must say, and he had given it long and careful consideration with his wife. Pulling out only meant saving the conversation for another day, and he felt he needed to get rid of this burden. Yet it was so pleasant, sitting here with the boy. Hux enjoyed his company immensely and he knew it would be such a shame to ruin the serene atmosphere with confrontation.

"So, what do you want to talk about exactly?" Calex asked, licking the sweetness off his fingers.

Hux decided there and then to take the plunge: "Calex, how long have you been with us now?" he asked gently, sipping his tea so as to avoid a sense of seriousness.

"Six years," Calex answered after a moment's thought. Yes, it must have been almost six years to the day. He too took a slurp of his tea, wondering where this conversation was leading.

"And how long have you been living in the city?" his old guardian prompted.

"I've been in Miss Kiberon's boarding house for almost a year." Calex knitted his brow. "What are you getting at, Hux?"

"Do you remember why you started living in the city?"

"Yes. You said it was time for me to become more independent."

"And what's the next step to becoming independent?"

"Working in the city, I suppose."

Calex realised the purpose of this talk now. He knew this day would have to come eventually.

Hux took a deep breath and set his cup down on the table. "Calex, what I'm about to tell you isn't easy, but needs to be said." He forced the words out of his mouth. "I think that it's time for you to move on. Once and for all."

"What do you mean?"

Calex was upset, Hux could see, and this pained him. The boy was almost a son to him and he could not help but feel a little of his sadness in his own heart. But he knew he had to continue.

"Your working here was never going to be permanent. It's just not normal for a Crimson to be working in the

Quilemoyenan countryside among Violets."

It was true to say that Hux's decision to have Calex live on the farm and employ him had always attracted a lot of attention. The other farmhands were fond of Calex but there was no denying that he stood out from the crowd. The sight of a Crimson ploughing the fields would often turn the heads of passers-by. 'Calex the Crimson farmhand' would sometimes feature in the gossipy chatter of the Tinklegrove village square, bathhouse and tavern. As if his race didn't make him stand out enough, there was also the fact that he was born abroad. The name of Kinsen was mysterious and obscure to the locals. His strange, exotic name with its 'ex' ending equally attracted attention, as did his unusual accent and manner of speaking. Nobody could argue with the fact that Calex had achieved an excellent command of his second language, but he would never have been able to attain the level of a native speaker. Never before in Tinklegrove's history had there been a riper topic for gossip than that of Calex Maro. Hux had long ago dispelled the chatter by telling the local folk everything they wanted to know about Calex, leaving little room for speculation. Of course, that didn't stop the young Kinsener from being somewhat of a celebrity in the commune. The chitter-chatter was almost always harmless but Hux had sometimes had to face the occasional words of criticism over his actions. Other farmers had told him that he had no business bringing a Crimson into the community and his presence was bound to cause problems. However, six years after his arrival, Calex had not once shown these expectations to be true. Calex listened to Hux's words with a sense of déjà-vu. He was very much aware of the unusual nature of his situation. He shrugged, expressing a deep-set frustration. "I know it's not 'normal' but I'm used to it. Besides,

I'm not bothered about what everybody thinks." He liked to pretend that this was the case, but his proud and agitated tone suggested otherwise.

"In a way, I'm not bothered by gossip either, Calex," admitted Hux. "You do a good job on the farm and that's all that matters from my point of view. But this isn't about me, it's about you. It doesn't seem right for you to work here forever. Your path spells out something different in this life. You know it's true."

"But I've never done anything else but this," Calex sighed hopelessly.

"You know that you can," Hux told him, but Calex stood up and walked to the window.

"Do you want to be a farmer?" Hux continued, getting to his feet. "To be the only Crimson in a field full of Violets? Is this what you want your whole life?"

"No, but…"

"But what?"

"I have no other choice!"

"You do!" Hux persisted, stepping towards him. "I'm not going to just cut you loose like that, dear boy. Far from it! I have an old school friend who's a priest at the Sacred Heart. I've talked with him and he says he could get you a job."

Calex was taken aback with surprise. He had never considered what it would be like to work at the Sacred Heart before. He contemplated for a moment then shook his head as if to reject the idea once and for all.

"I would have to lead Violets to their deaths. My gosh, Hux. It could even be you! I could never do it."

"A Crimson attitude indeed," Hux snorted. "Violets are honoured to die for the planet. It is the ultimate destiny of our lives. You see it as some pointless Crimson death, but for us it is the opposite. It is the most important and meaningful thing that could ever happen to us. It is a tradition that has been passed from generation to generation and it forms the core of everything we believe in. I anticipate the time I am chosen with elation... if I am ever chosen of course." Hux hated to think of the real possibility that the day would never come. The Violets of Quilemoyena considered dying of natural causes a huge disappointment.

"It's hard for us Crimsons to understand," admitted Calex.

"Well, that's what makes us so different, isn't it?" Hux exclaimed. Calex had always had a good relationship with Hux and he often forgot about what held them apart. The blue tint of Hux's skin was a stark contrast to his own but Calex seldom thought about it. It was at rare times like this he became aware that Hux belonged to another race with a culture in some ways very much unlike that of his own people. What could highlight this difference between them more than talking about the Sacred Heart and their attitudes towards being offered in sacrifice? Calex could think of very few ideas more terrifying than plunging into a pit full of molten rock. The idea of it being a great honour was a bizarre and troubling one.

The fact that Violets were offered in sacrifice while Crimsons went about their daily lives may lead to the thinking that Crimsons were the superior race and the oppressors of the Violets. The reality couldn't be more different: Violets felt themselves superior as they were more closely connected to the gods and the earth through their act of sacrifice. Their Violet blood had special properties that had the power to maintain life in all living organisms. Crimson blood could not provide the planet with its life force and they didn't want to have to offer themselves in sacrifice anyway. So both Crimsons and Violets knew their place in the world and respected each other, and for the most part, had nothing to do with one another. Calex and Hux's relationship was indeed an exception.

"Listen Calex," Hux said, seeing the boy's perplexed expression. "Working at the Sacred Heart is to work for the goddesses. If I were a Crimson, I would want no other place to work."

Easy for you to say, Calex thought.

"And what's more," Hux went on, "you have a privileged opportunity. Few people have a contact who's a priest of the Sacred Heart."

Struggling to feel excited about this, Calex gave a little grunt in response.

"This priest – Effarig," Hux enthused, "we've been friends since our school days. I'm sure you've met him. He's been round to the farm a good few times."

Calex shrugged his shoulders.

"Well, in any case, he remembers you. I've written down his address for you here. I told him you would drop by. Of course, you're almost an adult now, Calex, and I'm not forcing you to go. I'm advising you."

"Alright, Hux," Calex said, accepting the piece of paper from Hux's bluish, papery hand. He still felt reticent about going to the address written on it, though. The idea was going to take some getting used to.

"My dear Calex. It's time to return to the world you were born into," Hux encouraged. Then sensing the bond between them stronger than ever, he enveloped Calex in a firm hug. Affection came over him like a wave. He could not imagine feeling fonder of his own flesh and blood. "You'll be fine, my boy," Hux sighed. "You'll make me and Pentievra very proud." He almost said that Calex's parents would be proud too, but he was glad he stopped himself in time. Mentioning anything to do with Calex's past before he arrived in Quilemoyena tended to upset him.

"Oh, I almost forgot!" Hux took the money on the mantelpiece above the hearth: three thick coins of gold. "Here's what I owe you for your work this month... plus a bit extra."

A lot extra, thought Calex as he inspected the coins. He put them deep into his pocket.

"Thank you," he said earnestly. Calex felt so grateful to Hux for everything he had done for him but it was hard to express. It was at times when he considered what would have happened if they had never met that he felt truly indebted to him.

"Come back soon," Hux told him. "Any time you need help. We're always here."

"I know," Calex said quietly as he headed for the door.

"You will be in my prayers," Hux told him. From the window, he saw Calex walking out into the field to talk to his companions before leaving. He sat down in the comfy armchair facing the fireplace, reflecting on their conversation and pleased at how it had gone. He felt satisfied, optimistic, and that little hurt had been caused. It seemed certain that he had done the right thing. Looking out over his golden fields he began to pray for Calex's prosperity, but once again his prayer was interrupted. He turned around expecting to see one of his farmhands but was greeted by the sight of his silver-haired wife. He had been married to Pentievra for almost twenty-five years. There had been many young women who wanted to marry the charismatic and handsome Hux Windberry. On top of this, he was the heir to an eight-hectare wheat farm that had provided a comfortable life for his family for generations. Despite all the competition, it was Pentievra who had won his heart. She had not been a likely choice. As Pentievra had been blind from birth, the announcement of their marriage was met with many a raised eyebrow. For Hux, however, there was no doubt about it: Pentievra was the sweetest young woman he had ever met, with the kindest heart. She did not brag or boast about her conquest; and she ignored the spiteful comments from jealous women. Tragically, fate was cruel to the couple. They would have been wonderful parents – so they had always believed – but they had never been able to have children. After years of waiting they accepted their fate, which pained them immensely but had not destroyed their love.

"What's the matter, darling?" asked Hux, softly.

"Did you talk to him?" his wife asked in a near whisper.

"Yes," answered Hux in reflection. "It went well." He walked over to the doorway and put his arms around her. "He'll be just fine. You'll see."

They stayed like that for a while, thinking of the quiet, scared boy Calex used to be.

Chapter
THREE

In the warmth of the summer evening, the Chief Officer of the Sacred Heart was being escorted home by horse and carriage. The Crimson Fabian Zora knew that his house would be distinctly different when he got back. Not a remnant of her would be left, and a mass of tension would be relieved. Zora had already employed a new officer to replace his wife at the Sacred Heart. He told everybody that after being away to give birth to their first child, she had decided not to come back. It was an excuse that would suffice for the moment and one which was easily believable. In reality, Fabian had told his wife to leave the house with the newborn and never come back. When he first saw the child he was outraged. He needed some time to decide what to do next. In the end, there was no doubt about it: Hero and the child would have to disappear. Fabian's servant had delivered the message to his wife that morning, and she had been given the whole day to carry out his wishes while he was out of the house. By this time, she would be gone for good, and Fabian would be able to relax for the first time in two long weeks.

Fabian stared idly out of the window as the carriage made its way eastwards from the centre of the city. The candlelight that filled the interiors spilled out from the windows into the streets. Fabian detected an abundance of different odours; some of dinners cooking, others not so pleasant. The closer he got to his home, the less he was bothered by noise and pollution. The tightly-packed residential buildings which filled most of the city were replaced by elegant town houses. It was here, in the eastern side of town, where its wealthiest citizens lived. As a minister, Fabian Zora was expected to live in a lavish villa to reflect his high social status.

Fabian caught the eye of a young man in the street who had just entered into government. He recognised him from a recent meeting on the prolongation of the aqueduct, one of the meetings that all officials like himself had to attend. The young man had surprised everyone with his confidence as he participated in the discussion like someone with ten years experience. There were a lot of these ambitious young men in politics these days, thought Fabian irritably: arrogant, starry-eyed schoolboys who hungered for power. The greenhorn smiled at Fabian sheepishly from across the street. The minister averted his eyes, pretending not to notice him. He was in no mood for smiling and certainly not for the likes of that young fool.

Fabian started to reflect on his rather ordinary day at work. Like most jobs, his was more or less predictable. As well as participating in the sacrificial ceremony, Fabian had to ensure the smooth day to day running of the Sacred Heart. From time to time, there were official meetings and issues to be dealt with. Five years ago the rules had been changed concerning the sacrificial selection of the first ten Violets the officers came across in any given area. Before a governmental meeting was held on the subject, children and even babies could be taken. This was a tradition that went back generations. It was decided that only Violets over the age of fourteen should be accepted from then on. This was due to two reasons.

Firstly, there was a certain threshold of blood that was required every twenty-four hours. Ten adult bodies could provide this amount. If two of the eight sacrifices were children, the threshold would not be met. If this happened on a certain day, the planet would suffer and become unhealthy, like a human being who is malnourished. The resulting problems to the environment were of great consequence: large patches of arid land formed, and where plants died, the community was devastated by drought and famine. These phenomena had indeed occurred when the blood threshold was not met because children had been included in the sacrifice.

The other reason for the change in procedure was that children did not understand the significance of sacrifice. Those who were selected were often scared and reluctant because they were not yet old enough to understand such an honourable act. Tradition being of the utmost importance, it took a while to convince some government officials of the change. In the end, however, the law was passed and despite being a traditionalist himself, Zora accepted the decision as a reasonable one.

Despite the loss of ten lives a day, the Violet population remained constant. It was estimated that around 150,000 Crimsons lived in the city and 400,000 Violets lived in the countryside. 3,650 Violets were offered in sacrifice each year and of course there were natural deaths. And yet, the birth rate balanced it out. Violets had an average of four children instead of two, encouraged by the fact that pregnancy only lasted three months. As a result, the population remained at around 400,000 from one year to the next.

Today, a Violet woman of around thirty had given Fabian a golden locket at the foot of the volcano. She said she had had it since she was a child, that there was no use it going with her, and that he should give it to someone he loved. A typically open-hearted Violet gesture. Fabian might have appeared grateful but the locket ended up in his desk drawer along with various other trinkets that had been given to him by Violet sacrifices. Maybe he could have pawned it for a hundred demarit or so, but it's not like he needed the money.

Fabian would have liked to say that he enjoyed his job for a number of more admirable reasons. That on seeing the joy on the Violets' faces, you cannot help but feel joy yourself. Or that the Violets respect the officers so much that they share their last words with you. Or that at the Sacred Heart one can find spiritual fulfilment. Fabian knew exactly what he was supposed to say.

He had an inkling that he did feel this way when he started out, but ten years later the best thing about his job was the high salary to complement the affluence he had been born into. Nobody could pretend that it was hard work that had got Fabian his prestigious position. The Zora family was among the wealthiest and most influential in Quilemoyena City. Not that Fabian's school results were disappointing but his destiny to have an important job and high status had been planned out from the day he was born. Fabian had attended the Elite School of Quilemoyena (ESQ) whose graduates were guaranteed to become political ministers or to hold other prominent positions in government. His father, who had been the former vice-president's brother, made sure that his only son would land himself a top job as soon as he finished school. After a fair amount of hobnobbing, Zora Senior managed to secure the position of Chief Officer of the Sacred Heart for his son.

On one hand, Fabian could see how it was strange for Crimsons to be in charge of the Sacred Heart where a religious ceremony of prime importance took place. After all, it was the Violets who were the religious ones. Spirituality was built into the foundations of their culture and their hearts. They had the same fundamental beliefs as Crimsons, but their interest was so much stronger. Worshiping the gods was part of their everyday life and always at the forefront of their minds. Crimsons saw less point in worshiping the gods than Violets did. The gods existed, there was no question of that, and they had a certain amount of – but not absolute – power over the human world. Yet, the Crimsons felt no desire in their hearts to pray to or make offerings to them. They preoccupied themselves with the material world and their individual concerns. These feelings were partly to do with upbringing but mainly to do with blood. Violet people were quite literally connected to the planet. All living things were alive due to the blood of their ancestors. What ran through their veins was an essential component of what ran through the roots of trees and flowers. The Violet blood that pumped through their bodies was the same as that of the gods. If, for example, a Violet pricked his finger on a rose bush and a drop of his blood reached the soil, the whole flowerbed would bloom before his eyes. Crimson blood, on the other hand, had one purpose alone: to maintain the life of the individual in whose veins it flowed.

And yet, it was the Crimsons who were in charge of the running of the Sacred Heart. On a practical level, this made sense. The Violets lived outside the cities walls and worked with the land; The Crimsons lived inside the city walls and worked in the city. The one and only exception to this rule was the priests. These were Violet men and women who had chosen to dedicate their lives to religion out of adoration for the gods. They trained in the seminary in the east of the island. Being a priest was the sole vocation available for Violets within the city walls. Violet farmers and merchants passed through the gates to provide their goods but their visits were brief. Therefore, the sight of a Violet in the city was unusual, as was the sight of a Crimson in the countryside.

Fabian was feeling weary and let his eyes shut. He would be able to leave for his holiday villa on the coast of Serenah in just a couple of weeks from now. He would have time to himself on his private beach, facing the gentle lapping of waves. A good book, a glass of wine, and not a single person to bother him. Every evening: freshly-caught seafood on the terrace. A simple, easy-going life. The very thought of it was so alluring that he could leave this very instant. In fact, he planned to buy his ticket for the boat journey tomorrow which he knew would cheer him up, if only a little bit.

Fabian's work always finished around two in the afternoon. Today, he had eaten lunch afterwards with an old school-friend who now worked as the minister in charge of the island's roads. Over a roasted quail, they reminisced and caught up on each other's news. His friend inquired about Fabian's new-found parenthood to which he responded in a way that one would expect from a new father while quickly changing the topic of conversation. After lunch, Fabian did not want to go home as he needed to be sure that his wife would be gone when he got back. He walked to a common marketplace where he could blend in with the crowd. Here, he sat on a bench until the late afternoon, finishing his book Quilemoyenan Legends II, an anthology of poetry by the illustrious poet Suma.

As the carriage bounced over the cobbles, Fabian pictured his pretty and perfectly situated villa far away from the urban sprawl. The climate was sticky-hot here at the moment but at his Serenah hideaway there was a constant, refreshing sea breeze. He pictured the soft waves, the call of the gulls and the fruit trees in the surrounding hills, their branches heavy with ripe lemons and oranges.

"Where am I?"
Another person's voice came into his head. A teenaged boy's voice. The voice of someone waking from sleep at the crater of a steaming volcano, a voice laden with fear. "Where am I?" the voice repeated, more urgently. And then: "I'm so tired."
"And you will get to sleep soon." Fabian heard his own words coming back to him, tauntingly.
Fabian remembered how this boy had grabbed the bottom of his tunic, pleaded to him on his knees.
"Don't make me do this!"
The fruit trees, Fabian thought to himself, it wouldn't be long now before he were back among the fruit trees, their branches heavy with…
"I'm begging you!" the voice cried. And then there was the boy's face: Violet, with eyes that were red and streaming with tears. "I can't," he said "I can't do it."

"We're here, sir," announced the driver. Fabian had fallen asleep quite by accident, his head bouncing gently against the frame of the window as the carriage came to a standstill. The sun had almost set and the sky was dark blue, the moon a bright and perfectly sliced crescent. Fabian opened his eyes and groggily took a look around. "Ah, here we are," he acknowledged, handing the driver his payment.

Fabian's house was a testament to his status, its two-floored façade stretching out before him as he traversed the courtyard. The house stood at the top of the easternmost of the city's five hills, offering an unparalleled view of both the city and the countryside. As Fabian approached, the stones that ground under his feet signalling his arrival, his servant opened the iron-studded wooden door from the inside. The oil lamps had been lit so the hall was filled with a subtle, relaxing light. "Good evening, sir" the servant greeted him. Fabian stepped onto the mosaic floor made from thousands of tiny ceramic pieces. During the winter months, the hydrocaust system underneath it would send steam circulating through the pipes to warm Fabian's feet.

The walls were adorned with frescos featuring pastoral scenes of sheep, shepherds, cows and milkmaids which seemed to make up for the fact that Fabian had scarcely seen any of these things in real life. In the middle of the hall was a pool which collected rainwater from the opening in the roof above it. It had held a thin layer of water when he left that morning, but the sun had since dried it all up. At the very centre of this pool was a depiction of Fabian himself in bronze. This statue featured him about to throw a discus, one of his favourite sports. The pose showed off his muscular physique, although it was a rather exaggerated depiction. Although he was a strong man, Fabian did not spend quite enough time at the gymnasium to account for the awesome virility portrayed by the statue. He had commissioned this lavish treat only a few months ago, and it was still enormously gratifying to be greeted with it every time he entered the house. Fabian sat down on a chair, giving him a good view of the bronze sculpture, whose discus, he suddenly realised, was aimed at the marble statue of his wife at the other side of the hall. The bitter irony of this almost made Fabian shiver.

"Minister Tiger has invited you to dinner next week," his servant informed him.

"Who?" Fabian snorted, tearing his eyes away from the statue.

"Esroh Tiger, sir," the servant explained. "The newly elected Minister of the Water System."

Fabian rolled his eyes as he remembered. "Oh no, not him!"

'Tiger' was not this man's real name. Everyone knew that his surname was the traditional but unappealing 'Regit'. He had reversed the letters to give himself a name with more pizzazz. This was a controversial move for some but Esroh Tiger had the charm and wit to pull it off. The whippersnapper sucked up to everybody who held an important governmental position, and for the most part it worked. He had turned out to be the most popular and successful of the young, recently graduated politicians. There was talk of Tiger already being promoted by the end of the year. Minister Tiger's charisma had not worked on everyone however. Fabian saw a spoilt twenty-year-old who had just come out of the ESQ. He considered himself to be among those who saw straight through the young man's charming façade. Tiger was yet another power-hungry manipulator who did not give a damn about maintaining Quilemoyena's traditions. Why, the cheeky rascal had even changed his name! It was true to say that Fabian's name was not from the traditional Quilemoyenan naming system. His parents had preferred to give their son a more modern first name, and despite his family living on the island for five generations, his surname had its roots on the island of Serenah. However, if Fabian did have a time-honoured Quilemoyenan name, he would not disrespect the tradition by changing it.

"That little rat has everybody drooling all over him," Fabian spat as he got to his feet. "But I refuse to be one of them!" The servant raised his eyebrows at this heated response while Fabian continued to fume. "Minister Regit – or Tiger, or whatever he calls himself – knows I don't think much of him and that's exactly why he's inviting me to dinner: to butter me up like the rest of them!"

The servant spoke nervously: "I'll take that as a 'no' then, sir?"

"Yes, tell him I'm... washing my hair." Fabian gestured with his hand as if wafting away an annoying flying insect.

"Very well, sir," the servant concluded with a nod of his head. He occasionally bore witness to his employer's present mood – irritable, dramatic and slightly ridiculous – and dutifully hid his contempt for it. "In that case, I'll let him know that you won't be attending. Shall I tell the cook to prepare dinner for you?"

"No," Fabian decided. "I'm going to bed." He made his way to the square-shaped garden which was surrounded by the rest of the house. The doors around the garden led to different rooms.

"The plants are all dying out here," he called. "When's the gardener coming?"

"Tomorrow morning," answered the servant.

"Good," Fabian grunted, eyeing the shrivelling geraniums.

"Sir, it may be of interest to you to know that your wife is still here."

Fabian stopped dead. The servant looked uneasy. He had seen his employer lose his temper before and it was not an experience he wanted to repeat. He slipped out and headed for Minister Tiger's house to deliver the message, feeling that now was the ideal time to get out of Mr Zora's way. Fabian followed the path around the garden until he came to his wife's living quarters. From outside the door, he heard a female voice humming as if lulling a baby to sleep. Fabian barged into the room and the woman almost jumped out of her skin.

"We agreed that you would be gone when I came back." His voice was controlled but menacing. Hero looked up, holding a baby who was now asleep. Fabian did not look at it.

"I just wanted to talk to you," she said softly.

"What, in the name of the gods, is there to talk about?"

"The fact that you've jumped to conclusions without even giving me a chance to tell my side of the story."

"You can say what you like. It won't change a thing."

"Well, it's worth a try. Come on, Fabian. Let's sit down and talk about this."

At last, Fabian snapped. "Get out!" he shouted, knocking a ceramic vase off the table that smashed onto the floor. "I told you! This is finished. I don't want to see you ever again!" His shouting had woken up the baby and it started crying: a high-pitched, deeply unpleasant noise. Fabian clamped his hands over his ears as if the sound was causing him physical pain.

Hero tried again. "You have to listen to me!"

"No, I don't," barked Fabian. "That...thing and you are no longer part of my life. You are dead to me, Hero. You are dead to us all. Just go!"

"You will regret this!" Hero growled back, jumping to her feet. Fabian hit her hard and she fell onto the floor. After a moment of shock she leapt up, crying words of protest and choking on her freshly-sprung tears. She pummelled his chest which did not affect him in the slightest. He simply grabbed her hands in his and pushed her away. He caught a glimpse of the baby and a shiver ran through his body.

Nobody could know what had happened. The whole of Quilemoyena would talk about it and the name of Zora would be permanently destroyed. He could plan to have her killed, or even kill her himself and make it look like an accident. Although the thought had passed through his mind, Fabian felt that he was not capable of this. The easiest solution – and the one which left him with the least guilt – was to tell her to disappear without a trace. Despite his disgust and anger, he was still human. But now he laid eyes on the infant, he began to feel more hateful and violent than ever.

"Get out or I will kill you," Fabian said.

This comment left her in stunned silence and, without saying a single word, she gave in to his request. Fabian turned away from her and made his way to the main bedroom. It seemed much too big for one person. He shut the door behind him and despair finally took him over. Collapsing onto the floor he sobbed quietly, not wanting his wife to hear but unable to control himself any longer.

The next day, he would take anything belonging to or associated with her – statue included – and have them destroyed. He was still not sure whether he had made the right decision. If anyone saw the child she was carrying she would not only be sentenced to death, but publicly tortured and humiliated first. What is more, they would find out who she was and Fabian's career would be over, his reputation ruined. His life may well be at stake as well, he realised with sickening fear. He heard the great doors at the front of the house shut as Hero disappeared into the night with the infant: a baby neither Crimson nor Violet, but of mixed-blood: a brownborn.

Chapter
FOUR

$\mathcal{C}$alex could only afford to visit the bathhouse once this week and he had decided to go today. After the bombshell he had received that morning, he needed to unwind. The winds of change were blowing hard against him. Although it made him feel uneasy, he knew that moving on from the farm was necessary. Just because his life now was predictable and safe did not mean it was the best thing for him. Change was always difficult and stressful, Calex realised, and in a few weeks he would probably have settled into the new conditions of his life. Despite these acknowledgements, Calex was struggling to feel enthusiastic about working in the city. The fact is, he loved being in the great outdoors. During his early years, he had lived in a spacious house surrounded by fields. Such an opportunity did not exist for him anymore. The main issue behind this was the divide between Crimsons and Violets in Quilemoyena. While the Violets inhabited the island's countryside, the Crimsons occupied its buzzing urban centre. Calex knew without a doubt which one he preferred. He occasionally wished he were a Violet, and today he had done more than ever before. If he were blue-blooded, Hux would let him stay. As a Violet, he could fit in with the others on the farm and not feel an outsider whenever they spoke in groups.

Calex supposed he was going through some sort of identity crisis. He had received greater access to the Violet world than most Crimsons. Some people never even got the chance to speak to a member of the other race. Calex was in the unusual position of standing on the bridge between the two different cultures. It was a bridge that very few stood on. Even on the island of his childhood, where there was no great city wall that separated Crimsons and Violets, mixing with a member from the other race was not common. In Kinsen, so far from here, Crimsons and Violets lived in both towns and countryside. Indeed, Calex's parents had lived and worked in a soap-making workshop on the outskirts of a rural village. Young children of both races played with each other in the streets but they soon realised that there were fundamental differences between them. By the age of ten, they would grow out of being colourblind: Violet children would play with Violets, and Crimson children with Crimsons. There were no negative feelings towards the other race, but it was as if there were an invisible force keeping them apart.

Here in the bathhouse, the steam was so dense that he saw the other men in the room as fuzzy, pinkish shapes. Calex had been in here so long that he felt as if his brain were starting to melt. Yet his lungs and skin felt refreshingly clear and he hoped that soon his troubled head would too. As he stood up he suddenly felt so dizzy that he almost fell, clambering out of the side room and into the main hall. Here the steam had more space to disperse and it was easier to see. Lying on stone slabs around the pool were men whose skin was being massaged with olive oil and scraped off with a special tool. This instrument was cleaned in water, washing away the dirty oil, then the worker would continue on the next patch of skin. This was the standard cleaning procedure used for centuries in Quilemoyena. The idea of soap was still yet to catch on in these parts. In fact, Calex had not seen a bar of soap in years. Calex looked at the pool which was busy as usual with men discussing issues of both business and pleasure in water that came up to their waists. Calex did not bother to head over there himself. He was only here today to get clean and lose himself in the steam.

This basic bathhouse was near to Calex's residence and a single one demarit coin gained entry. The feeling of getting squeaky clean always gave Calex an enormous feeling of satisfaction, especially after a long day spent in such unpleasant humidity.

Every now and then, however, Calex liked to treat himself to a few hours in one of the city's more up-market bathhouses. Like the typical resident of Quilemoyena City, he was fond of their fancy features and frills. Calex rarely lusted for luxury, but an afternoon spent in a grand bathhouse was the little touch of lavishness he occasionally awarded himself when he had the money; the kind of bathhouses that took foreigners' breath away with their elegance and grandeur, sending them back home to their families speaking of the wonders of these Quilemoyenan bathhouses, among the many other exemplars of progress on which the island prided itself. Thanks to its volcano, natural hot springs were bubbling just under the island's surface and these were exploited in the many bathhouses at residents' disposal. At last, Calex decided that he had had enough. He grabbed one of the towels from a large pile, wrapped it around his waist and went to get dressed. He had casually arranged to meet a couple of his friends that evening after a sloppy dinner at Miss Kiberon's. A drink or two at the smoky and overcrowded tavern was a typical way for him to pass his time after the sun had set.

Before long a mug of ale was making its way over to him, splashing over the sides. His friend thumped it down in front of him and Calex thanked her. She took a puff from her long pipe and gave him a wink. Her name was Rumel and she was a carpenter. She made beautiful little figurines out of wood which she sold on the market. They were delightful little forms – squirrels, trees, a girl and boy holding hands – and she told the punters they brought good luck. Whether this was true or not, Rumel did not know, but it sold her figurines nonetheless. She had even made her own pipe. Her hands were tough and masculine, looking almost as if they belonged on another body.

Calex took the first sip of his ale. It was bog standard stuff, nothing special. The son of soap makers, Calex had a sharp nose for fragrances. He detected a tiny hint of liquorice but sadly this was overpowered by the taste of river water. The ale was thin and bland, most probably the tavern's home brew.

"What's on your mind Calex?" she probed, noticing he was a little distant.

It was no longer the revolting taste of the ale, nor his future for that matter. He had banned himself from thinking about that for the rest of the day before it drove him totally crazy. In fact, he had no intention of mentioning the news to his friends.

"I was just thinking about Allirog Redips," he admitted. The five-hundred-year-old story of Redips had become the stuff of Quilemoyenan legend. Even Calex had learned about him at school as a child in Kinsen.

"What about him?" probed his male friend, a large,

hairy man called Drazil. Calex shrugged and rubbed his eyes. It had been a long day and he still felt dizzy from overdoing it at the bathhouse. Perhaps after an ale or two he would perk up. Drazil spoke again, eager to start a conversation. "Well, the way I see it, he was just an ordinary man wanting to make his mark on the world and earn a bit of fame. The biggest con in history if you ask me."

"That's a very cynical attitude," contended Calex. The ale was no longer necessary to perk him up. Suggestions that Calex's childhood hero was a fake were more than enough to do the job.

"And yours is a very naive attitude," quipped Rumel. "There is no reason to believe that he reached the other side. They just found those words carved into the boat after it capsized."

"What did it say again?" Drazil searched himself. "Something like: 'If I do not make it home, know that it is no great loss for humanity, for I cannot describe the wonders I have seen."

"More or less," nodded Calex who considered himself well-informed on the subject. "And, by the way, it's glory not wonders."

"What makes you believe it?" Rumel's tone was cynical.

"It's a matter of faith," he replied. "I believe that Allirog Redips is the only human being to ever sail that ocean and find out what's on the other side. Five hundred years later and nobody since has been able to achieve what he did."

"Some have tried," recalled Drazil, "but none have made it. It's a perilous voyage. Ale's a bit warm isn't it?"

"That's the thing!" Calex cut in, eyebrows furrowed. "It is a very long voyage, but not a perilous one. He had food, water, everything he needed. Then, with less than a day's sailing to go, the boat capsized. There was something else going on. I believe the goddesses had a hand in it because they didn't want anyone to know what's there."

Drazil held up his hands as if to say 'enough'. "Calex, why do you always choose to have these heavy-handed debates with us when we come out to have a few drinks," Drazil concluded, gently mocking him.

"You started it!" Calex answered back with a chuckle. Drazil and Rumel clapped their mugs together and drained them in one gulp. Then, Rumel leapt up onto the table in her typically extravagant fashion and made an announcement to one and all.

"My friends!" she bellowed, and the chatter died down. "Let us make a toast to Quilemoyena, our beloved homeland with its rich, fertile soil and peace-loving people!" Shouts of "hurrah!" and "hear hear!" came from each corner of the tavern.

"To Quilemoyena!" cried Rumel, and the whole tavern cheered. Calex smiled, a little embarrassed but impressed by the confidence of his friend. He never took part in these displays of patriotic fervour and wondered if the time for this would ever come.

When Calex finished his drink, and while Drazil and Rumel were on their fourth, he said his goodbyes and headed to the door. A man with a thick white moustache stood up, blocking his way, then stumbled to the ground.

"Not again Harry!" roared one of his similarly drunk friends. "That's the third time this week!"

"Here, let me help you up." Calex bent down to give the fallen man a hand.

"Get your hands away from me, you dirty foreigner."

"I beg your pardon?" Was it still obvious just from one sentence? Calex thought his accent was barely noticeable these days.

"You give me a hand then what? What do you want in return? My house, my money, my job?"

"What are you talking about?" Calex demanded, feeling the need to stick up for himself instead of walking away. The white-moustached man repeated Calex's words, exaggerating his accent. He was laboriously bringing himself up to his feet, evidently in the advanced stages of drunkenness.

"Why don't you do everyone a favour and just go back home?"

After this last comment, Calex felt his blood beginning to boil although it was not the first time he had come across such racist bigotry and it would certainly not be the last. Quilemoyena was where the sacrifices which benefited the whole planet took place, and this made many of its inhabitants arrogant. Many Quilemoyenans felt that other islands and their inhabitants were backward and inferior. It was indeed true that no settlement compared to Quilemoyena City in terms of size and technology. Its political system too was relatively advanced and well-organised. Other islands looked up to Quilemoyena as a model for their own society and Quilemoyenans were well aware of this. The island happily welcomed tourists, but foreigners living on their shores was a subject of hostility for many natives. Some were anxious that they were using up resources but many of them were just instilled with a firm sense of superiority. The strong feeling of national pride in the hearts of many Quilemoyenans made them antagonistic towards those from elsewhere. In his everyday life, most people treated Calex like one of them but once in a while he had to put up with racial abuse.

"This is my home," Calex bounced back. "I've lived here for years. You don't know the first thing about me."

"I know one thing: I don't like you and I think you

should..."

"Oi, Harry!" called his friend. "Leave the kid alone. He's just a harmless Geshtie."

"I'm not from the Geshtin Fields. I'm actually from Kinsen," Calex corrected him.

"Same bloody thing," mumbled the friend, gulping his ale.

"Hey, what's going on here?" Rumel heard the ruckus and had come over.

"Oh, he's a friend of yours is he?" Harry attacked. "You should know better, after all that you said about being proud of Quilemoyena. Our beloved homeland, you said. And then you go mixing with the likes of him. What a load of rubbish!"

"Peace-loving people, I said. Now, that is a load of rubbish. Clearly." Rumel tried to pull Calex away from the situation and get him to come back to their table. Calex, not wanting to pursue the argument, accepted willingly.

"Oh, you're walking away now, are you? You coward."

"I'm not a coward," Calex retorted. "I just have no time for the likes of you." He hoped that was the end of it but he could not help but hear a final insult behind his back.

"Geshtie coward," the man said venomously.

"For the last time," began Calex, turning back around to face him, "I'm not from..." But he was cut short by a blow to his nose, causing him to stumble back into the next table.

Chapter
FIVE

*N*ight had fallen on Quilemoyena City. In the absence of human traffic, cockroaches and rats claimed the street for themselves. They licked their way around piles of rubbish and carried edible waste back to their dens. In the weeds and bushes that grew at the sides of the roads, invisible crickets sang. Further up the walls, mosquitoes flurried around the recently-lit street lamps. Wandering around outside the tavern was a stray dog looking for scraps of leftover dinner. By some incredible stroke of luck, it came across a chicken bone with some meat still clinging to it. It fought another dog and some rats for the opportunity to devour it. The cockroaches, meanwhile, did not bother to compete with the larger beasts, occupying themselves with nothing bigger than breadcrumbs.

Not so far away, Hero held her baby tightly to her, wrapped up in its blankets. She made sure that his face was hidden from view. Her forehead was swelling and her eye still ached. It was the first time her husband had hit her. Her long auburn hair was messy, and a couple of strands stuck to her freckled face, dried on with tears.

Hero did not have a clue where to go or what to do. There was nobody she could trust. Her husband and her parents alone knew her secret and they had abandoned her. One other person knew: the midwife, who Fabian had ensured would keep quiet due to a large sum of money and some unpleasant threats. Hero had been born into a life of privilege, always surrounded by people and possessions. For the first time in her life, after nineteen years of comfortable living, she had nothing and no-one. The realisation that she was utterly alone was so terrible that she was yet to fully accept it. Her life was now so different from before that reality seemed like a dream. To be precise, she was living a nightmare, realising one minute at a time that she was not going to wake up.

For the little that Hero knew, leaving Quilemoyena City seemed like a smart move. With its heaving population it was the most dangerous place to be. Despite finding it difficult to think straight, she began to formulate a plan to escape to the countryside and find somewhere to hide. She would take it one step at a time. Hero had wandered west, as it was unlikely that she would be recognised at the city gate in working class side of town. She walked in the shadows whenever possible, taking light steps and staying close to the walls. There was a lot of darkness to hide in but eventually she came to a patch of light. She heard the music of an accordion mingled with sounds of talking and laughter, and presumed it was a tavern. As she came closer, she saw the ale-drinking patrons through the windows and saw the sign above the door: The Lusham Locks. The typical late night rowdiness was beginning to stir. Two men merrily left the building, unleashing a roar of banter and waft of ale as the door opened. They wobbled across the street, arms around each other's shoulders, to the building opposite. There, they were greeted by a women wearing very little in the way of clothes who warmly invited them inside. The heat was sweltering, but Hero doubted that was the reason for her attire. She continued to stand there, obsessively rearranging her hair, and Hero kept on walking. She quickened her pace, looking down at the cobbled ground.

As she passed the door of The Lusham Locks, Calex Maro walked out alone.

"Hello, my dear," cooed the woman, hands on hips. "Is that your blood on your face or somebody else's?"

Calex touched his lips and looked at his fingers: a few drops of bright crimson. "It must be mine," he deduced with surprise, beginning to taste it in his mouth.

"Maybe I can find someone to make it better for you," the woman purred. Calex blushed, smiling as he turned away, part embarrassed and part apologetic. Hero could not help but take a look at the young man as he walked parallel to her. His hand was wiping away the blood and he had an upset expression on his face. Hero soon regretted her curiosity because she caught his attention. He returned her gaze and she quickly averted her eyes, turning to go down another street to get out of his way. Before she could, he spoke to her: "That road's blocked," he said. Earlier in the day, Calex had overheard his neighbours talking about a balcony that collapsed that very afternoon. The debris had blocked the whole road and as far as Calex knew, it was still being cleared away. This kind of thing happened far too often as greedy landlords tended to choose the cheapest building material available. Inevitably, this lead to angry tenants pestering the reluctant landlords to fork out hundreds of demarit in hospital bills. This time, fortunately for the landlord and his wallet, there was nobody on or underneath the balcony when it gave way.

"Where are you going?" Calex asked the young woman, wanting to make himself useful.

"The nearest city gate," she replied.

The coldness of her tone did not dissuade Calex. "It's a bit difficult to explain how to get there," he said. "I know how to get there myself but I think it's too complicated to give you directions."

"I'm not asking for any," Hero said bluntly. "I can find my own way."

There was a small fountain at the corner where the two roads met. Calex splashed water over his face, even though he was no longer bleeding. It felt refreshing in the evening heat.

"I tried to help a man who fell over," Calex told her. "He was drunk and hit me. Life's much easier if you mind your own business, don't you think?" Hero did not answer. She noticed that he had a light foreign accent, which she could not quite make out. He started to walk over to her and she stepped back into a shadow.

"Are you meeting someone at the gate?" he asked. It seemed unlikely now that he had taken a proper look at her: she had a bundle on her back as if she was going somewhere and she was holding something else in her arms: another bag, perhaps.

Hero hesitated as she tried to find the words to answer his question. "Yes, I mean no. I mean, I'm fine... I..." The mysterious object in her arms wriggled and began to make noises. Hero felt a pang of panic and clutched the baby to her chest.

"You've got a baby," Calex beamed. "I'm good with babies. Can I see?"

"No," Hero snapped, stepping back. To her relief it was a false alarm: the baby was not going to cry after all and promptly fell back to sleep.

Calex began to apologise: "I didn't mean to…"

"Life's much easier if you mind your own business," Hero interrupted, repeating his words. "Don't you think?"

"Alright, I'm sorry," came Calex's defensive response. What's her problem? he thought. He turned back to the fountain for another splash of water, leaving her in peace. When he looked up, however, she was still standing there. She had a guilty look on her face, as if she had realised that she had been too harsh on him. Indeed, she felt bad that she had to be so rude to someone who was friendly and polite. She never usually behaved in such a way. Her terrible ordeal was transforming everything that had gone before. There was an additional reason for her staying put: she did not know how to get to the gate. The western side of the city was unfamiliar to her and with nothing but oil-lamps weakly lighting the streets, they all looked the same. They seemed to be empty too, except for the young man who said he knew the way to her destination. Hesitantly, she approached him. "Could you show me the way to the gate?" she asked. "I think I'm lost."

"I thought you said you could find your own way," Calex said, surprised by her quick change of heart.

"I was wrong," Hero said awkwardly.

Calex shrugged. "I suppose I could spare ten minutes," he said, with less friendliness than before. He started to lead the way and she walked alongside him. The silence between them was uncomfortable. Hero felt it was necessary to attempt to redeem the initial impression she had given to him.

"I've had a really hard day," she said as a kind of indirect apology.

"That makes two of us," Calex added without smiling.

Hero noticed the kindness and sincerity of his face in spite of the darkness. "You're not from around here, are you?" she observed, trying to keep to small talk.

"No," he answered with a little annoyance. How come people always picked up on his foreignness – the fact he was different – before anything else?

"Where are you from?" she pushed.

"Kinsen," Calex answered matter-of-factly.

"That's a long way from here!" she exclaimed. He did not respond.

"Look, I'm really sorry for being rude," she attempted at last. "All mothers are very protective of their babies. It's just a natural reaction. I didn't mean to snap at you."

"Forget about it," Calex insisted, the edges of his mouth curling into a slight smile. They came to a marketplace where the stalls stood bare, ready to be stocked up with goods the following morning. The only signs of movement were the squeaky dash of rats and rummaging of stray cats through the waste. The nearby residents were all sleeping and somewhere unseen, a dog barked. Meanwhile, an elderly homeless couple were warming their hands over a makeshift fire.

"This is the square where the Rock Festival takes place," Calex told Hero, warming up a little.

"The what?"

"The Rock Festival. Where they display different rocks."

"Oh yes. I've heard of it but I've never been," she said. Of course not, Calex told himself. He could tell how posh she was from her accent and the way she held herself, not to mention her pompous and arrogant manner. Her clothes looked new and well-made, and she wore a long black cloak with a fur hem at the bottom, purely for decoration. No, Calex deduced, she would never mix with the masses in the western side of the city. Just to fill the silence he was going to tell her about last year's Rock Festival, where reddish igneous rocks from the Sacred Heart were the central attraction, but he was interrupted.

"Could you spare a couple of coins for an old woman?" The homeless woman who had seen them entering the marketplace was not one to let an opportunity slip away.

"I've got nothing on me," Calex replied honestly.

"Me neither," Hero added, just as truthful as Calex. He assumed from her apparent status that she must have been lying. They tried to keep walking but the old woman stood in their way. She wore an assortment of colourful rags and her hair was a matted, greasy nest on top of her head. They could smell her foul breath from where they were standing.

"Trouble," was the word that came from her mouth. "You've got trouble, my dear. Hard times ahead of you."

"Leave me alone!" Hero exclaimed, moving away with a jerk as the woman's hand reached out to her.

"What have you got hiding under there?" the old woman croaked. Hero hurried out of the square and Calex followed. They heard the old woman's shrill chuckle behind them.

Calex snorted with amusement. "That's Quilemoyena City for you," he joked. "Sends everybody stark raving mad!" Hero was too shaken to respond. "What's the matter?" he asked, seeing she was upset.

"Nothing," she mumbled. Calex led her down a few more narrow, winding streets, dimly lit by lanterns. Calex told her about the collapsing balcony incident, telling her that sort of thing happened all the time.

"All the time?" Hero echoed.

"More often that you'd like to think," Calex said. The gate, which was lit either side by beacons, came into view. Hero doubted very much that she could have found it by herself. When Calex came here every morning on his way to the farm, there was always a queue and he would have to wait his turn to pass. At night, it was desolate save the two guards.

Hero began to panic again as she imagined, for the umpteenth time, what could happen to her if she was found with the child. The Minister of Justice would not stop the people of Quilemoyena City from tearing her to pieces. She did not know how they would kill her, but she knew they would be a lot less sympathetic than her husband.

Quilemoyena was not merciful in dealing with criminals. Making an example out of them by punishing them harshly and publicly was seen as the best way of deterring future crime. People guilty of petty misdemeanours were put in the stocks for a day or two for the public to pelt to their hearts' desire with rotten vegetables. Capital punishment was treated like a spectacle, with crowds gathering from all around to watch the event. Murderers were branded with hot iron and hung, as were those who committed significant theft, rape or other crimes considered to be serious. The government deemed it important that the rest of the public learned from these examples in order to keep the city streets as safe as possible. It was fair to say that there was a sadistic element to these violent punishments. People often joked that the money for them should come not from the Minister of Justice's budget, but the Minister of Entertainment's. Being only nineteen years old, Hero had never thought about how she would die. If she had, she would have imagined herself as an old woman in a warm bed. But she would never have thought that it would be in a public arena in agony with a rope around her neck, begging futilely for mercy. After her demise, the baby would be kept as a trophy, lifelessly displayed for one and all on the streets of the city.

"I'll go alone from here," Hero said to Calex, the cold tone returning to her voice. "Goodbye."

"Bye then," Calex replied, a little surprised by her abrupt farewell, and he turned around to walk home. What a strange girl, he thought.

Hero walked up to the gates, a large and rather foreboding stone structure with huge wooden doors. The two guards stood together bantering and certainly not doing any work. The job was coveted by lazy men who looked as if they could hurt you if they could be bothered. There really was little else to it.

"Good evening," said Hero, making eye contact with both of them. She was trying hard to conceal her nervousness with a slight smile.

They were not so cordial in response. "Proof of identification," said one of them.

"I didn't know you needed that," Hero said with surprise.

The guard sighed and rolled his eyes. "Obviously if you're wanting to pass through you need to have your papers with you," he said. Hero knew little about the policy at the city gates. If truth be told, she rarely had any reason to go through them. However, she knew that they were usually wide open to let traffic pass freely.

"You don't always need to check I.D., do you?"

"Not during the day, no," said the second guard. "We don't have time when there are long queues. But it's the middle of the night and there are some dodgy characters about."

"Do I look like a dodgy character to you?" Hero retorted, becoming impatient. "I'm just visiting a friend outside the city walls."

"Isn't it a bit late for social visits?"

"Do you really have to ask so many questions?"

"Not really, no," confessed the first guard. "But we'll still need proof of identification."

Hero had nothing of the sort on her. She had left the

house in a hurry, having thrown nothing but a few clothes into her bag. Completely without a clue of what to do next, a figure emerged from the shadows.

"Darling, I'm here. Sorry about this, gentlemen. I tripped over a paving stone back there. Did you forget your identity papers again, sweetheart?"

It was the young man who had just helped her. She was overcome with relief, and bewilderment.

"Are you the lady's husband, sir?"

"Yes I am," Calex replied convincingly. Hero did not say a word: this Calex could obviously play this game better than she could. The guards took a look at his identity papers complete with fingerprints.

The first guard read his details aloud: "Maro, Calex... Citizen of Kinsen... Inhabitant of Quilemoyena for... almost six years now."

"You come through here every morning, don't you?" noted the second guard. "I had no idea you were married to such a lovely lady." Calex raised his eyebrows and cocked his head as if to say 'well now you know' then put his papers back in his pocket, their permanent home.

"We'll open the gate this time," the first guard informed them, "but remember to carry your papers with you next time, madam."

The guards unlocked the doors, stood aside and let them pass, both of them giving Calex a cheeky wink while Hero was not looking.

A long, dark road stretched out in front of them. In the distance, they saw some light coming from the handful of cottages dotted about the landscape. The gates creaked behind them and made a bang when they shut, then the enormous key turned in the lock. When they had walked far away enough from the gate for the guards to hear her voice, Hero turned to Calex to speak..

"I thought you'd gone," she told him in a near-whisper.

"I heard you get stopped by the guards so I waited to see if you would have any problems," Calex told her.

"That's so kind of you," Hero said, rather amazed by what he had done. He could have had no idea how much trouble she was in and how much she needed someone to be kind to her. "Thank you," she said, with all her heart.

"You're welcome," Calex replied. His smile was full of warmth and for a moment Hero forgot about the terrible situation she was in. She looked up at him – he was quite a lot taller than her – and smiled back.

"Your name is Calex, right?" she said. "I heard the guards read it from your papers."

"That's right," he confirmed. "Calex Maro."

"That sounds very Kinsonian," she said, giving a laugh.

"What about you? What's your name?" Calex asked.

Despite the feeling that she should not give her real name, Hero found herself telling him anyway. Calex did not seem like the kind of person who cared much for politics, but it was possible he had heard of a minister with the surname of Zora, so she only gave her first name. What harm could that do?

"I suppose I'd better go back through the gate again," Calex sighed. "Can you think of any good excuses to tell the guards?"

"I can't make up stories as well as you," she admitted.

As Calex started to turn around, something stopped him. It did not seem right to interrogate her but it was hardly responsible to leave a woman and her baby in the middle of nowhere in at night.

"Are you sure you know where to go from here?" he said with concern. "I feel bad about just leaving you like this."

"Don't. Seriously, I can manage," she reassured him

with a smile. He did not quite believe this statement but he did not want to force his company on her either. After all, she was an adult and she could make her own decisions.

"Well, alright," Calex said. "It was nice meeting you and..."

Calex's voice trailed off. His eyes had become fixated on something: the object lying in Hero's arms. She had let her guard down, having become too relaxed in Calex's company. When she looked down at the baby herself, she saw that his face was in full view. There was little light but it was not dark enough to conceal his colour. When she looked up at Calex, his face expressed shock and confusion. Her smile faded and she felt a chill flow through her like ice.

Chapter

SIX

$\mathcal{C}$alex's look had frightened Hero. She became aware that she and the baby were alone with a stranger outside the city walls in near darkness. She felt extremely unsafe, regretting the moment she started to talk to him and realising it would probably turn out to be the beginning of the end.

"What are you going to do?" she asked, stepping back. The tension and secrecy he had recognised in her before seemed to make sense now. "I know what I should do," Calex said cautiously. The baby's skin appeared a purplish-brown due to the blood underneath it. Although he knew it should disgust him, he found it strangely fascinating.

"Neither Crimson nor Violet," he reflected, somewhat blown away. "Incredible. I've never seen anything like it."

Hero thought of bribing him then remembered that she barely had anything on her. Money could get her practically anything she wanted in the past. As a child she was never short of toys and the finest foods. As an adult she and her husband could buy or do what they wanted without money being a problem. But she had left her life of affluence behind her. Her husband held the purse strings and he was obviously not going to give her anything. Their money was tied up at the bank and the small amount of loose change she had found around the house didn't amount to much. In hindsight, she should have brought some of her jewellery to use in place of money. She had some splendid necklaces, bracelets and brooches. Not just coloured wooden beads on a string, but gold and silver worked into the shape of flowers and animals or set with crystals and intricate enamel designs. Yet she had not had the time to think about this, the same way she had not thought about the identity papers, and now it was too late. But then she remembered something: she was wearing one piece of jewellery. She used the thumb of her right hand to feel if it was still there.

"Take this," she said, removing the ring from her finger. It took some effort as she had not taken it off since her wedding day. "It's worth a lot of money." She held it out to Calex and he saw it was indeed a valuable object: a band of solid gold encrusted with three rubies.

"Why would you give me that?"

"In return for keeping quiet."

"I'm not the sort of person you can bribe," Calex said proudly. He held up his hand as to say 'no' and Hero put the ring back on her finger, feeling a little reassured by the integrity of his response.

"He's yours, isn't he?" Calex asked, his voice still calm.

"I am his mother, yes." Hero willingly answered his question. She saw no point in hiding the truth now.

"So this is why you're out here?"

"That's right," she admitted. "My family have disowned me. I no longer exist to them. My husband has told everyone I know stories to cover up the truth."

"And he's the one who threw you out into the street to-night?"

Hero nodded.

Calex contemplated the new information, letting it sink it. He knew he should steer away from this type of person like anyone else would. Crossbreeding, if it could be called that, was the most unspeakable taboo. Anybody responsible for it – either Crimson or Violet – would have to be mad or possessed by a malevolent, supernatural force. And yet this woman seemed neither. Something did not fit, and Calex was eager to unravel the mystery.

"Are you going to report me to those guards over there? If so, just get on with it. Don't play games with me." Hero was trying to appear tough but Calex could tell how scared she was.

"I'm no policeman," he told her with a shake of his head, "and anyway, I don't think you deserve it. There are things you don't want to tell me. That's normal. I haven't known you for very long. But I have a feeling that you deserve help."

Hero could not believe her luck. More than anything right now she needed somebody to be on her side. "I appreciate that," she said humbly.

"So, where are we going then?" Calex asked. "I mean, where are you going?"

"Far into the countryside," she told him, gazing out into the darkness. "I have to keep away from other people."

Calex shook his head in disapproval. "That doesn't sound like a good plan. It's not safe out there. How do you expect to survive beyond several days?"

"Well..." She shrugged hopelessly. "What else can you suggest?"

An idea floated into Calex's head. Something warned

him that what he was about to say was not wise but he found himself saying it anyway: "Listen. I know some people who you could stay with for a while. A couple who helped me when I was in trouble."

"I can't stay with other people. What if they saw the baby's face?"

"Hux is always out on the farm and his wife is blind. There would be no risk with her. You would just need to be careful around Hux and the farmhands."

"They're Violets." Hero realised. The idea did not disgust her in the slightest; she just found it strange. This Calex had obviously had some untraditional relationships with members of the Violet race. "How long do you think I could keep the game up?" she asked.

Calex speculated. "Maybe a week or two. It all depends on how careful you are. From there, we could find another solution. Don't ask me what." Hero nodded and even smiled a little. Calex told her it was an hour's walk but that he knew the route very well. They started to make their way but the further they went from the city, the darker it became. The beacons at the gate could be seen for miles around but they were the only significant source of light.

"Would you like to hold him for a while?" Hero asked. It was a request for help dressed up as a favour. Her arms were tired from the baby's weight.

"What? Me?" Calex exclaimed. "No. No, thank you."

"I thought you said that you were good with babies," Hero reminded him.

Calex smiled shyly, remembering the words he had blurted out earlier without thinking. "Well, maybe I am. It's been a very long time."

The last time he had held a baby was at the age of five when his younger brother, Irendex, came into the world. This was perhaps his earliest memory. At their family home, his mother was holding the newborn as his father gazed at his sleeping face. Calex sat at the other side of the room, excited about the new addition to the family but jealous that he was taking up all his parents' attention. He remembered the moment when his mother passed the baby into his waiting arms, so afraid that he might drop him. He was transfixed by his brother's impossibly smooth skin, heavy head and chubby limbs. Then the infant opened his eyes and Calex noticed that they were bright green just like his. This memory sprang to mind as Hero passed her baby to Calex. He nervously took him, feeling the warmth and weight of this strange object for the first time.

"What's his name?" Calex was captured by a sense of wonder.

"I haven't decided on one yet," came Hero's response. Calex handed the baby back to his mother with a nervous smile.

The road was fairly flat, straight and well-maintained but it was hard to navigate in the dark. To make matters worse, the moon had been obscured by clouds, blocking out any moonlight that could have helped them to see where they were going. Walking was a struggle and after about half an hour, they decided to lie down among the shrubbery and sleep. They found a comfortable spot near the road soon enough. If there was one thing they had to be grateful for, it was the heat. Having been so hot during the day, the temperature was now very pleasant indeed.

"I'm sorry I don't have a horse to get you there quicker," Calex said with a yawn as he settled down into the grass.

"Never mind. It's nice to get some fresh air," Hero found herself saying, noticing that her good spirits were coming back at last. She was well aware of the fact that this was the first time she was to sleep outdoors in her entire life. She laid the baby down gently, not in an expensive cradle of pinewood and silk, but in a patch of grass. He did not seem to notice the difference. Hero untied the cloak from around her neck to use as a blanket. She then took off the bundle that she was carrying on her back – some clothes wrapped up in a piece of linen – which could serve as a pillow. Before lying down, she pulled out one of her dresses and suggested Calex use it to rest his head on. He accepted gratefully, whilst claiming he would have been perfectly comfortable anyway.

Hero felt relieved to rest her head at last and instantly began to nod off. "Calex, do you think we'll be safe here?" she mumbled.

"I think so," he answered her. "But let me know if you hear anything, all right?"

She murmured a weary 'mm' in agreement then quickly fell asleep while her baby continued in its slumber. Meanwhile, Calex stared up at the sky for a while. There were cloudless patches where he could see the stars shining. He picked out the constellations he recognised and made ones of his own. The unfamiliar nature of the situation he was in prevented him from settling down. As long as he thought about the mixed-blood baby and the young mother by his side, he would never have been able to get to sleep. Involuntary, the thoughts that came to distract him were of the events that took place in the tavern earlier that evening. As his eyes shut, he remembered the white-moustached man's drunken face and his razor-sharp words. Calex was less bothered about the punch as he knew that when men got drunk they tended to do such things to each other. It was not the first time something like that had happened and it would surely not be the last. Fortunately it very seldom went beyond a few angry words and Calex almost always managed to put on a brave face and walk away. But that was not to say it did not hurt him. As a matter of fact, these comments and threats always got under his skin and stayed there for a long time. He supposed he should be grateful for the few friends he had. Quilemoyena City may well have been full of strangers who did not care if he lived or died, but people like Rumel and Drazil made the city seem a little smaller and more bearable.

He awoke groggily as the sun began to rise, three or four hours later. The birds had already begun to sing and the clouds had blown away, the low sun turning the sky pink and light purple. Calex felt enchanted by waking up this way. What a privileged opportunity it was to see the break of day in all its glory. After all, it was not every day that he woke up in a field. He rubbed his eyes and gave a joint-cracking yawn, experiencing the discomfort that comes with not having a good night's sleep.

He sat up and regarded the landscape, its softly rolling green hills scattered with sheep. Now that it was light, Calex noticed a couple of fumaroles gently emitting vapour into the air from the bowels of the earth. This was not a rare sight in the countryside of Quilemoyena. There were other islands in the known world that were home to volcanoes, all of them with impressive mountain ranges. Quilemoyena was unique in the way that it was unusually flat for an island situated on a hotspot. The signs of its volcanic activity were evident all over the island however, not just at the Sacred Heart. The sight of fumaroles was not uncommon, their red and yellow-tinted rocks releasing steam from unseen depths. There were all sizes, from the tiny to the enormous, many of them with barriers built around them as they were extremely hot and contained unstable ground, occasionally spitting up fiery-hot mud. Many smelt so bad that nobody, not even wild animals, dared come near. Quilemoyena also housed a number of geysers, whose spurting waters attracted Crimson visitors from the city as well as Violets who considered them sacred. The island's many bathhouses owed their existence to the naturally present thermal springs.

Calex's hands slid into his deep trouser pockets. The morning was cool and he knew it would not stay like this for long. It was going to be another scorching hot day: that was for sure. There were his identity papers in his left pocket. In his right, there was a piece of paper neatly folded up. He took it out and unfolded it. It was a poem by Suma that he had recently copied. His handwriting was so messy that only he could read it:

When the sun sets on one's day
And his soul shall fly away
To the gods' own keeping place
Its new chance it shall await
To come again into this world
A little boy or little girl
To step once more through life's door
With no memory of what went before

Calex sometimes looked at young children and wondered if they were the souls of his family reborn. But even if they were, what would it matter? His family as he knew them were probably gone. The idea that the same souls might pass him in the street from time to time gave him little comfort. In any case, there was no way to know if it was really them. The soul stripped down was believed to be pure; containing no personality, no talents, no characteristics. The development of these things in a person depended on their upbringing and the personalities of their parents. A budding poet

was probably no wordsmith in a former life. A gifted
guitarist was not necessarily a maestro of the last generation. Even if there were certain similarities passed on
from one life to the next, all memories would be lost.

Calex read the poem aloud, enjoying the rhythm, then
folded and put it back into his pocket. The paper was
breaking up, the folds weak and fluffy, and it would not
last much longer. A swallow dived down and collected a worm in its beak. In an instant, it had flown away
again. Why do they move so fast? Calex contemplated.
Perhaps it was because they had such short lives. They
had to do everything quickly, just to fit it all in. He reflected on this idea. It was not until he noticed the sound
of Hero's breathing that he remembered she was there.

As she still lay sound asleep, he took the liberty of regarding her face for a few moments. Her lips were slightly
parted and her chest moved gently to the rhythm of her
breathing. How strange it felt to be looking at a stranger
in such a private situation as sleeping. But as no one
was around, he found no reason to stop. He noticed the
bruise on the left side of her face and wondered if it was
there before or if it had formed overnight. It was as if
his gaze woke her up. As she opened her eyes Calex
promptly averted his, peering into the vastness of the
sky. She began to orientate herself. "Where am I?" she
murmured rhetorically. She looked towards the person
to her side. His was a nice face to wake up to, open and
smiling. She gave a stretch and rubbed her eyes.

"We ought to keep moving," Calex said. "I think we
should get to our destination before farming begins. I
don't want to interrupt Hux's work."

Hero nodded and then suddenly felt an acute sense of
dread. But her eyes quickly found the sleeping baby
and she relaxed again. "He's so tiny," Calex marvelled.
He gazed at the infant's plump face, admiring his serene

63

look and skin as soft as any newborn's, only marred by its colour.

"He was only born two weeks ago," Hero pointed out. The baby stirred and started to cry in long, high-pitched wails, and Calex simultaneously lost his sense of admiration.

"I need to feed him," she said awkwardly. "Calex – would you mind?"

"Oh no, of course not," Calex excused himself, beginning to blush. He hesitantly stood up and began to walk towards a nearby group of trees, wondering if he could find anything that could serve as breakfast. He soon came across a tree of bright red apples, and plucked two of the plumpest from it. He hesitated about taking a third one: did babies eat apples? No, he realised, they drink milk and that was the precisely the reason why Hero asked him to go away. I'm too young for this, Calex thought to himself, realising the ridiculousness of his prior assumption. The feeling that he was being catapulted into adulthood had plagued him since the morning before. Calex felt scared and reluctant, although there was an element of excitement as well, like a dancing glimmer of sunlight in a dark cave. Adulthood brought with it new possibilities, and Calex was intrigued as to what exactly these might be.

Calex rejoined Hero and her baby and they made their way back to the road. As neither of them had slept very well, they did not speak much except to exchange pleasantries. They finally came to the Sector that the Sacred Heart calls '210'.

The Sacred Heart divided the countryside into five hundred blocks of around a kilometre squared each. The numbers spiralled out from around Quilemoyena City. 'Sector 1' was at the city wall's northernmost gate. 'Sector 2' was next clockwise and the spiral continued from there. Windberry Farm was towards the north-west, closer to Quilemoyena City than to the coast, and was situated in the 'Sector 210'. However, the Violets paid no attention to this system and ignored the little wooden signposts that were dotted all over the island. It was understood that the segmentation was for the Sacred Heart alone. Violets had their own place names. For example, the village where Hux and Pentievra lived was known to Violets as Tinklegrove.

Windberry Farm came into view, and Calex and Hero headed for the farmhouse which was isolated among Hux's many fields. The inviting-looking house had two floors with stone walls largely cloaked in ivy and a thatched roof. To one side of the house, there was a pen full of clucking chickens and a vegetable garden with lettuce and rhubarb plants, along with peas and beans which crept up poles. To the other side, there was a grassy field where Hux's grey horse stood grazing lazily next to its stable. At the end of this field was the outhouse, which had its own water pump. Behind the farmhouse was a courtyard with a large barn. As well-equipped as any Violet could hope for, the courtyard housed its own water-well. All around were fields of wheat as far as the eye could see, the wind moving the heads like a golden ocean. There were a few farmhands dotted around, already hard at work and filling pony-drawn carts with freshly-cut wheat.

With their feet hot and aching, Calex and Hero arrived at the front door of the farmhouse at last. Calex knocked enthusiastically and the door opened promptly with a noisy creek. A fond smile appeared on Calex's face as he set eyes on Hux. He felt the usual rush of comfort at seeing him. His old guardian's expression was one of surprise, as well as a little amusement. "Well, this is unexpected!" Hux admitted.

"Well, here I am," Calex chirped. "I'd like to introduce someone to you. Hux, this is Hero. Hero, Hux."

Hux inspected her as they shook hands. Her skin was pale and freckled, her face framed by ginger tresses. She looked tired and drained, her eyes sinking a little, but she was undeniably pretty. Her expression was calm and friendly; her mouth smiling but not too much. Hux could not remember seeing Calex with a Crimson girl before. This Hero must have been a couple of years older than Calex and this made him seem more mature. Seeing them next to each other like that made Hux smile fondly. It was another reminder of how Calex was growing up.

"It's nice to meet you, my dear," Hux said. She had a lovely presence, he decided. He noticed the bundle in her arms which he presumed was a baby. How strange! How did Calex know this girl? He was sure the answers to his questions would come soon enough.

"So, what's going on, my boy?" he asked. "Are you in trouble already?"

"No," sniggered Calex, a little too confidently, "of course not."

"You see?" Hux said to the girl. "That's Calex for you. Never in trouble. Always a good lad."

Calex looked down with thinly-concealed guilt. It was the first time he had seriously doubted that being there at Hux's doorstep was the right thing to do. He knew how much Hux loved and trusted him. He could do nothing wrong in Hux's eyes but this situation could lead to disaster; the destruction of his reputation forever. Calex asked himself: was he betraying his dear guardian? It annoyed him how Hux loved him so much. He felt, shamefully, that he did not deserve it.

"So, what are you doing here exactly?" Hux asked. "Don't tell me it was just to say hello."

"Actually," Calex began, knowing it was too late to turn back, "I have a favour to ask of you."

"Go on, my boy."

"Well, Hero is from the island of Serenah and she has come to visit some friends," he fabricated. "But there's been a mix-up and they've gone on holiday for a few days themselves."

"Oh dear," Hux chortled, "that's unlucky." Hero nodded in agreement, noticing that Hux seemed to be falling for the story.

"So," Calex continued, "I was wondering, if it's not too much trouble: could she stay with you for a few days?"

"My dear Calex," Hux sighed, still smiling. "It must be hard work carrying around a heart of solid gold all the time." Hux had no choice but to say yes to Calex's request. Hospitality was highly valued in the countryside of Quilemoyena. Not welcoming a suppliant into your home and providing them with food, water and shelter was severely frowned upon, not only by one's neighbours but by the goddesses themselves. If Hux had said no then he would have to fear that next year's crop might fail. And Hux was indeed a pious man.

"Of course I can offer my hospitality," he concluded.

Chapter
SEVEN

Space was not a luxury in the countryside like it was in the city: it came as standard. Hero was surprised at how spacious the farmhouse was. This impression was enhanced by the fact there was very little furniture. The entrance hall contained no more than two wooden chairs either side of a small table with a vase of flowers from the farm as well as Hux's guitar that leant against the wall. Hux and Pentievra, typically for Violets, had few possessions and every room was tidy, uncluttered and sparsely decorated. They could have moved in yesterday.

The young Crimsons walked through the hall and into the kitchen. There was a large oven at the back where a fire was burning to heat up the stoves. Hux's wife stood peeling potatoes and putting them into a large pot of water.

"Hello Pentievra," Calex called cheerfully.

On hearing his voice she dropped the potato she was holding and called out his name in surprise. Calex went over and hugged her. He adored Pentievra. She had shown him affection when he felt lonely, and she had always been there when he awoke in the night with bad dreams. He tried not to think of this as he introduced her to Hero and repeated the fabricated story to her. Fortunately, Pentievra was not interested in details. She was simply delighted to have a guest and the opportunity to take care of a baby. "How exciting!" she exclaimed. "You're very welcome here, my dear."

"Thank you," Hero said. She already liked Pentievra a lot.

"Calex, show her the bedroom, will you?" Pentievra continued. "And I'll prepare you both some breakfast."

"You really don't have to..." came Hero's polite response. But Pentievra had already got to work. "Don't be silly," she said, taking two eggs from the basket. "Of course I do."

"Yes, Hero, she does. Don't tell her that!" Calex received a friendly slap on his arm for this comment and left the kitchen chuckling. He led Hero down the corridor and upstairs to the spare bedroom. This is where Calex had stayed until he began to live in the city. Nobody had slept there for almost a year but the bed was made up and there was a towel over the chair.

"It looks like they were expecting someone," Hero observed.

"They're always ready for guests," Calex told her. "It's a Violet thing, you know."

Hero lay the baby on the bed and untied the cloak from around her neck. Then she sat herself down, the bed creaking a little under her weight. Calex had not noticed it when she had the cloak on but it was obvious now: Hero was carrying quite a bit of weight on her belly and yet her arms and legs were slender. She looked tired.

The room was much less than she was accustomed to. There was no finery, no ornaments, nothing that did not have a function. The colours of the rug, blankets, bed-sheets and curtains were mismatched, and yet the room felt cosy to Hero; unfamiliar but not unpleasant.

"It's so peaceful here," Hero sighed. Calex said nothing in response, looking through the window into the wheat fields and listening to the birds. The baby was awake and looked up at his mother, peering unfalteringly at her face. His eyes were big, dark and lovely. She reached out her finger and he squeezed it with his whole hand.

"It's so strange," Hero began. "I can't believe he's here and yet it feels like he's been here forever."

Calex nodded, not really understanding what she meant. Then he was distracted by a smell coming up from the kitchen. "Can you smell that?" Calex beamed, his eyes lighting up. Hero detected it too: the mouth-watering, smoky scent of bacon.

Calex headed for the door but Hero was hesitating. "It's alright," he reassured her. "There's no-one else in the house. You can leave him up here." They were soon sitting at the kitchen table. Pentievra let a fried egg slide from the pan onto each of their plates and then she served the bacon which continued to sizzle before their eyes.

"Fantastic!" Calex exclaimed, tucking in immediately. Hero added her thanks before starting to eat her meal in a more civilised fashion. She was impressed by Pentievra's ability to find her way around and even cook without the use of her eyes. As Pentievra had been born this way, she was used to it and her other senses were heightened. She had the ears of a fox and an excellent sense of direction.

"You two enjoy your breakfast" Pentievra said. "I'm just going upstairs to prepare a cot for the baby."

"No," Hero spat, almost choking on her food. Pentievra turned to her with alarm but on seeing the Violet woman's cloudy, sightless eyes Hero remembered there was nothing to fear.

"Sorry," Hero said. "I just... don't want you to go to any trouble."

"My dear!" Pentievra chirped. "It's no trouble at all."

After they had finished eating, Calex and Hero went upstairs and found Pentievra laying the baby down on the makeshift cot. It was actually a wooden box on the bedside table, the kind of box one would use to transport vegetables, but filled with blankets and very comfortable-looking and safe. The room smelled slightly unpleasant and the source of this seemed to be the screwed-up towel beside the cot.

"I changed him," she informed Hero. The baby's lower half was wrapped up in a new towel and he was wriggling happily, stretching out his new limbs. He too liked Pentievra, it seemed.

Hero had said thank you so many times it was starting to get embarrassing. She managed to find different words to express her gratitude. "That's very kind of you to do that," she said.

"I adore babies," Pentievra exclaimed. "They grow and change so quickly. And every time they learn to do something new it's so delightful. There's so much to look forward to. You'll see, my dear."

"Do you have any children?" Hero asked. Calex bit his lip, anxious that this question might upset her. Luckily it did not, although her voice was tinged with an old sense of sadness.

"No, dear," she said wistfully. "I would have had five or six if I could. I would have loved it..." Pentievra's voice trailed off. She was daydreaming and her eyes glossed over. An old, impossible dream was coming back to her. Hero was searching for something appropriate to say but she was at a loss for words.

"But that's something you youngsters have to learn," Pentievra said eventually. "You can't always have your own way."

Hero smiled sympathetically. So that's why they took Calex in, she thought.

"Anyway," Pentievra continued, the chirpy tone bouncing back into her voice. "I think it's time you fed him, my dear."

"But he's fine. He's not crying," Hero said.

"You shouldn't wait until he cries. By then he's desperate."

Hero was pleased Pentievra couldn't see her blush. Would Pentievra think she didn't know what she was doing? She had been a mother for half a month and her sense of who she was had transformed. Now there was another human being who relied completely and utterly on her. It was stressful but exciting, and she felt she had more purpose in life than ever before. Yet very little had prepared her for her new role. Friends with babies and small children had talked of their experiences while she was pregnant and Hero had listened attentively. However, nothing could have prepared her for the reality of having her own child to take care of. Since he had been born she had had no support or guidance. She had felt terribly isolated and alone, but now there was Pentievra. It seemed like things were falling into place.

"I'm sure I'll be able to find something we could use as a bath for him. Maybe one of the troughs for the animals from the barn. I'll give it a good clean first, of course."

"Don't you want me to get it for you?" Calex called after her as she left the room.

"Stop fussing!" she said, wandering off downstairs.

"That's Pentievra," Calex said to Hero. "Fiercely independent."

Hero was looking out of the window again.

He realised that he probably had that same lost and empty look about him when he first came to this place. The feelings of anguish and loss felt fresh again as he looked at her face. It may have been many years ago but Calex remembered well those first few days on Windberry Farm. Hero was not at peace and there was nothing he could do about it.

"I've got a lot of things to do in the city," Calex told her, feeling it was time to leave.

"Alright," Hero said with a weak smile. She took off her ring again and handed it to him. Calex shook his head and opened his mouth to speak but Hero stopped him: "It's to say thank you," she said.

"I told you," Calex protested, "I can't accept that."

"Please," she insisted. "It's my wedding ring. I want to get rid of it."

Calex understood now. He reluctantly took the ring from her fingers and put it in his pocket which was deep enough to ensure it would be safe. Calex got up to his feet, searching for the appropriate words to say before leaving.

"Well, take care," was what he came out with. A bit pathetic, he thought instantly. "I'll see you soon," he added. That offering was not much better but he did not want to seem too keen.

Calex shut the bedroom door behind him and walked down the stairs. Hux, who had been outside with the farmhands, approached him in the corridor. He ushered him into the living room with its great fireplace.

"What's the matter?" Calex said in an anxious voice.

"Nothing Calex," Hux said quietly. "I was just wondering if there was something you wanted to tell me now that we're on our own."

"Something to tell you?"

"Yes, you know. About the girl."

"Well, what about her?"

"I don't know."

"I suppose you're just surprised I have Crimson friends, aren't you? Well, that's what you wanted, isn't it? For me to go back to the world I come from and all that."

"Calex, calm down. There's no need to make this difficult. It's just that you've never asked us a favour like this before," Hux admitted.

"So?" Calex said, nervousness seeping through the veneer of calm.

"Hero seems like a lovely girl but it all seems very strange. You've never mentioned her before."

"Oh right. So now I have to talk to you about everything?" Calex retorted, starting to feel annoyed.

"Alright, my boy," Hux said, sensing Calex's irritation. "I just wanted a bit of reassurance."

"Well, what do you want to know?"

"How long you've know her for, where you met..."

"We met in a tavern in the city."

"A tavern? Oh, Calex."

"What?"

"And where is the father of that baby?"

"I don't know." Calex felt exasperated.

"You don't know?!"

Calex felt his heart rate quicken. "I know but it's a bit sensitive and it's not for me to say. As you said yourself, Hero is a lovely girl and she just needs a place to stay for a while."

"You said a few days!"

"Yes, a few days. Look, Hux. Can't you just trust me?"

Hux sighed. "Of course, my boy. I trust you." Foolish decision, thought Calex. He couldn't bear to look Hux in the eyes. He could have been getting Hux into serious trouble, risking as much as his life to help this girl. And the truth was that he barely knew her. It was crazy to put Hux and his wife in so much danger, after all they had done for him! The feeling Calex had that he was a bad person loomed heavily over him. However, one thing was for certain: it was too late to turn back.

"Go and see Pentievra," Hux said, squeezing Calex's shoulder. "She wants to talk to you alone."

In the kitchen the stove was getting hot again and Pentievra was preparing a pie. The metal trough that would serve as a bathtub for the baby was already sitting on the table. Pentievra would take it upstairs later but first she needed to prepare lunch for Hux and the farmhands. She was rolling the pastry when Calex came up behind her. He laid a hand on her shoulder.

"Calex." She said his name without needing to hear his voice first.

"I looked for you before I left yesterday," he said softly. "Where were you?"

Pentievra set down the rolling pin and took a deep breath. "You know me, Calex. I'm a bit of a coward. I just hate saying goodbye."

"Goodbye? Why would you have to say that? I'm always going to be around."

"I know," she sighed, turning around to face him. "But if I had my way I'd have you living here with us forever. But we must do what is best for you." Pentievra put her arms around Calex and hugged him very tightly. Seconds went by and she still did not let go. When she did, Calex saw her blind, drifting eyes welling up with tears.

Hux insisted on taking Calex back to the city walls on horseback. He rode with the skill of a man who was born to work with the land and animals. Calex thought of how he could never control a horse like Hux could. The skill came so naturally to the Violet man. The more Calex thought about Hux's words of the previous morning, the more he realised he was right. It's time to re-turn to the world you were born into, Hux had said. Your path spells out something different in this life. You know it's true.

At the West city gate, Calex jumped down from the saddle. Hux's horse, despite being an enormous beast, was obviously happy to be relieved of his weight. Calex thanked his old guardian for the lift, and with that, Hux took off towards the horizon. Calex watched him go, feeling burdened by the secret he kept.

Back in his stuffy room, Calex remembered that he would have to visit the priest Effarig later that day. Despite his reservations about working at the Sacred Heart, he was determined to make a good impression. After all, it was the only job opportunity he had. He lay awake on his bed and the late morning sunlight poured in through the window and warmed his face. The street outside was typically busy and full of the sounds of screeching infants and boisterous animals, but he managed to block them out and lead his thoughts elsewhere. He reflected on the previous night, remembering the blow he received to his mouth. Biting on his lips, they felt a little sore and bruised, but not too bad. As he lay, feeling his lack of sleep catching up with him, he began to recall memories buried deep in the past. Knowing he could not stop his mind thinking what it wanted to, he let them come.

Calex was on a boat watching his brothers playing on the deck.

"I caught you so you have to walk the plank," said Malfex, two years older than Calex. The youngest brother, Irendex refused to give in to the boy who towered above him.

"I challenge you to a duel," he announced. The boys

grabbed a couple of wooden walking sticks from nearby and began to poke and parry each other. Suddenly, Malfex gave Irendex a mighty blow but he refused to fall down.

"Get on the floor, loser," he commanded. "You're dead!" A familiar voice interrupted their game: "Boys! What are you doing with those sticks?" It was their mother. "Give them back and apologise to this lady and gentleman this instant!"

"Sorry," they choroused, being more annoyed that they had to stop the game than embarrassed. They handed the sticks back to the elderly couple sitting on a bench.

"Now, boys," said their mother. "Go and play another game that doesn't interfere with other passengers on this boat." The boys obeyed and scurried off to look for more fun. Maybe their father would have some ideas. Meanwhile, their mother walked up to her other boy who stood nearby.

"Cal? Don't you want to play with your brothers?"

The curly-haired boy of eleven silently shook his head. He was gazing over the side of the boat at the deep, near-black sea. "When are we going to be there?" he asked her.

"Tomorrow morning," she replied. The boy put his hands out, catching the raindrops that began to fall from above.

"The sky looks angry this evening," Calex said sullenly.

"Just a bit of rain, that's all," his mother reassured him.

"Why are we going to Quilymayner, mum?"

"We're going on holiday, darling."

"But why to Quily... Quilymayener?"

"Well, they're supposed to have some lovely seaside ports over there. We're going to do a tour of the north coast."

"Your mum just wants to see the Sacred Heart." Calex's

father had come out onto the deck and squeezed between his wife and son, putting an arm around each of them.

"That's not true!" Cara dismissed his words but she could not deny that she had some curiosity to see the legendary place, if only from a distance.

"What's the Sacred Heart?" asked their son.

"Well done, Malfex," Cara sighed. "You're going to have to explain now."

"It's where the sacrifices take place, son," Calex's father said, giving his wife a look as if to say 'see, there's nothing to hide'. Sure enough, Calex had heard a little about the sacrifices in school. Cara did not want her son to ask any more questions. It may be a fact of life but it did not seem an appropriate subject for an eleven year-old boy.

"Even I feel uneasy with it," Cara admitted to her husband, quietly.

"Well, you shouldn't complain," he told her. "You wouldn't be here if it wasn't for them doing what they do."

"That's true and I'm not complaining but I still find it unsavoury." His parents continued their conversation as Calex looked into the overcast, darkening sky. Even then he knew that it did not look like 'just a bit of rain'.

In the present, Calex was feeling very drowsy but warned himself not to fall asleep. There was business to be done. But he found that he was unable to rest anyway, as his mind had become stuck on the young woman, Hero. He had taken the ring out of his pocket and was fingering it. The way the rubies sparkled when they caught the sunlight did not cease to impress him. He found that the ring fitted on his long, thin fingers perfectly. It looked rather feminine perhaps but it was safer on his finger than in his pocket or anywhere else.

As he sat up, Calex took a deep sigh and felt a sort of thrill whiz through his veins. He was impatient to talk to the girl; break through the cloud of mystery that surrounded her and find out about her past and her secrets. He felt as if something had woken up inside of him and he knew that had to see her again.

Chapter
EIGHT

When Effarig Taog was a young boy, he and Hux Windberry were inseparable. They sat next to each other at school, and played together by the babbling brook and woodland surrounding their homes. Their mothers used to joke that they could not bear to leave each other's side in case the officers of the Sacred Heart came, taking one and leaving the other behind. They were, for all intents and purposes, brothers.

Effarig and Hux were now nearing sixty and the years had changed their smooth skin to rough, and their brown hair to grey. They were no longer the best friends they once were long ago. Hux was always expected to take over the family farm and at the age of sixteen he did so as his father was taken for sacrifice. Hux invited his best friend to join him in running Windberry farm, but Effarig had other plans. For some years he had felt his calling was to become a priest. On the day Effarig left Tinklegrove to train in the seminary in the east of Quilemoyena, both boys were heavy with sorrow. The days of always being together were over, and their childhood had come to an end. Effarig donned his red robes three years later and his visits back to Tinklegrove became less and less frequent. He had his own house near the seminary where he returned after work in the city. Like all priests and priestesses, he lived a celibate life. A life of solitude, but not one of loneliness.

Effarig and Hux were always glad to see each other and got along well, but it was nothing compared to the old days. The raucous laughter of the past was now a polite chuckle, a subtle reminder of their days as boys, running hot and carefree through the sun-dappled shade of the forest.

Now at the end of the day, Effarig's back was aching and he looked forward to sitting back and relaxing in his comfy armchair. He was still dressed in his dark red woollen robes, although he always removed his round hat of the same colour and hung it behind the front door when he came in from work. Dinner had been satisfying and a book would keep him entertained until bedtime, although he usually fell asleep in the armchair a few minutes after sitting down. He scanned his bookshelf, hoping to revisit one of his favourites. He was in the mood for something easy and undemanding. His hand reached for his volume of Little Geshtin – a History in Drawings.

It stopped in mid-air as a knock on the front door made him freeze. Who on earth could that be? He opened the door and saw a young Crimson man before him. Effarig's eyes narrowed, recognising him but unable to remember who he was. Fortunately, the visitor spoke before Effarig was obliged to ask his name.

"Good evening, Mr Taog," he said politely. "I'm Calex Maro."

"Ah!" exclaimed Effarig, realising it was the lad his old chum Hux had taken under his wing. "Do come in."

"Thank you," Calex said, wiping his feet on the mat.

"I've come because Hux told me..."

"Yes, about the job. I hadn't forgotten. I was expecting your visit sooner or later."

Calex looked around and became acquainted with his surroundings. Effarig's house was a cosy, dimly lit abode cluttered with books. The shelves being full, there were a few piles of books on the floor, and cups of tea finished days before could be found about the room. Order was important at the Sacred Heart but it certainly did not extend to the priest's home.

A glowing log crackled in the fireplace. As the evenings were so balmy at the moment, Calex assumed Effarig had lit the fire for the comforting sound and smell.

"How is the old boy?" Effarig asked.

"I'm sorry? Oh, you mean Hux? He's fine, just fine."

"And Pentievra?"

"Very well, too."

Without asking if he had already eaten, Effarig started to reheat some leftover wild boar and roast potatoes. Calex had not skipped Miss Kiberon's lacklustre stew that evening, but he did not see that a second, and much more hearty, dinner could do any harm. He devoured it in front of the fire, chatting with Effarig as he did so. The priest reminisced about the old days while sipping on a glass of local red wine, glad to have the young Crimson's company. Hux had been quite the joker at school, it seemed. Effarig recalled one day when he and his friend got up early to catch butterflies before school, then let them loose in the classroom before the teacher arrived, delighting and frightening the other children in equal measure. Despite having his fun, Hux was a good pupil and rarely got into trouble, clever enough to make the teachers oblivious to his antics. Hux was often the centre of attention and Effarig the quiet one, but they were seldom seen apart. Hux had been his dear friend and Effarig's heart was filled with warmth as he remembered those now-ancient episodes from their schooldays.

Calex had momentarily forgotten why he was even there. Effarig soon reminded him:

"Well, Calex," he said, already fond of the lad. "I'll do everything I can to get you into the Sacred Heart. Posts for auxiliaries crop up every now and then. I promise I'll speak to Mr Zora about you tomorrow."

"Who's Mr Zora?" Calex asked, wiping the gravy from his mouth.

"Fabian Zora is the Chief Officer of the Sacred Heart. A very important man," Calex blushed a little, feeling he should have known that. He had not been particularly interested in politics and who was in charge of what. One reason for this was that as a native of Kinsen he would never be able to vote anyway, not even when he turned eighteen next year. More significantly, the power games between rich kids, as Calex saw it, were no concern of his.

Effarig told Calex a little about the work conditions of auxiliaries. The salary, although fairly low, would at least come from a reliable source, providing him with the security he needed. The job was six days a week but on the positive side, he would have afternoons after one o'clock off every day. Calex's reaction was positive: it did not sound like a bad start for a first job in the city. His plate empty, Calex stood up to clear the table.

"Oh, don't you worry about that," Effarig protested, taking the plates away. "Now, how about some apple crumble?"

Calex's eyes lit up. Dessert was non-existent at Miss Kiberon's boarding house. What a joy it was to be back in the countryside again.

The next morning, Calex woke up late for the first time

in ages. He had no farm to get to, no seeds to sow, no crop to reap. He was as free as a bird, and he had to admit that it felt good. Soon, he hoped, he would be starting his new job but while he could he would enjoy these lie-ins. He stretched his arms and legs, rolled over and fell asleep again, managing to ignore the racket from the street below. He was among the privileged few who had no work to attend to, and he was extremely grateful to be among them. Little did he know, this lie-in would be the only one he would have.

He was finally woken up to the sound of knocking at his door and a high pitched voice squawking "Maro! Calex Maro!" Calex opened his eyes groggily, still stuck in a dream about fruit crumble: peaches, pears, plums, figs were abundant. He rubbed the sleep out of his eyes and found himself in a dingy box with no fruit whatsoever. He stumbled to the door, the lack of the shadow telling him it was midday or later.

"Sleeping into the afternoon?" Miss Kiberon exclaimed, her eyebrows rising up her apple-shaped face. "Aren't you living the life of luxury!"

"I'm surprised myself," Calex said honestly. He waited for his landlady to say something but she simply stood there, her eyebrows not descending a millimetre.

"Yes?" Calex said finally.

"The rent, Maro!" Miss Kiberon exclaimed. "The rent!"

"Ah!" said Calex, and went to find the money. He now had more than enough after receiving his generous pay packet from Hux.

"You didn't think I'd just come to say hello now, did you?" Miss Kiberon snorted.

"Well, that might have been nice." Calex placed the coins in her waiting hand, thinking about how pleasant it would be to have a visitor, someone in the City to just come and ask him how he was. Miss Kiberon stood and counted the coins carefully.

"Very good," Miss Kiberon concluded, making her way towards the stairwell. "By the way, the next rent is due in four days. Let's try and make it on time this month, eh Maro?"

"Of course," Calex said, adding in a near whisper: "Kiberon."

The landlady stopped and turned around. "What did you just say?"

"Miss Kiberon," Calex told her.

"Watch your manners," she retaliated, coming back towards him. "Or I'll not give you this letter."

"What letter?"

"I'd almost forgotten," she said, pulling it out of her pocket. "It arrived for you about fifteen minutes ago."

Calex's heart jolted with excitement. It must have been news from the Sacred Heart. Sensing his enthusiasm, Miss Kiberon held the letter up in the air, out of his reach.

"Next month's rent please, Mr Maro," Miss Kiberon said proudly. Calex sighed, pouring more coins into her free hand.

"Thank you," Calex said, exasperated but relieved to have the letter in his possession. As the door creaked shut behind him, his hands hurriedly opened the letter, letting the envelope fall to the floor as he skimmed through:

Dear Calex Maro,
I spoke with Mr Zora this morning. You're in luck – one of our auxiliaries is leaving this week. Mr Zora says that he will meet you tomorrow and, providing you make a good impression, you can start work right away. I persuaded him to give you a chance despite your unusual background. Please turn up at the Sacred Heart gates at eight o'clock tomorrow morn-

ing.
Best regards,
Effarig Taog
P.S. Enjoy the cherries!

He could barely believe the news. The mission of finding
a job in the city, which had at first seemed so daunting,
had been remarkably easy in the end. Calex was glad he
was to start right away so he would not have the time to
get bored or anxious about his future. Of course the job
was not yet secured, but if all it took was giving a good
impression Calex felt confident he would succeed. He
re-read the letter and frowned when he reached the end.
What was the postscript about the cherries referring to?
Was there a joke or double meaning he was missing?
Calex did not want to spend any more time cooped up
in his tiny bedroom. He trotted down the stairs with
a spring in his step, greeting the neighbours he usually ignored on his way. He passed Miss Kiberon in the
hallway and noticed she was eating something, holding
the stalk to her mouth. Looking through an open door
was her desk and on it he saw a basket of ripe, deep
red cherries. Not wanting to give Miss Kiberon another
reason to hate him, Calex tried to forget about the stolen
gift and walked out into the sunshine.
He began to wander through the busy streets of Quilemoyena City. It was so rare that he found himself able
to stroll aimlessly. This was another privilege of the un-
employed – how lucky they were! There was time to notice the goings-on around him that he usually ignored:
the petty arguments of husbands and wives; the playing of children too young for school; the rushing about
of people heading towards destinations unknown to
Calex, each individual absorbed in his or her own private world. Calex felt like a ghost observing others, neu-

tral and unstressed. In a shop-lined street, a man was having a shirt fitted in the tailor's, a woman was having her hair cut, and a group of maintenance men who worked for the aqueduct were fixing a fountain that was spitting water. A number of people were clearing away the debris of the balcony that had collapsed a couple of days before. Calex soon found himself at his friend Rumel's workshop which she shared with several other professionals of the carpentry and woodwork crafts trade. Calex suddenly sneezed, a reaction to the sawdust abounding in the air.

"Calex!" Rumel exclaimed, putting her chisel to one side. "What are you doing here? Why are you not on the farm?"

"I'll explain at the Lusham Locks tonight," he replied, as if explaining would take a long time. The others looked up from their worktables and, seeing that he was not a customer, looked straight down again. There was one other woman in the workshop, sandpapering a chair that her workmate had just built. It was not unusual to see women working in Quilemoyena City, as in the countryside, but it was fair to say that women with the status of wife and mother were a more common sight. Besides, Rumel's situation was a little different from the norm as she lived with another woman. Such circumstances were not frowned upon as such, but not paraded in the streets either.

Rumel had at least fifteen more statuettes to make before the end of the day, half in upmarket mahogany and half in a cheaper wood from the forests near the city walls. Her list of orders was pinned onto the wall behind her. Judging from the size of the list, business was clearly booming as residents of Quilemoyena City found that the ornaments made suitable gifts as well as decorations for their own homes. As Rumel continued her chiselling, Calex's eyes scanned the shelves which held Rumel's finished work. A well-built lumberjack yielding an axe, a pretty milkmaid milking a cow, a wise professor with a book in his hands: Crimsons seemed to love the models of professionals in action. Which one is me? thought Calex. Which one will I become? Calex contemplated the appeal of these figurines. People liked to see everyone in a role, which reflected their deep-set desire to find a role for themselves. The verb 'to be' was used to describe one's job and therefore was an essential part of who one was. The need to fit in and to find one's place in the world was of prime importance to every Crimson. Calex wondered if everybody became who they were born to be, at least eventually.

"Are you listening to a word I'm saying?"

"Sorry?" Calex said, spinning around.

"I said I'll meet you in the Lusham Locks after dinner."

"That sounds good. See you then."

Calex met up with Drazil and Rumel that evening. This time though, he only had one mug of ale and went to bed early. Tomorrow morning would be important and he wanted to be at his best.

*S*everal nights of little or no sleep were beginning to take their toll on Fabian Zora, yet he was determined to hide his chagrin from the rest of the world. He went to work as usual, making an effort to seem his normal, confident self. Even though he often felt like snapping at his colleagues and being left alone, he knew he had to suppress these feelings. He must act as though nothing had changed. When Fabian left the Sacred Heart every day, he sank away into the darkness of his bedroom. There, he would mope around, read, sleep and think. The thinking part was involuntary. He would have been much happier if he were blissfully unaware of the recent misfortune that had invaded his life. Still, he had bought his ticket for the boat journey to Serenah where he would relax at his seaside villa. He was counting down the days until the date shown on the ticket which gave him something to look forward to. The ticket sat on his bedside table, and the simple act of looking at it made him feel better. However, there was another ticket which he kept out of sight. This was the return journey back to Quilemoyena, which he frequently had to stop himself from tearing up and throwing in the bin. Zora had shown his face in public to maintain a sense of normality in his life, and to prevent anyone from thinking something was wrong. He swam, worked out and received massages at the bathhouse, he attended the dinner parties of the ministers he could stand, and he made his presence known at the theatre. Yet he had little motivation for these activities. He simply wanted the solitude and oblivion of his dark bedroom. This had been going on for several days. Fabian had started to wonder how long he could keep up the act.

He presently found himself in his office at the Sacred Heart, facing a fresh-faced young man referred to him by one of the priests. This Calex Maro was clearly trying to make a good impression. Fabian found it difficult to echo his friendliness and enthusiasm. He really did not feel like showing this lad the grounds and introducing him to the job.

"I see no reason why you shouldn't start right away," Fabian declared after asking Calex about his past. It was certainly an eyebrow-raising one. Fabian did not really feel comfortable with the unusual relationship the boy had with Violets and the countryside but he couldn't be bothered to be fussy. He would have preferred an ordinary boy who was Quilemoyena born and bred but Calex would have to do. At least he was polite and seemed able to follow instructions. Plus he was used to active work. Auxiliaries had to accompany the sacrifices up the volcano, day in and day out. That required physical fitness and after years of farm labour, Calex certainly was up to it.

"I think the work here will suit you," Zora added.

"It is not work, sir, it is a great honour," gushed Calex, thinking that perhaps he was taking his enthusiasm a little too far.

Fabian Zora clapped his hands together and stood up. "Now, if you would like to follow me," he announced. "I'll give you a brief tour."

Calex was genuinely excited about this part. The Sacred Heart, behind its high-set brick walls, was not seen by ordinary people but its beauty was renowned by all. He followed his boss to a small, dark room. As they entered, he noticed a small bath and racks full of shoes. Fabian explained that everyone – officers, priests and auxiliaries – had to remove their footwear and wash their feet before entering the courtyard as the grounds were sacred. Calex's realised that this meant walking up the volcano, which was surely fairly rocky, barefoot. Fabian told him that he would get used to it and said that he would soon be rewarded by a pair of extremely tough feet that could walk on any surface. Calex slipped off his worn leather sandals while his boss removed his elegantly long suede boots. On catching a glimpse of Fabian's tough-soled feet, Calex could see what he meant. Both of them placed their shoes on the rack and proceeded to wash and dry their feet.

They then continued through the corridor which gave way to a hall. Calex smiled with pleasure when he saw the impressive fountain in the middle, whose waters were spurting out of four stone deers' mouths. They walked towards the great wooden doors, which were opened by two auxiliaries as they approached. Sunlight burst into the hall and Fabian and Calex walked through.

The view was nothing less than incredible. Calex had never seen a place so pristine and orderly in his life, not to mention splendid. Marble reliefs lined the wall, depicting scenes from Quilemoyena's history. Calex was delighted to see a depiction of Allirog Redips on his boat, with silver and sapphire detail for the waves. Another relief featured the goddess Quil rising from the sea, her wavy tresses cast in solid gold. Other reliefs depicted scenes that Calex recognised from the history of the island by the poet Suma. Every child – even those from Kinsen – had read the famous book at school. There were many statues as well for Calex to feast his eyes on, mostly depicting the three holy sisters: Quil, Emo and Yena. Gods not associated with the island of Quilemoyena were also depicted albeit less prominently. For example, Lusham, the protector of the Geshtin Fields was portrayed on the wall in relief with encrusted rubies for his long red hair.

"Hardly anybody has the pleasure of witnessing these beautiful works of art," Calex observed in wonder.

"They are not for people to ogle at," responded Fabian. "They are in honour of the goddesses." Although charmed by these luxurious creations, Calex thought of the taxes that went to pay for them. He could not help but think that the money would be better spent elsewhere, such as on making the streets of Quilemoyena safer.

All these statues stood on the mosaic-floored courtyard that was bisected by a path made of marble. This path, which was covered by a red carpet, led up to the base of the volcano. Calex's eyes looked up to its summit, which was around two hundred metres higher than the ground where he stood. The top of the volcano could be seen all over the island, even when it was just a dot in the distance.

Fabian led Calex to the left side of the courtyard where there was a large circular table made of dark, polished wood. This was the Table of Choice. On the surface of this table was inscribed a map of the Quilemoyenan countryside divided into Sectors. A ball was thrown out onto the table every morning by the priests. Where the ball stopped was where ten sacrifices would be taken from. It was the officers' job to go to that place in the morning and bring the first ten Violets they came across back to the Sacred Heart. Here they would be sacrificed at midday when the sun was directly overhead.

A young priest-in-training appeared to the side of Fabian and informed him that the priests were ready to use the table. When the priests cast the ball, the whole area had to be cleared as they needed total peace and concentration to connect with the goddesses and to be driven by divine influence. Fabian led Calex out of the courtyard.

Calex passed the three priests as he walked through the doors, and recognised one of them as Effarig. Calex wanted to stop and thank him for his help in getting the job but he knew this was not the right time. Instead, he gave the priest a warm smile and Effarig winked back.

"And what will my job be, sir?" Calex asked as they walked down the corridor. His new boss seemed distracted and not particularly interested in talking to him. He explained, briefly and vaguely, that as an auxiliary, Calex would be among those whose job it was to keep the courtyard immaculately clean. He would have to polish the artworks and the floor. When the priests came out to use the Table of Choice, he would go inside to pray until the sacrifices arrived. When they did, he would escort them up the volcano for the final walk. Every sacrifice received his own escort.

"How long does the final walk take?" Calex enquired. Fabian told him that this walk from the base to the crater would take about fifteen minutes, depending on the pace of the sacrifice. In general, he explained, the older they were the slower they walked. The final prayer began when all ten sacrifices were at the top and in position around the crater.

They were now back at the door to Fabian's office. "Well, that's the important part covered," Fabian said, concluding their meeting. "Get to the Prayer Room at eight tomorrow morning." He passed Calex a scroll. "Everything you need to know about this job is written there. Read it well before tomorrow."

Calex bade his new boss goodbye and turned to leave.

"Oh, don't forget your shoes," noted Fabian as he disappeared into his office.

Calex slipped on his leather sandals and walked towards the front door. He almost sighed aloud as he looked at the meaningless symbols on the scroll. Calex had never got to grips with the Ekans alphabet, the traditional alphabet of Quilemoyena. Nowadays, people tended to use the standard alphabet of the region, the Kreen, which was also used in Kinsen alongside their own traditional alphabet. Calex could read his mother tongue in Kreen script, as well as the Quilemoyenan language thanks to the help of Hux and Pentievra. The Ekans alphabet was employed less often nowadays for reasons of practicality. It featured a mass of complex symbols, owing to the fact that combinations of different letters had their own characters, and it took years to master. It was not surprising, however, that an official document like this would use it. In the local bookshops, there were nowadays as many books written in the Kreen script as there were written in the Ekans script. Many of Quilemoyena City's residents, especially the older ones, sneered at this fact. They felt that the Ekans alphabet was an exclusive, traditional element of the island that distinguished it from others. They would nostalgically reminisce about an earlier time when all books were written with the Ekans alphabet. The people who defended the Ekans alphabet tended to be the sort of people who frowned upon Calex. They were the patriotic and chauvinistic types, and many of them, rather ironically, didn't know how to read the Ekans alphabet themselves. The elaborate system featured twenty symbols for different vowel sounds, and these vowel symbols were fused with consonant symbols in a huge amount of combinations.

There were, therefore, other people who argued that adapting to overseas trends and using the Kreen alphabet was necessary for Quilemoyena to move ahead in the modern world. There was another camp of people who mourned the slow death of the Ekans alphabet but were secretly relieved about its demise for reasons of practicality. The conflicting feelings of national pride and the desire for convenience sat uneasily together.

For Calex, who had not received any formal education since he arrived in Quilemoyena, these squiggles meant nothing. It wasn't too late for Calex to learn to read the alphabet, of course, but how could he possibly manage that before tomorrow? He found it surprising that neither the priest Effarig Taog nor Fabian Zora had thought to ask. If they had brought it up he would have told the truth, even if it had cost him the job. But it seemed that as he had come this far it would be a shame to confess he wasn't able to read the Ekans alphabet and find himself jobless and back at square one again.

After the day's ceremony had come to an end, Fabian had to leave for a government meeting. The Assembly Hall was not far away but he went there by carriage nonetheless. He had time for a hearty lunch beforehand in a nearby restaurant: grilled steak with peppercorn sauce and a slice of caramelised apple and carrowbean tart, all washed down with a large glass of red wine from Serenah. The meeting was to be on the renovation of certain temples in the countryside and the financial concerns surrounding the issue. Many ministers and political figures were arriving, especially those in posts linked to religion and architecture. Some simply came out of interest but Fabian Zora was obliged to attend. Also present were many priests, which meant that the Assembly Hall was in the rare position of housing both Crimsons and Violets. The central space where speeches were given was surrounded by ascending seating. Fabian sat towards the back where he could daydream without anyone noticing.

The massive amphitheatre steadily filled up to maximum capacity and the chatter died down as a priestess stepped onto the podium to start the proceedings. As his eyes wandered around the hall, Fabian noticed that the Minister of the Water System, Esroh Tiger, was there. He was looking smug, giving little waves to people he knew and showing off how well-connected he was. Why in the name of the gods was he at this meeting? And what was that dreadful cape he was wearing? Fabian squinted and saw that it was made from... tiger fur! How pathetic! That cape must have cost a small fortune as tigers were only known to live on the island of Rosenbale, over two thousand kilometres from Quilemoyena. How it annoyed Fabian that the young politician relied on these cheap gimmicks to win him popularity! That wealthy, arrogant pig had everyone eating out of his hand. Fabian's stomach flipped at the idea that Tiger could end up as President within a decade. As much as it pained him to think about it, things certainly seemed to be heading that way. In spite of his condescending attitude towards him, Fabian found that he could not take his eyes of the fellow. The young man's presence was simply captivating. Not that Tiger was especially handsome or even interesting to look at. He just had so much magnetic charisma that everyone he spoke to felt like they were being addressed by some sort of demi-god. Despite looking at him from a distance, Fabian saw the light in that kid's eyes: eyes that anticipated a bright future which he approached without care or fear. Did that same light emanate from Fabian's own hazelnut-brown eyes once? Either he had lost something or it was not there in the first place but this Fabian could never know. Suddenly, Fabian realised that Tiger's luminous eyes were looking into his own, that friendly smile on his face aimed at him! In reflex, Fabian averted his gaze, a little embarrassed that Tiger would know that he too could not help noticing his presence. A few seconds later, an explosion of laughter came from Tiger's direction. Fabian froze – were they laughing at him? No, he realised, Tiger was just being himself with his superb social skills: impressing people with his insight, charming them with his wit, saying the right thing at the right moment, and throwing them into the clutches of joyful laughter. It dawned on Fabian that the tiger-fur cape was not an ostentatious show of wealth after all. It was merely an ironic gesture: Tiger was gently mocking himself and everyone had understood this except for Fabian. His joke was irreverent and fun, demonstrating a refreshing absence of the self-seriousness that one would expect from a young politician. And then, it hit Fabian like a lightning bolt: everybody loved Esroh Tiger and that is why he could not stand him. The boy had a gift with people, and what a gift! Tiger was popular and (as much as Fabian did not want to admit it) likeable and easy-going. His annoyance had given way to aching jealousy. The insecurity he had barely given thought to before had been unearthed.

In a state of utter depression, Fabian sought solace in the anticipation of his holiday. As the priestess droned on, he pictured his villa in Serenah, his own personal paradise. He saw himself on the ferryboat, the wind ruffling his hair. Then he saw the land approaching, and those sweet, familiar fruit trees. Fabian sighed and closed his eyes, not letting them open for a very long time.

Chapter
TEN

Feeling pleased about starting his new job in the morning, Calex decided to indulge himself that afternoon. His newfound sense of security gave him a warm feeling of wellbeing as he walked the short distance to the Riverside Bathhouse. He paid two five demarit coins at the entrance and stepped through the door for the men's baths, while the women entered through the other door leading to their quarter of the bathhouse. In the changing room, Calex undressed and left his belongings on one of the shelves which were guarded by the bathhouse staff. Security was not guaranteed but Calex was not worried: the bathhouse's clientele were mainly affluent and Calex did not really have anything worth stealing anyway. He walked out into the main hall and was greeted by one of the most stunning views in Quilemoyena. The mosaics that adorned the high walls and floor were one thing, but the glass dome ceiling was like nothing else Calex had even seen before. (Glass was a fairly recent invention and was in short supply). It was not Calex's first glimpse at this marvellous architecture, but it never failed to impress him every time he saw it. The large swimming pool occupied the main hall but was of little interest to Calex. He disliked swimming and always avoided the pool, for reasons he did not care to contemplate. Around the pool were many different tubs which exploited the island's natural hot springs. The hottest was at forty-five degrees Celsius: unfiltered spring water straight from the depths of the earth. It was impossible for most people to stay in there for more than a couple of minutes and they always came out looking as red as lobsters. Other tubs were at forty, thirty-eight, thirty-five and thirty-two degrees. After soaking in these hot tubs, it was common to take a dip in the tub at nineteen degrees for a shocking sensation swiftly followed by a sense of well-being. The Jacuzzi tubs, both hot and cold, forced water out of several holes, providing a sort of massage for those inside it. The 'herbal tubs' were filled respectively with tea leaves (brown), rosemary (green) and carrowbeans (red). Bathing in these tubs was said to be good for the skin, the saltwater bath likewise. Finally in the main hall there was an area where water fell from a great height, landing on the backs of people underneath and creating a powerful massage.

A wide and graceful marble staircase led up to a second floor where one could find a variety of saunas. The temperatures of these varied from fifty to seventy-five degrees Celsius and staff ensured that these temperatures remained constant. There was even the 'Arts Sauna' where a member of the bathhouse staff recited poetry. Chatting was permitted in all these saunas, except for the 'Silent Sauna'. There was also a large steam room and an 'Ice Room' which was currently closed to the public. During winter when ice was available, the shelves were filled with ice and people could relax in the nude in freezing conditions. In the relaxation rooms, people could sleep or read a book from among the many on the shelves. One of these rooms had small bags of carrowbeans hanging from the ceiling, and the other had sprigs of thyme, creating pleasant, refreshing aromas. In the 'exfoliation area', the common oil scraping ritual was being practised and massages were also provided, as well as shaves, haircuts, and hair removal by plucking. Finally, a café where tea, bread and cakes were served ensured that one could stay in the bathhouse for hours. It was indeed possible to arrive at six in the morning and leave at eleven at night and Calex had done this on a number of occasions himself.

"I don't know which is hotter," said a voice that made Calex look up, "in here or outside." Calex acknowledged the comment with a nod, searching for a witty response but finding none. The heat was melting his brain. "Been in here for long?" the young man asked him.

"Don't know, don't care," Calex said amicably. Now it was the other's turn to smile in agreement. He sat down next to Calex on the wooden bench and a bathhouse worker came in and tossed a wooden ladleful of water onto the coal. The temperature suddenly shot up and Calex exhaled slowly as new beads of sweat replaced the old ones.

"I'm Elidocorc," the young man said, reaching out a hand which Calex shook. He was not used to strangers making conversation; it was not the way in Quilemoyena City. He was pleasantly surprised by the friendliness of this fellow who seemed to be a few years older than himself and wore a permanent smile on his face.

"I'm Calex," Calex said.

"From?"

"I'm from Kinsen."

"I knew it! You've got the look."

"Really?" Calex said, genuinely surprised. Nobody had ever said that before, although maybe people often thought it and this Elidocorc certainly seemed more open than the average resident of Quilemoyena City. Calex was pleased that Elidocorc did not press on with his questions as he hated to talk about his past. For others, it was just small talk but for him, it was the greatest source of misery that he knew. Calex was happy to listen to other people's stories however. Elidocorc explained that he lived with his parents and younger brother and sister by the banks of the River Emo, five minutes' walk from the bathhouse.

"I can't wait to get my own place," Elidocorc complained. "My parents drive me up the wall. Always hassling me... do this, do that. It isn't enough that I make an honest living, I have to work for them too. You know what I mean, right?"

"Sure, I know what you mean," Calex shrugged.

"So, do you have bathhouses in Kinsen?"

"Of course," Calex said with a grin. "We're not savages, you know."

"I don't know much about Kinsen," Elidocorc admitted. Of course, thought Calex, Quilemoyenans don't know much about anything except Quilemoyena. Their pompous 'centre of the world' mentality meant that they often forgot that other lands even existed and they certainly knew nothing about foreigners' ways and customs. To put it simply, it was the national attitude to think that Quilemoyena was the best and other islands were backward and undeveloped. This outlook annoyed Calex but amused him sometimes as well. Occasionally he met another foreigner, and they could talk about it, but for the most part Calex let Quilemoyenans go about their ignorant ways and he kept his thoughts to himself. "So, what's Kinsen like?" Elidocorc said, and Calex smiled, finding him naive but endearing.

We make soap, and it's a whole lot faster and more practical for cleaning yourself than that oil scraping method you lot use! This is what Calex wanted to say, but he resisted the temptation.

"It's a very flat country, farmland mainly. It rains a lot..."

"You're not really selling it," Elidocorc interrupted.

Calex shrugged. "Well, it's just... home."

He surprised himself with this last comment. He had not thought of Kinsen in that way for a long time. There was little of interest on the island. The weather was often dark and wet, the food bland, and even the national musical instrument, the Bikoflay, sounded like the screech of a cat whose tail had just been stood on.

He hoped Elidocorc would not ask him any more questions although it seemed inevitable. To his relief, however, Elidocorc changed the subject: "I'm supposed to be meeting a girl tonight," he said with an element of boastfulness. "That's why I'm here. I want to look my best."

"Where are you taking her?" Calex asked, his green eyes twinkling.

"Just for a mug of ale or two," Elidocorc replied. "What about you? Have you got a special lady in your life?"

Calex blushed. "Not really. Well, I have met a girl, actually." His heart started to pound. Hero, the mysterious redhead. It was only two days since he had met her but it felt like too long. He had not spoken of his secret crush (if that was indeed what it was quickly becoming) to anybody, nor of the events of when they met. And here he was telling this stranger. This Elidocorc certainly had a knack for making him open up.

"She's... got a baby." That was the first thing he decided to say about her. After all, it was the point about her that he found the most unusual and troubling. Of course, this was topped by the fact that the baby was of mixed-blood, the derogatory term for which was brownborn, but he certainly was not going to share that with Elidocorc. Calex sighed – he knew very well that she was an unsuitable candidate for a girlfriend.

"She sounds like bad news," came Elidocorc's response. "I wouldn't get involved with her if I were you."

"It's too late," Calex said dreamily. "I want to see her so badly."

"What's stopping you?"

"I don't want to look too keen. I've decided to go and see her in a day or two."

"Have you kissed her yet?"

"Hey, come on!" Calex laughed, his face reddening even more in the heat of the sauna. "Enough of these questions! I just don't want to dwell on her too much. I'm supposed to have other things on my mind at the moment."

"Like?"

"Like my new job. I'm starting tomorrow."

"Really?"

Calex nodded. "I'm pretty nervous about it."

"So what's the job?"

"Well, it's at the Sacred Heart," Calex said tentatively. He still felt uneasy with the idea of working there. Despite his efforts to get used to it, he wasn't yet entirely comfortable with the sacrificing of Violets. It was harder for him than most Crimsons as he had lived and worked with members of the Violet race. Although it was far from being against their will, he couldn't shake off the feeling that escorting them to their deaths would be traumatic for him.

"I'll be an auxiliary," he added.

"That's what I do" Elidocorc blurted out, startling Calex. "I'm an auxiliary at the Sacred Heart too!"

"What a coincidence! Isn't that strange?"

"Yes," said Elidocorc, shaking his head disbelievingly. "I suppose it is!"

Calex relaxed into the heat and his wooden seat. So here was yet another friendly face to greet him in the morning. He felt more comfortable than ever about the new job and let himself doze off for a while, till his head was perfectly clear and empty of thought.

Chapter
ELEVEN

Calex awoke the next morning determined that his first day of work at the Sacred Heart would go well. Get to the Prayer Room for eight, Mr Zora had said, although he had neglected to tell Calex where exactly that was. By the time Calex worked out where to find the Prayer Room, he was the last of the auxiliaries to arrive and his confidence was immediately knocked. He was kicking himself for turning up late, if only by a couple of minutes, recalling that one of the farmhands at Tinklegrove had once told that turning up on time was most of what there was to a job.

The room was mostly bare and, thankfully, dimly lit. The auxiliaries, all Crimsons like Calex, sat crossed-legged in a circle on straw mats, waiting for the Violet priest or priestess to arrive. Calex mumbled a shy, self-conscious introduction and felt many eyes scrutinising him as he awkwardly sat down next to the now fully-clothed Elidocorc. He was grateful to see his friendly face again. After a minute or two talking to the young man he met in the bathhouse, Calex regained a little of his confidence.

To his relief, Elidocorc told him about many of the procedures without him even having to ask. The Chief Officer did not seem to have much time or patience for him the day before and there were many things that Calex felt unsure about. His goal for the day was to not draw attention to himself by doing things incorrectly, and it seemed that Elidocorc would make achieving this a lot easier. The experienced auxiliary explained how they took it in turns to read aloud a prayer every morning, in the Ekans alphabet of course. Calex seized up, wondering how he would find an excuse when it was his turn. Over dinner the night before, Calex had tried to get some tips from the others in the boarding house. Unsurprisingly, he couldn't find anyone who seemed to want to help.

Calex's confidence had been going up and down constantly but now his optimism was hanging by a thread. The sense of enthusiasm he had woken up with that morning was quickly trickling away, like milk in a hole-ridden bucket.

Who am I kidding? he thought to himself, He had made himself out to be an intensely pious young man whose dream had come true in getting to work at the Sacred Heart. The real Calex was indifferent at most to religion, and praying and cleaning were certainly not his favourite things in life.

How long can I keep up this act? he thought.

He wondered how he would react when the sacrifices made their jump into the volcano. The idea of it certainly seemed both repugnant and frightening. On a positive note, the job would pay his rent until something better came along or until he figured out what he really wanted to do. That is unless he got sacked for not being able to read the Ekans alphabet, of course.

This is ridiculous, thought Calex. What am I even doing

here?

A priestess arrived in her red robes and round hat. She held a large book in her hands, protected by a thick, hard cover. The auxiliaries stopped chatting immediately and got to their feet.

"Good morning," she greeted them, gesturing for them to sit back down. Then she turned to Calex. "Cherissné," she greeted him. Mr Zora had obviously told the priestess there was a new auxiliary from Kinsen and she wanted to show off her rudimentary knowledge of the language.

Calex smiled and blushed in the same instant, his eyes darting straight to the floor.

"Nice to meet you too," he slurred, speaking to the straw mat. He had been hoping to conceal the fact he was different – foreign that is – but now everyone knew. A few eyes looked at him again, considering where he was from. Only one of them recognised the language.

"You're from Kinsen?" asked an auxiliary next to him under her breath.

Calex nodded sheepishly in response.

"My name is Lee Retsbol," said the priestess to the newcomer, "You will meet all of us priests and priestesses over the next few days, I have no doubt. Now, a prayer." The priestess handed the heavy book to Elidocorc. "Number 61," she told him. Elidocorc opened the book three quarters of the way through then flicked through a few pages to find the right poem. He then cleared his throat and read aloud with the gravitas of a celebrated actor:

A Violet's heart beats strong and fast
To hear the bells arrive at last
Onto the cart to not return
His mortal shell to surely burn

Through the gates of the Sacred Heart
The blessed end to every start
His purpose he shall now fulfil
When sacred blood shall flow and spill
They are the grass, the sea, the sky
For these things they were born to die

The other auxiliaries joined in with the last two lines as they were the same for every poem. Calex mumbled along with them. So theatrical was Elidocorc's 'performance' of the poem that Calex wondered if he should clap.

As they walked out into the courtyard, the priestess told Calex that he would be sweeping the red carpet today, and if he did it well he would soon be allowed to polish the Table of Choice. Calex got the impression this was something he was supposed to feel excited about, and responded accordingly. The work began and the auxiliaries applied themselves to their tasks. The manual labour that Calex had done before was out in the fresh air and lush green of the countryside. The success of his work contributed to the livelihood of Hux and Pentievra, whom he cared about. Here in the city, the work had no interest for him at all. He daydreamed his way through the cleaning task, thinking of the myths depicted in the artworks surrounding him. Calex looked dubiously at the carpet he had swept, wondering if it was actually dirtier now than it had been before. He seemed to be brushing bits of grit and dirt around rather than away from the carpet. How could cleaning be so difficult? He thought it was supposed to be something anyone could do.

Noon arrived soon enough and the gates opened to let in the horse-driven carriage. The auxiliaries gathered by the gates together as it entered, hearing the bells bouncing on the horses' reins.

"Here they come," Elidocorc pointed out to Calex. "Try not to look surprised, okay?"

Calex had every intention of blending in but could not hide his sense of fascination as he watched the unfamiliar scene of the ten Violet men and women getting out of the carriage; some laughing, some crying with overflowing emotion. One of the sacrifices insisted on shaking the hand of everyone he saw, another kissed Calex's cheek then fell down to her knees before him. Calex gasped and instinctively took a step back.

"Just stay calm and professional," Elidocorc said to Calex discreetly. "You'll get used to it."

Two serious-looking officers were also dismounting the cart and they went over to join Fabian. He too was in the courtyard for the ritual but his mind was elsewhere. His thoughts had begun to wander to his wife and the baby again and he felt heavy with sadness.

The auxiliaries paired up with the sacrifices, choosing whoever was closest. Calex found himself with a middle-aged woman who seemed quiet and reserved. Apparently, the sacrifices had different ways of appreciating the last moments of their lives. Calex smiled nervously and she gave an equally shy smile back. He picked up on the fact that talking was permitted between the pairs of sacrifices and auxiliaries but he was certainly content to continue in silence. A small band of musicians had appeared and they began to play. At first, the music seemed solemn and stately and held no interest for Calex. Soon though, the violinist being to play a bittersweet melody and Calex looked over to the musicians and felt quite moved. He thought it was only right to make the occasion special for these people.

The procession began, the priestess Lee Retsbol leading the way up the volcano and the pairs - sacrifice and auxiliary - walking one behind the other. He noticed that a few of the sacrifices were holding hands with or had their arm around the auxiliary who was escorting them. He was pleased that his Violet woman - his sacrifice - was more reserved. For his first day it would be perfect. Then soon after they left the carpet and were walking up the rocky path, everything went terribly wrong. Calex received a heart-stopping blow in the place where it hurt the most. He shrieked despite himself and fell down, consumed by an incredible pain. It was several seconds before he realised what had just happened. The perpetrator of the attack, his sacrifice, had left his side and was heading fast towards the gates.

"Stop her!" Fabian Zora shouted to his officers, but they were unprepared for such an event. The sacrifices being willing, they never had the need to carry weapons. The Violet woman banged with all her strength against the gate that had been locked and bolted. She screamed frantically for it to be opened but the guards caught her and dragged her away while she wailed and kicked like an animal. Everybody in the courtyard had stopped and was staring at the spectacle. Fabian gestured to the priestess to continue the ceremony without the woman. It was important that the sacrifice took place at the same time every day, or as close as possible, and noon was approaching fast. The priestess, auxiliaries and other sacrifices carried on the final walk to the crater as Calex still lay on the ground recovering from his injury.

Fabian had gone over to speak to the woman and the two officers joined him, unsure of how they would protect him or each other. Calex, who had been completely ignored, pulled himself to his feet and joined the onlookers. The Chief officer opened his mouth to speak but it was the woman, held still by the two guards, who spoke first.

"Curse you and your institution of murder!" she growled. "My children will return home from school today to find their mother has gone forever! I didn't even get to say goodbye!"

Fabian was speechless. He was instantly reminded of the similar event with the teenage boy, Elias String. Fabian could hardly believe it; the nightmare seemed to be repeating itself. Lightning was indeed striking twice. Fabian had been so certain that he was making the right decision when he sent Elias String to his death. He felt that he was just following the rules. But now, he was not so sure. After all the guilt that he had felt over Elias String, things were not so black and white any more. Or not so Crimson and Violet, came the voice of irony in Fabian's mind.

He made an attempt to use Violet reasoning with her: "You have been selected today as a sacrifice," he told her. "This is a wonderful blessing."

The woman spat at him fiercely, her bad aim landing on his left foot. Fabian had never been spat at before in his life and never thought it would be something he would have to deal with. Was he losing his grip?

"W…Why don't you want to take part in this ceremony?" Fabian said.

"I want to live," the woman said. The Chief Officer took a deep, troubled breath. These were exactly the same words that Elias String had used. The officers noticed this too and gave each other fearful, knowing looks.

The woman started to sob. "I want to go back home," she pleaded. "Just let me out of those gates and you'll never hear anything from me ever again! I'd act as if nothing had ever happened."

She could continue her life in peace and Fabian would never have to think about her again. It was a deceptively simple solution. But the logical side of Fabian's brain told him something else. It reasoned that she could not be trusted to keep her mouth shut. More likely than not, she would talk to other Violets and cause trouble. What would they say? Maybe they would laugh at her but maybe, just maybe, they would take her seriously. Fabian could see this leading to something terrible: an uprising of Violets against sacrifice. Uprising. The word struck terror into the Chief Officer's heart.

True racial hatred between Crimsons and Violets that had never existed before because everybody accepted his or her role. Quilemoyena had not known war for hundreds of years. It was in no way prepared for public unrest. The city and countryside had justice systems overseen by the government, but there was nothing like a military with trained soldiers, not anymore. There was tales of violent warfare in faraway lands; armies that fought on battlefields for their leaders who craved power. Crimson and Violet blood had even been shed in this fashion on the island of Quilemoyena, but that was all hundreds of years ago. Those times were long before the modern, civilised world with its aqueducts, sewerage system and bathhouses. Long past were the days of fighting for rulership and the need for an army. Quilemoyena's political system had been in place for as long as anyone could remember. The minor problems that arose were dealt with in governmental meetings. Why, there was no need for violence in this day and age! This was a time of peace that felt to every Crimson and Violet like it would last forever.

Fabian needed a second opinion, a different perspective. The priestess Lee was standing with Effarig, who had come out into the courtyard on hearing the commotion. Fabian headed over to them to talk quietly.

Effarig sighed. "We need to stub out this problem before it can grow." Lee nodded her agreement beside him.

"That means?"

"That means you can't let her go," Effarig said regretfully.

"So what you're saying is we should force her to jump? Like Elias String?"

Effarig swallowed hard when he was reminded of that boy's name. "Give her a choice," he said. "Either she can jump into the volcano of her own accord or we kill her ourselves. I hope she chooses the former."

"In any case," added Lee, "we're running out of time."

"But we're not murderers," Fabian said with horror. "That's not what we do here at the Sacred Heart. It's not who we are."

"Of course it's not," said Effarig. "But it's either that or unleashing chaos. As the Chief Officer, the ultimate decision lies with you, though."

"These difficult choices are what being in charge is about," Lee quipped.

Was there a hint of contempt in her voice? Fabian recognised that Lee was deliberately patronising him. And yet, he knew how his situation must seem to others. He had been born into privilege and so far his role as the most senior figure at the Sacred Heart had been about the prestige, salary and status. Now Fabian had to learn the burden of the job, behind all the perks. It was to make the decisions that no one else wanted to make, to feel the weight of responsibility that others would rather pass on to someone else.

Fabian saw the hope in the Violet woman's face. She thought she stood a chance and Fabian could barely look her in the eyes.

"Look, you are going to have to... die today," he said, trying to conceal to her and his staff that he was out of his depth. "Either the way it was intended by tradition or by our hand. It's up to you."

Good, thought Fabian, give her a choice, some ownership of the decision.

But it didn't seem to help. The woman started crying again: desperate sobs that the onlookers could not bear to witness.

Suddenly, a voice cried out: "She's got a knife!"

Fabian's heart stopped beating as he watched the knife hurtling towards him, aimed at his chest. His reflexes sprung to action and he whacked the woman's arm aside in the nick of time. The weapon fell down on the mosaic floor and Fabian grabbed it before she could. Within an instant, the woman's hands were clamped around his thick neck, her thumbs digging into his throat and crushing his windpipe. Fabian choked violently but he managed to push her away from him without much effort. The officers held her back and a string of curses erupted from her mouth while Fabian gasped to get his breath back, staggering to his feet.

"There's no time left!" Effarig said desperately. "Do it, Fabian. Do it quickly. Get it over with!"

The hand that held the knife was shaking uncontrollably. Fabian felt so awful at that moment. He would have preferred to put the knife to his own throat.

"No!" screamed the Violet woman, held in place by two officers. One of them pulled back her hair with his spare hand, exposing her neck to the blade.

The rational part of Fabian's brain was dictating to him again. You know what you have to do, it said without a shred of emotion, it's your job. Rather clumsily, he slit the woman's throat. Violet blood spurted out in a shower, with a force that surprised everyone who witnessed it. It fell on Fabian's tunic and the courtyard around him and continued to flow from the wound after the initial burst, quickly staining the mosaic floor a bright, startling shade of blue. Gasps of horror erupted and then an eerie silence fell as the officers and priests hung their heads. The woman had died almost instantly, crumpling to the ground unconscious, which offered Fabian a tiny amount of consolation in the face of the wretchedness he was feeling.

They would need to throw the dead woman's body over the crater of the volcano straight away. A Violet's blood was of little use unless it was fresh. The moment that life left the body, blood started to quickly deteriorate, losing the properties that made it so precious. The volume of blood required for the day had not been attained so it was sure that the planet would surely suffer over the next few days: flowers would wilt, rivers would lessen in volume, leaves would be a paler shade of green. The priests and officers would have to join together to pray for forgiveness for this. They hoped the goddesses would be lenient.

Feeling as disgusted as Fabian, the two officers tied a cloth around the woman's neck, stopping any more blood from escaping. One of them tried to soak some of the fallen blood into her clothes.

"Oh stop it, you idiot," said the other, losing his patience, "We don't have time for that."

The other officer lost his cool too. "This is disgusting," he exclaimed. "I can't do it."

"For goodness sake!" Fabian scolded them. "Pull yourselves together and get moving."

They obeyed, lifted the body up onto their shoulders and began the walk up to the summit where they would join the auxiliaries and priestess who were still there.

Fabian spoke sternly to the small congregation of priests in the courtyard. A pair of officers who had been inside the building on archiving duties had emerged to see what the commotion was about. Fabian didn't look happy to see them.

"All of you, listen to me. You will continue to carry out your duties as usual and you will not, under any circumstances, mention what happened today to anyone outside these walls. If I find that anyone has gone against my orders, his dismissal from the Sacred Heart will be the least of his worries. Is that understood?"

"Yes sir," they chorused solemnly. As the workers began to disperse, the Chief Officer looked to the crater of the volcano, where the auxiliaries still were, including his newest recruit.

"One last thing," he said to his staff. "When Calex Maro gets back down here, send him to see me straight away." And with that, Fabian Zora retired to his office.

Chapter
TWELVE

Elias String: that was all Fabian Zora could think about. How could he ever forget what had happened, so similar to what had happened today? Violet sacrifices who were unwilling to go to their deaths.

The memories of that day came back to Fabian Zora in the aftermath of another traumatic episode at the Sacred Heart. The similarities were startling. He hastily removed his tunic which was splattered with Violet blood. The feeling of nausea felt sharper than ever and his heart was thudding. Covering his mouth with his hand, he hoped that he would not be sick. He sat back in his chair and took deep breaths. It was impossible not to relive the day's events, the memories lucid and horrible. What was the reason behind that woman's reluctance? Was there any link between her and Elias String? Did the gods have anything to do with this? Only one thing was clear: Fabian Zora had a big problem.

And as if his life couldn't get any more difficult, he now had blood on his hands. He had never thought that he would kill another human being.

The knock at the door he had been expecting arrived soon enough. He quickly slipped into the spare tunic that he kept in the cupboard and wiped his face, regaining his professional demeanour.

The door opened. "You wanted to speak with me, sir?" Calex said, his voice anxious.

"Yes, I did" Fabian confirmed. "First of all, how was your first day?"

Calex was momentarily lost for words. He could hardly answer this question truthfully. It had been a traumatic shambles and nothing seemed worse than having to come back the following morning. He had just witnessed a violent murder which is definitely not what he had signed up for when he accepted the job. As well as this, he was still in a considerable amount of pain from the kick he received earlier, which nobody at all had bothered to ask him about, much to his frustration.

"It was great," Calex forced himself to say. "As I said, Mr Zora, it's a great honour for me to work here."

"You heard what I said, didn't you?" his boss jumped in. "It's very important that you don't mention what you witnessed to anyone. The others know how important this is but you're new and I just wanted to check that was clear. Can I trust you, Calex?"

"Of course, sir," Calex said, brushing a lock of hair behind his ear. As he did so, Fabian noticed the ring on his finger. It had not moved since Calex put it on several days before. He had considered what to do with it. Pawning it would be his preference but he was worried that Hero would change her mind and want it back.

"Where did you get that ring?" Fabian demanded.

"I found it," Calex lied quickly.

"I could swear..." Fabian grabbed Calex's hand and gazed at the ruby-encrusted ring. It could be another, of course, but it might just have been Hero's wedding ring.

Calex may well have found it in the street if she had angrily tossed it away that night. It would be a sheer co-incidence but not impossible. Calex, meanwhile, could not understand why Zora was acting so oddly. He wait-ed for his boss to give him back his hand, allowing him to leave at last.

"Excuse me," Fabian said eventually, letting Calex's hand go. "I must be mistaken."

"That's all right, sir." Calex grinned nervously and left to join his colleagues who were on their way home.

"See you tomorrow morning," Fabian said, wrapping up their little talk. Calex hurried to put his shoes back on and get out of there, which is what he wanted more than anything else.

"Hello again, Calex," said the young man passing him in the corridor. It was Elidocorc with a bowl of hot water between his hands. He was apparently on his way to see Mr Zora too.

"Oh, Elidocorc," Calex said, his voice trailing off as he didn't know what to say next. To ask him how he was would seem a silly question considering the day's events.

"I saw what happened to you earlier," his colleague said with concern. "That must have really hurt. Are you alright?"

Calex felt comforted that somebody had asked at last. Elidocorc seemed friendly, open and kind; quite unlike what Calex had come to think of as a typical resident of Quilemoyena City. Perhaps they would end up becom-ing friends.

"I'll be fine," Calex reassured him warmly. "Thanks for asking."

"I'm glad to hear it," Elidocorc said, giving Calex a wink as they parted ways.

The Chief Officer's door was open and Elidocorc slipped

into the room with the bowl of hot water between his hands.

"I've brought this to help you get cleaned up, sir."

"Thank you. Just leave it here, Elidocorc."

"We've washed away the blood in the courtyard," the auxiliary informed him as he posed the bowl on the desk. "Let me take your dirty tunic, sir," he offered. "I'll make sure it's clean by tomorrow." He took the woollen garment and turned to leave.

"Wait a minute," Fabian stopped him. "You know that's not all I want with you. Take a seat."

The auxiliary nodded. There was no look of surprise on his face because it was not the first time. He knew exactly what his boss wanted. He checked that the corridor was empty and the door firmly shut before taking a seat opposite Mr Zora. Elidocorc was an auxiliary like the others but he had another role at the Sacred Heart as well.

"I presume you've met our new auxiliary," Fabian said in a low voice.

"I'm one step ahead of you, Mr. Zora," the young man said proudly. "I followed him to the bathhouse yesterday. Already managed to find out a few things about him."

Fabian's eyebrows rose with surprise. "I'm impressed, Elidocorc," he said. "Excellent work."

"Just doing my job, sir," Elidocorc replied smugly and he leaned in for further instructions.

Chapter
THIRTEEN

Ten days had passed since Hero had arrived at Windberry Farm. The harvest was in full swing and Hux appreciated the extra help, even though Hero was a lot slower and less skilled than the others. One of the farmhands taught her how to use a scythe so that she could reap the wheat. It had taken her more than a week to master the technique, but now she felt that she could handle it quite well, swinging the tool back and forth as the wheat fell down around her. The fallen wheat would be gathered vertically and tied up by a piece of string. These so-called stooks were gathered with the help of oxen and collected into the barn. Hux's workers would begin the threshing process of separating the stalk from the grain in a few days time. Until then, Hux would continue to pray that it would not rain. Hero was discovering another world. She had never experienced the hard physical work of a farm labourer before, nor had she ever mixed with Violets. Rounding them up for sacrifice didn't count. In the past few days she had become fascinated with their way of life, finding their attitudes so different from those she was used to. She saw how they were a deeply religious people and loved working with the land. Their dedication to nature and lack of interest in materialism intrigued her. They demonstrated an alternative way of living and, so she had begun to think, a superior one. People seemed so much healthier and happier than those in the city.

Hero could not believe how much she had been missing out on during her sheltered existence in which she had only ever spoken to Violets in passing. In the fresh-air greenness of the countryside, her life which Crimsons would consider privileged did not seem so privileged any more. She had been taught about dates and details in history and complex mathematical equations; about politics, languages, and science. She knew how to dress for every kind of event, which hairstyle, colours and styles were in vogue. An educated, sophisticated young woman from Quilemoyena City's upper class. Hero Zora had never felt she was lacking until the day she arrived at Windberry Farm.

People out here in the countryside – Violets – valued a different kind of knowledge; practical knowledge that served them from day to day: knowledge of the soil, of seeds, of animals. "Soil is the great connector," Hux said to her one day out in the fields. "We Violets contribute to all that is nature through our sacrifice. This soil is what binds all of us."

"Not me, though," observed Hero.

"Yes, you too!" exclaimed Hux. "When Crimsons die they are buried and eventually they will become the soil too. We are all connected by the soil, my dear."

Hero would put a lot of effort into her work, building up a sweat and exercising her little-used muscles. The women farmhands around her were country girls seemingly as strong as tree trunks with broad shoulders and arms that could be mistaken for men's. Hero, a fragile-looking Crimson with delicate, feminine gestures, had a way of walking and moving that stood out like a sore thumb. The farmhands would sing while they worked, joining together in a happy, sometimes rather unsoundly chorus. Hero enjoyed listening to their unfamiliar rustic songs and chants. Unsurprisingly, the others wanted to know where she had come from and what she was doing there. Everything she said was in accordance with Calex's fake introduction of her to Hux. She was from Serenah (luckily Calex had chosen an island where they spoke the same language so Hero wouldn't have to put on a foreign accent all the time) and a misunderstanding had led to her having nowhere to stay. The farmhands found it strange that she had ended up on this farm instead of in the city with her own kind, but after raising an eyebrow, they thought little else of it. A pair of extra hands in the fields could only be a good thing.

Every now and then Hero would take a break from her work, enjoy the delights of the summer and listen to the sound of birds chirping and wheat being cut nearby. The Violets would approach the outsider curiously, and she would do her best to make conversation with them. The farmhands' children were the most curious of all, giggling and whispering whenever she came along. "You talk to her!" "No, you!" they would say but Hero would usually come and talk to them first. The children would be intrigued by her skin colour and Hero reached out her arms so they could inspect and touch it. At first, she was shy but she soon got used to it.

Although she wanted to spend more time with the baby, Hero felt she had to pull her weight on the farm. Pentievra was more than happy to help look after her little one while she worked. Having never been able to have children herself, she welcomed any opportunity to look after other people's, although it sometimes awoke old feelings of sadness about her own infertility. The baby cooed and cried like any other baby would and without the use of her eyes, Pentievra had no way of knowing that he was not a normal Crimson infant. In the evenings, Hero helped cook and clean which lightened the load on Pentievra. While Hux played cards with his chums downstairs, Hero would help Pentievra with her needlework or read aloud to her. Pentievra was grateful and was quickly becoming fond of the girl. Hero was finding making up stories tiresome though and certainly didn't enjoy deceiving her hosts. Everything she had told them about her past was a lie and she could never completely relax in their company. What's more, she would soon have to leave this place. She had already been there more than 'a few days' and she risked starting to look suspicious.

Hux and Pentievra went to the village temple at least twice a week and Hero, newly-curious about every aspect of Violet life, expressed an interest in what went on there. Pentievra suggested she find out for herself, and stayed at home with the baby on one occasion while the young Crimson and Hux headed to the daily service. Hero felt like a fish out of water in the packed temple of Tinklegrove but she was getting more and more used to feeling that way every day. There were hymns and prayers organised in a traditional manner. Hux knew the words off by heart, as did the others in the congregation. Hero listened to them and looked up at the stained glass windows of blue and purple. Towards the end of the service the offering took place, accompanied by the choir. The offering was not one of money, although people could give freely to the temple if they wished, but of blood. Pew by pew, the members of the congregation came to the altar where the priest stood with the temple's most valuable object: a sharp knife with an elaborately jewelled handle. One fingertip of each Violet was cut to allow a few drops of blood into the offertory bowl. The other priest then handed the Violets a small square of cotton to hold against the cut to stop the bleeding. The Violets then made their way back to their seats to make room for the others. Hero was of course the only one who didn't stand and make her way to the altar. The idea of someone cutting her fingertip made her squirm. In fact, at one point she feared she might be sick but when she looked away from the altar and up at the stained glass window she soon felt better. The filled bowl was an offering to the gods and it would sit on the altar, two candles burning either side of it until the following morning. As Hux sat back down, Hero looked at his hands and saw that there were faint marks on two of his other fingertips that were healing. Hero had never noticed these marks on Violets before but from now on she would know what they meant.

Hero had been thinking a lot about her past in recent days. In her mind, she spent much of her time in her parents' house where she had been born and brought up. She remembered the toys she held dear: a ten year old girl's paradise that was a dolls house to the simple wooden blocks of her earliest years. To her grown up eyes, those blocks provoked no excitement, which was only to be expected at her age, but to a toddler they were fascinating. Only a tiny remnant of that fascination was left, like a fine layer of fairy dust in her adult mind. How sweet it was that her own child would feel that curiosity and joy from such a simple thing. She hoped she would be able to relive it all through him. Hero's father featured only briefly in her earliest memories. Mr Reed was seldom around and never seemed to take much of an interest in his only child. Hero returned his feelings, or lack of them, and had never felt close to her father. While many of the city's wealthy worked for the government, Hero's father was a trader of precious stones. He had lived for his work, and as a result, was rarely at home. Mrs Reed, Hero's mother, on the other hand, was always around. Always around to tell Hero what to do, how to behave, how to think. As a skinny slip of a thirteen year old, Hero's anxiety about her appearance was made worse by her mother's constant nagging.

"Midnight blue is out of fashion, darling. And that dress is far too big for you. You can't go out like that. Let me find you something else."

The dress her mother gave her to wear instead was lighter in colour and more figure-hugging, drawing attention to what Hero felt were her funny-shaped legs and embarrassingly flat chest. She caught a look at herself in the mirror and thought herself plain.

"Let's put a little black around your eyes, Hero. And for goodness sake, stop frowning!"

It's just as well I'm done with them! thought Hero but she could not entirely convince herself. Her parents had cut their ties with her, and although they were not perfect, she could not pretend that it had been for the best.

Hero remembered how she had loved the family dog. With no brothers and sisters to play with, and being home-schooled, the cocker spaniel brought her a great deal of comfort. She would gaze out of the window on rainy days, stroking him as he lay curled up on her lap, his hair a similar shade to hers. He was so soft, his small heart beating hot and fast against her face when she hugged him. Like so much else from her previous life, he was gone now.

One day, Hero found herself alone in the house. Her back was hurting from the hard work she had been doing in the fields and she was taking the morning off. Pentievra had gone into the village and Hero could enjoy the whole house to herself. Pentievra had picked some flowers from the garden that morning and at her request Hero was arranging them into vases. She took the prettiest peonies for the most frequented rooms, mixing them with a few other flowers Pentievra had brought in. She saved the duller, dryer ones for her own bedroom. She trimmed and arranged the blooms for her hosts' bedroom – a rich bouquet of pink of purple – and carried it to the stairs. She was surprised to hear voices in the nearby room with the fireplace. Hero had been certain she was alone in the house. She put her ear towards the door and moved closer.

"That's some nasty sunburn you managed to get, my boy. I told you to stay in the shade."

"I forgot."

"And now look at you. You're like a blueberry. You drink up that glass of water and stay here because I've got to get back to work."

"I don't feel very well."

"Well, you'll know for next time then, won't you! I'll be back to check on you in a bit."

"Tell me a story, dad."

"I don't have time for that, boy."

"Oh come on, dad. Please."

"Alright then, if you promise to be good and keep out of the sun."

"I promise."

"Good. Now, let's see what old Hux has got on this bookshelf. Oh, this looks good. Poetry for Under Eights."

"I'll be eight next month and then I won't be under eight any more, will I?"

"Good point. So we'd better make use of this book while we can. Now let's see... Ah! Here's one I know:

A long time ago but not far away
A child was born on a sunny day
but the sun shone not upon his face
because he was a brownborn
A brownborn, a brownborn.
Because he was a brownborn.

The mother said "Out! With this child away."
Not even wanting to see his face
and only the servant girl would stay
to take care of the brownborn
The brownborn, the brownborn.
To take care of the brownborn.

The baby was sick from its very first breath
With pale, sullen eyes it seemed hours from death
and only the servant girl was left
to save the life of the brownborn
The brownborn, the brownborn.
To save the life of the brownborn.

For the baby sheep's milk she got
in her arms she gently rocked
but his heart had already stopped
and that was the end of the brownborn
The brownborn, the brownborn.
And that was the end of the brownborn.

The boy was falling asleep, his eyelids suddenly heavy, and his father went over to kiss his forehead. Hero heard the book being put back on the shelf and footsteps heading towards the door. Her hands holding the vase of peonies were trembling. Whether the story was a true one or not, it had shaken her to the bone. She put the vase down on the nearest surface and hurried up the stairs, just before the farmhand came out. In her bare room, the baby was sleeping soundly in his makeshift bed, or so she thought. On coming closer she saw his eyes were open and looking around. Those big brown eyes fixed on her and he started to move his arms. Hero scooped him up into hers and kissed his tiny face. He was such a good little boy, calm and alert. A great tear fell down Hero's nose and onto the baby's chest, disappearing into his blankets.

"I'll be with you until the end," she whispered.

She sat crying helplessly with the baby in her arms for a few minutes before something caught her attention. In the corner of the room, on the left of the window, the wooden skirting board had come loose. There seemed to be something hidden behind it, that should have been pinned between the skirting board and the wall. Hero slipped her fingers between dust and cobwebs to pull out a folded-up sheet of paper.

She unfolded the sheet and found a profusion of drawings. They were the drawings of a pre-teenager. The main drawing represented an adult couple and three children all holding hands. Smaller drawings around it represented the same people. The person responsible for these drawings obviously did not have the artistic skill to bring these figures to life as he wanted to. There was writing too at the bottom of the sheet in a foreign alphabet. Thanks to her study of languages, Hero recognised it as the traditional alphabet of Kinsen and was now sure that it was Calex who had done the drawings. The Kinsen language and traditional alphabet was not something she was familiar with, however, and no matter how much she looked at it she wouldn't be able to work out what Calex had written.

The creak of the door opening made Hero nearly jump

out of her skin. She leapt up and turned around, putting the sheet of paper behind her back.

It was the boy from downstairs, the farmhand's son.

He stood in the doorway, staring at her. He had probably never seen a Crimson before, Hero presumed, judging from his stare.

"You know, it's not very polite to stand there looking at me like that," she told him.

"I heard you crying," the boy said after a moment.

Hero shrugged. She couldn't deny it and changed the subject.

"Why aren't you at school?" she said, sniffing.

"It's the weekend," answered the boy. "Dad always brings me to the farm at weekends."

Hero had lost track of what day of the week it was. "Why don't you go outside and play with the others?" she asked the lad.

"I got sunburnt," he said. His skin was a deeper shade of blue than usual, especially on his forehead and nose. "My dad says I've got to stay inside."

"Ah yes. Well, maybe we should go downstairs and find you something to do then."

"Is that a baby?"

Hero walked towards him, blocking his view, then led him out of the room with a hand on his shoulder.

"I've got some flower arranging to do. You can help me with that."

"Boring!" chimed the boy.

"Come on, I want to get it done before Pentievra comes home."

At the bottom of the stairs, Hero wiped away her tears, blew her nose and dabbed her forehead with cold water so as to maintain the impression to anyone she might cross that everything was under control. She got back to work on the peonies with the Violet boy at her side. Two

questions played on her mind as she did so:
Who was the young man from Kinsen?
And when was he coming back?

Chapter
FOURTEEN

$\mathcal{T}$he next day as Pentievra was going about her chores, she heard the door open unexpectedly. "Who is it?" she called, and at the sound of Calex's voice her face broke into a beautiful smile.

"Hero's so happy to be here," she gushed five minutes later as they shared a pot of tea. "And she's really been helping us out on the farm." Calex was delighted to hear this news and to see that his plan had worked out well. He felt pleased with himself.

"Is there any news about those friends she came to stay with?" Hux asked, a little less enthusiastic than his wife. Calex hesitated, having completely forgotten about the story that he had fabricated. "It's been more than a week now," Hux pressed.

"I know," Calex began, rapidly searching for words. "There have been some problems with her friends getting home but they should be arriving in a couple of days."

Hux frowned with a look of suspicion. "Calex, if there's something you're not telling me... "

"Be quiet, Hux," Pentievra chipped in. "Hero's a lovely girl and we're happy to have her here."

"Thank you Pentievra," Calex said, getting to his feet. "And don't worry, Hux. She'll be out of your way in a day or two." He realised that he would need to think of a new plan quickly before things could turn sour. Yet as soon as he walked into the open, sensing the relaxed atmosphere all around him, he quickly put this issue on the back shelf of his mind. Stepping into the fields, he noticed that about two thirds of the land had been harvested now. Friendly waves were exchanged with some of the farmhands and it was not long before he found the person he was looking for.

"Hold it higher," he called as he approached Hero who was wielding the scythe to and fro. "And bend your knees a little bit!"

"Calex!" she called, putting down the tool and wiping the sweat from her forehead.

"It's good to see you!" He did not let on just how pleased he was to see her. Great would have been a more appropriate word. He shuffled his way towards her through a patch of wheat that was still standing. "I'm not working today," he told her, "so I thought I'd come and say hello." The late afternoon sun made their faces look almost as golden as the wheat.

"Well," Hero said, "hello." They chuckled together.

"I wanted to see if you were alright," he said.

"As well as could be expected," she shrugged, laying the scythe against the trunk of a nearby oak tree. "Thanks again for helping me. I'm just sorry we couldn't have met in happier circumstances."

"Me too," Calex agreed.

"You're wearing the ring!" she noticed with surprise.

"Yes, it's the safest place for it."

"Why don't you sell it?"

"I thought you might change your mind and want it back."

"No," she shook her head vehemently. "I never want to see it again."

"It might come in useful just in case of..."

"Really," Hero interrupted. "I don't want to be anywhere near that thing."

"Alright," Calex said, resigning at last. "I take it nobody has any suspicions."

"About the baby? Not at all," Hero replied. "I've only let Pentievra anywhere near him, and that's just because she's blind."

"Good," Calex said with a nod. "Pentievra tells me you're happy here."

"I'm hardly happy, Calex. I'm trying to give that impression, though. I'm glad they're convinced."

Calex seemed disappointed.

"I'm sorry," Hero said, realising that she sounded ungrateful. "I appreciate you bringing me here. But I can't forget my problems overnight."

Calex smiled, understanding now. "Of course not," he sympathised.

They sat down in the space where the wheat had just been reaped. The bottom of the stalks that stuck out of the ground felt sharp and quite uncomfortable, but they both wanted to sit.

"They told me about you working at the Sacred Heart," Hero explained, changing the subject. "How do you like it?"

"It's... exhilarating," Calex said sarcastically.

"What do you do exactly?" Hero asked.

"Cleaning, mostly," came Calex's deadpan response. "A lot of cleaning."

After the dramatic events of his first day, things had gone much more smoothly and nothing unusual or remarkable had happened at all. The routine was quickly becoming tedious and repetitive. It had got to the point when Calex was excited to find bird droppings on a statue: there would finally be something substantial to clean. If Calex had learned something, it was that it was indeed possible for one to clean something until it could be cleaned no more.

"What about escorting the sacrifices?" Hero pushed.

"Yes, well, I do that too." Calex flicked away a spider that had started to crawl up his leg.

It was not hard to detect his lack of enthusiasm. "Not your dream job, then?"

Calex sighed. "I don't know what my dream job would be. But I know that being an auxiliary is boring. It's probably more interesting to be an officer."

"It is."

"How would you know?"

"I was one."

"Really?" came Calex's astonished reaction.

"Yes," she confirmed. "You know Fabian Zora?"

"Well, of course. He's my boss."

"My name is Hero Zora," she said, not wanting to have to spell it out.

Calex caught her drift. "Don't tell me...!" he spluttered. "No wonder he was so harsh on you. If anyone knew the wife of the Chief Officer at the Sacred Heart…"

"Exactly." Hero emphatically stopped his train of thought. Calex understood so much more now. The mystery was not fully unravelled but he felt as if he had just undone a big knot. Yet, he found this discovery rather depressing. His shoulders sank down as he sat silently next to Hero, mulling over his thoughts.

So, the mysterious husband who had thrown her out into the street was none other than Fabian Zora, a man with more power and wealth than anyone else Calex knew. He had got the impression that Hero was from a privileged background but he had underestimated just how much exactly. She was the wife of the Chief Officer of the Sacred Heart!

Calex thought of this man's formidable presence and long, elegant woollen tunics. Not to mention his lusciously thick beard. Calex could not grow a beard if he tried. He knew very well that the best that he could do was a little fluff on his chin. Comparing himself to Fabian Zora was like comparing a cat to a lion.

He searched desperately for some positive points that could make a girl be interested in him. His teeth may not have been the pearliest of whites nor the straightest in line but they were in good condition and all still there. He had been victim to a spotty phase but it was never as bad as some of his peers and it seemed to have passed now. He was tall with lean, well-defined muscles and, so Pentievra and the other farmers' wives liked to tell him, a face that would make hearts break. Although, on second thoughts, how seriously should he take the complements of little old ladies? Calex could not seem to drag his mind away from the cons. He had no particular skills or talents (as far as he knew), a sorry excuse for a formal education and no money to speak of. To make things worse, Hero was surely a year or two older than his seventeen. A look of dejection solidified on his face. It was hopeless – how could Hero ever be interested in him?

"He's hiding a big secret every day, isn't he?" A touch of resentment escaped in Calex's words. Hero shrugged in response. "How did you two meet?" Calex pushed. Hero had no desire to talk about her relationship with Fabian. She had brought it up on the spur of the moment but now she regretted it. If she had answered Calex's question, she would have said that she and her future husband met at the theatre two years ago. There was no hiding of the fact that their parents were setting them up. In terms of social status, they were the perfect match. Hero and Fabian got along fairly well and soon announced their engagement. Their parents were delighted and Fabian was relieved as he was nearly thirty and his peers were already married with children. After the wedding, Hero started her first job as an officer of the Sacred Heart. She soon began to find her new husband short-tempered and aggressive but she did not complain. She had comfort, security and an interesting social life.

"Enough about that." Hero ordered as she pushed away the memory of her first meeting with Fabian Zora. She quickly changed the subject of conversation. "Did the others tell you? We're having a big picnic next to the barn."

"Oh, really?"

"All the farmhands have brought something to eat. I pressed some apples and made some juice." She smiled proudly. "I'm sure you'll be able to join us."

"Well, I haven't contributed to the harvest."

"I'm sure it doesn't matter. Come on!" She took the scythe and they started to walk down to the barn. The other workers had already left the field and were laying the table. A walnut cake and a sunflower seed loaf were already there and Pentievra was bringing out Hero's apple juice in a big glass jar.

"It took about a hundred apples to make that," she told Calex. "They don't go very far, do they?"

"Calex!" called one of the workers, "be a gentleman and carry that scythe!" Calex apologised to Hero and took the heavy tool from her hands. She objected, of course, saying that she was a strong farmhand now and such assistance was not necessary. Laughing and teasing each other like this, anyone would think they had know each other for a long time.

Suddenly another thought came to mind and Calex's smile disappeared. "I don't want to dampen the mood but we need to talk about the plan," he muttered. "Hux is starting to get suspicious."

Hero was about to respond when Hux approached them. "You will join us, won't you Calex?" his old guardian encouraged.

"I'd love to," Calex responded, "but I haven't brought anything to eat."

"It doesn't matter," Hux chucked. "You can do the washing-up!"

The farmhands, both men and women, gathered at the long wooden table that had been brought out from the barn. There was a married couple among them who had brought their toddler along. Calex sat alongside them and saved a seat next to him for Hero, who had gone upstairs to check on the baby. The Violets sat chattering and laughing together, excited about the feast to come and the fact the long day was over at last. Finally, they quietened down to say grace, joining hands around the table. Hero made it back just in time.

All eyes closed and Pentievra's voice could be heard: "Oh, goddesses Quil of the land. Bless this food and make us worthy of it. We remain at your service to nourish these fruits of the earth. They are, as we are, yours. Forever."

After a few seconds of solemn silence, everyone reopened their eyes and Hux got to his feet with a glass of wine in his hand. The others also took their glasses that had been filled with sweet red wine from local grapes.

"I'd like to make a toast," Hux announced, "to a fine harvest." The farmhands piped up in agreement, raising their glasses high.

"It's been a good one," someone called out.

"It certainly has," Hux agreed. "I have to say that I was worried a couple of weeks ago. I wasn't sure if you would be able to make it in this blazing heat."

"Me neither!" called out someone else.

"But you soldiered on like the hardworking, loyal Violets you are and I am very pleased with all of you," Hux continued. "At least the gods have been kind in keeping the rain off our heads and I see no reason why the last of the wheat shouldn't be in the barn by tomorrow."

"Can we eat now?" came another voice, which received a few laughs and calls of "yes, hurry up! I'm famished!"

"Alright, alright," Hux chuckled. "A toast – to another successful harvest at Windberry Farm!" Everyone clinked their glasses together, took a sip of the wine then proceeded to fill their plates with food. The table was abundant with delicious pies and salads, mouth-watering roast chicken and fresh walnut bread. To finish on a sweet note, there were cakes adorned with carrowbeans and fruit that had been picked from the surrounding orchards: peaches, apricots, pears and cherries. It was a colourful feast for the eyes as well as the stomach. Calex picked out Pentievra's famous potato pie and cut himself a generous portion. He shovelled a slice onto Hero's plate as well.

"What's that you're giving me?" she asked.

"It is from the kitchen of the gods," Calex answered. "That's all you need to know."

The Violets had no qualms about talking incessantly and eating at the same time. Calex was used to this kind of gathering among countryside folk and knew that the conversation always revolved around farming. One of the farmhands asked Hux why he did not invest in some equipment to allow him to mill on the farm itself rather than sell the wheat to be ground for flour elsewhere.

"Why change things?" Hux argued. "I have a routine that works and a good relationship with the miller. We've been working together for twenty years. I see no reason to change a thing."

"If it ain't broke, don't fix it," added Pentievra.

"But you could make a lot of money, Hux!" encouraged the farmhand who had come up with the suggestion.

"For what purpose?" retorted Hux. "I'm happy; I have everything I need! Please excuse my bluntness, Calex and Hero, but I am not one of these Crimsons in the city who just want more and more and more. Don't be influenced by their mentality, my friends. This way of thinking has taken over the city and now seems to be making its way into the countryside. Don't lose sight of what is important. I have enough in my life. I have no desire for anything more."

The farmhands looked towards Hux as if he were something in-between a priest and a teacher. His words had made Hero think about how Calex was different. It had not taken her long to realise that he seemed to break the mould and now it made sense: Calex was down-to-earth like these Violets. He was not interested in accumulating financial wealth; she remembered how he had flat-out refused to take her valuable ring. True wealth, according to Hux, was wealth of character and everything material was just for convenience and decoration. The way Calex was today was the result of his upbringing with Hux. How could Calex avoid his influence after six years on Windberry Farm? Perhaps, Hero thought, Calex did not realise any of this. She was here because of him, his kindness and his generosity. She silently reflected and admired him as she sat by his side, not sharing her thoughts with anyone.

The farmhands' conversation quickly moved on to a

lighter subject, namely comparing the harvest to those of previous years. A couple of years ago it had rained non-stop for days and the farmhands winced with the sour memory of it. Last year, the yield had been reduced when a large area of the crop was infected with a bacterial disease, depriving the grain of sufficient nourishment and leaving it worthless. Hux was often asked why he was so preoccupied with growing wheat as opposed to other crops. It was a risk in that wheat was more prone to diseases than other grains and people often suggested he grow more reliable cereals like corn or barley as well to cover his back. Hux always responded with the same reason: his family had been growing wheat for centuries and he saw it unnecessary to break with tradition. There was never a lack of demand for wheat, Hux argued, as it was always needed to make bread, biscuits, cakes and ale. The stalks too were valuable as they could be used to make straw-filled mattresses (the most common type in Quilemoyena), thatching for roofs, baskets and rope, and many other things that the farmhands took it in turns to name in what became a sort of game.

Calex and Hero ate quietly, half listening to the banter, half daydreaming in their heads. Neither of them spoke as the last lettuce leaves left their plates.

"How do you two know each other?"

The voice came from across the table and Calex looked up hesitantly. "We've known each other for ages," he mumbled in a way that suggested there was nothing interesting to say on the subject. "It's a long story."

"Well, we've got plenty of time," Hux intervened. Calex gulped hard and avoided Hux's penetrating gaze.

"Well, I don't know where to begin really," he offered, sinking away into his chair. Fortunately, Calex's lacklustre reaction had made the farmhands quickly lose interest in this topic and someone called out another question:

"So, what are you doing now?"

"You mean, as a job?" Calex asked, his voice betraying his anxiety. He was starting to get sick of being grilled by questions. "I work for the Sacred Heart," he admitted reluctantly.

All the Violets stopped talking and Calex felt their eyes fixing on him. Embarrassed, he looked down at his plate once more. He tensed up, feeling sure that their reaction was going to be a negative one. Yet suddenly they burst into cries of encouragement and congratulations:

"You've done well, Calex, really well."

"Talk about taking a step up in the world!"

"We knew you were cut out for great things."

Calex smiled with relief and was grateful for these words. *Imagine if they knew that Hero was an officer and her husband is the Chief Officer,* he speculated, *they'd probably jump on her.*

The blazing sun sat low in the cloudless sky and continued to glare down upon Windberry Farm. Stark shadows gradually crept up the side of the house as late afternoon became evening. Hux brought out his guitar and started to strum a well-known Quilemoyenan countryside song; the melodious chords making the others stop their conversations and turn towards the source of the music. Calex hummed along while the Violets who had better singing voices sang aloud, led by Hux whose voice was tuneful if not pitch-perfect:

Oh, the golden harvest!
The wheat-heads rise in August.
With our sickles cut them down we will,
And commence our jolly chorus!

Hero did not know the song at all, but she listened attentively and smiled with appreciation. Wanting very much to contribute something to this wonderful feast, she poured out the apple juice. Her effort was successful: despite a few pips, the juice was sweet and delicious. It was only when everyone began to stack all the empty plates that they realised how dark it had become. The lack of sunlight was, of course, no reason to bring the festivities to an end. Pentievra brought candles out of the house. Meanwhile, crickets set the bushes alight with their buzzing song, accompanying the jolly strumming of Hux's guitar. Calex and Hero felt relaxed and full of good food. They listened to Hux's skilful manipulation of the instrument, enjoying the pleasant and peaceful atmosphere and feeling no pressure to speak. Across the table, the toddler had fallen asleep in his mother's arms and she was rocking him gently to the rhythm of the music.

"I'm going to check on the baby," Hero whispered to Calex as the current song came to an end.

"I'll come with you," Calex said, getting to his feet too and realising that the wine had gone to his head. A couple of the farmhands exchanged winks across the table and Calex blushed and got away from them.

They made their way around the house to the front door, leaving the party behind them. A gust of wind played with the wheat that still stood, making a loud shh sound. Above them, the sky was cloaked in the purest of blacks, pinpricked with brilliant balls of light. The almost-full moon reigned supreme in the sky, its mountainous reliefs visible to the naked eye. It was a cloudless, fogless night and the moonlight radiated down with its full strength.

Calex had seen many a night like this out here in the countryside but he knew that it would be unfamiliar to someone from the city, where a clear view of the sky was always obscured as absolute darkness in the streets was unheard of. "Look up," he said, knowing that she would be impressed.

Hero gasped. Not only could she see the brightest stars but those further behind as well. There were truly hundreds – no – thousands of them. Hero could not tear her eyes away. The vastness of this galactic landscape was breathtaking. The moon itself was so bright that it burned its shape into her retinas.

"In the city there's always a lot of unnatural light and pollution," Calex told her. "You could never see the stars as bright as this."

"I never knew this kind of sight existed," Hero marvelled. "And I had no idea that the moon could provide so much light."

Hero's expression was one of pure enchantment. Calex considered telling her about something else he knew she would love. He had discovered this place in his early days on Windberry Farm and often went back there after dark without anyone knowing. It seemed so special that he had never wanted to tell anybody. Until now.

"Come with me," he said, making his decision to share the secret for the first time. "I've got something to show you." He led her through the field opposite Windberry Farm and into a patch of vegetation where there were many trees and bushes.

"Calex," Hero laughed. "Where are we going? I can't see anything. What's this all about?"

He did not answer as there was no need. They suddenly found themselves enclosed by hundreds of miniature green stars. At first, Hero was completely bewildered but then she realised that the light-bearers were suspended in bushes. Calex waited for her reaction, full of anticipation.

"I don't understand," she said.

"They're glow-worms," Calex whispered.

"Oh, I see," Hero murmured, transfixed by the insects. "I think I've heard of them."

"You city folk!"

"What?"

"Nothing."

Hero giggled and pushed him fondly. "You're making fun of me."

"No, no. Not at all," Calex said with mock-seriousness. Hero spent a few moments gazing into the bushes, impressed by the bright light that the glow-worms emitted from their tails, but Calex was distracted. In his imagination it was easy to picture his hand reaching for hers, making contact with her warm flesh and joining their solitary forms together in the dark. Yet in real life, something stopped him, something made this impossible. What was this obstacle? Politeness, perhaps, or fear of rejection. Considering the paralysing embarrassment that could pursue, it did not seem worth the risk. Calex tried to push this urge to hold her hand away as they headed back towards the farmhouse.

"It's been a lovely evening," Hero sighed. "I'm glad you came."

Calex smiled wholeheartedly. "Me too," he admitted.

"But you wanted to talk about my staying here, didn't you?"

"Ah, that," Calex said glumly.

"Have you had any ideas?"

"There's no one who I could ask to help you except for Hux and Pentievra," he said with a shrug. As much as he liked the idea of having this girl in his room, he knew it wasn't in her best interests. "You would be welcome to stay with me but you know that you're not safe in the city."

"You're right," Hero sighed.

"Let's think about it," Calex said encouragingly. "We still have some time."

But he, for one, could not think about that now. He felt strangely distracted: the girl, the moonlight, the coolness of the air...

They entered the house by the front door and made their way up the stairs. It was difficult to see as nobody had lit the lamps yet and they cautiously found their way to the bedroom, the wooden floor creaking underneath their feet. Sure enough, the baby was sleeping on his blankets. His tiny breaths could be heard in the silence. Calex could barely see Hero but he felt her movements and the warmth that radiated from her body. Maybe he had been wrong earlier. Maybe she could be interested in him after all. It would have been easy to brush her long hair back and kiss her, to drown himself in the smell he detected from here. He resisted, of course, grateful that he had not drunk a second glass of wine. If he had, nothing would have stopped him. He caught a glimpse of the bed he had slept on for six years that was hers now and sat down on it. It creaked under his weight, he noticed, which had never been the case all those years ago. He remembered how Pentievra used to sit here until he fell asleep. When he first arrived on the farm he had trouble settling down. He was groggy all day and strangely wide-awake at night but Pentievra's presence in the bedroom made it much easier. She stayed with him until he was fast asleep. There were no books to read to him. Nobody at the farm was literate and, in any case, Pentievra was blind so she sang to him instead. Her songs would send his mind off on an adventure and soon he would be singing along with her, until his voice trailed off with sleepiness. Her gentle hand would stroke his hair until the blanket of slumber came over him. She would unlace his fingers from hers and put his hand under the covers so he wouldn't get cold during the night.

Calex's eyes fell upon a sheet of paper that lay on the table opposite him. A forgotten piece of paper, finally unfolded after many years of going unnoticed. Hero turned and found him inspecting it. Calex remembered how he felt when he did this drawing, full of nostalgia and love for his family. A boy desperately trying to rec-reate them, to bring them back to him.

"I found it," Hero told him, "and Pentievra said it must be of you and your family."

The laid-back, comfortable rapport between them evaporated.

He was going to ask why she was sneaking about the house, but instead he gave voice to what upset him more: "You told Pentievra about this?"

Hero nodded, realising she had taken a step too far.

"What did she tell you?" Calex demanded.

"Just the truth about what happened."

"Well, what the heck does Pentievra know about the truth? Nobody knows the truth. You can't imagine how much it tortures me. I don't want to talk about it. I don't even want to think about it!" He turned away from her.

"I'm sorry," she tried. "I didn't mean to upset you."

"Why was Pentievra talking to you about that anyway?" he rejoined, more sad than angry now. "As if my life is something to be gossiped about, something to entertain other people."

"Come on, Calex. It wasn't like that. I'm sorry. I shouldn't have said anything." He felt her touch on his arm, but only briefly as he had started walking away. The front door slammed behind him and the baby started to cry.

*C*alex wanted to get away from here. Windberry Farm did not seem like his home. So where was home? His residence in Quilemoyena City felt temporary, with the impersonal neighbours and ever-bustling urban life. Yet he could never feel at home in this countryside, surrounded by a race of people not his own. So, Kinsen? The place of his childhood. No, he could never return there. Being there without his family would tear him apart, stirring up memories he would rather suppress. Yet the memories of that night were not so old that they seemed like dreams. They stuck in Calex's mind, only having become a little less clear and vivid over the years.

The ship's mast had been struck by a single bolt of lightning and started to burn, while waves of fury tore at its very foundation. Water and flames began to consume the wooden vessel, and screams and cries for help built up in crescendo. Calex had lost sight of his family, having become separated from his mother. Still, he stood where she had left him so that when she returned he would be there. But minutes went by she did not come for him. The boat was coming closer and closer to its complete destruction. Calex then had to make a decision. Should he move to a safer place? Or should he wait for his mother to come back?

The choice was made for him. A roaring wave swept him into its wrath, dragging him overboard and into the sea. Calex was underwater for what seemed like a very long time and swallowed so much water it made him feel terribly sick. By this time, the boat was falling apart. He saw it in the distance, the last of the flames being snuffed out by the sea. He saw and heard the passengers fighting for survival.

Using the dregs of his energy, Calex found a piece of wood bobbing around as if it was seeking his attention. He put his arms over it and rested his head. Staying alive was the only thing that mattered now. The waves continued to rage and he was at their whim. The cold of the water did not bother him so much as keeping his head above it. He held tightly onto the wood for some time, knowing how close he was to death. The rain poured as if it had not rained for years and the thunder sounded like the voice of a thousand giants. There were many times that Calex thought that the storm was coming to an end, but after a few false alarms he began to give up hope. Every muscle in his body felt sore, his head pounded and his stomach was sickeningly full of brine.

Then, hope came. The rain began to get lighter and the waves seemed to lose their angry momentum. A new fear came over Calex: a cold fear of isolation. He had become separated from all human life in the middle of a deep and barren ocean. Being the middle of the night it was pitch black and he could not see a thing. All he heard was his own coughing and the mild swish-swosh of the water. He clambered up onto the plank of wood, using all his might to lift himself up, desperate for rest. He lay on it and threw up, removing the seawater from his stomach and lungs. Then he began to cry, for he had never been so scared. He heard his cries echo through the night to no avail. For the first time in his life, there was nobody to help him. Then eventually, through lack of energy and in a pit of despair, he fell asleep.

When he awoke he felt the sun on his face and solid ground beneath his feet. His clothes were still clinging to him, his body caked in brine. Opening his eyes, he saw three or four Violet men leaning over his face. "'E's alive," they cried as he began to blink. It was real, thought Calex returning from dreamland, it was all real. The world suddenly seemed so bleak and cruel.

"Quino'fae mon yoter unt galm?" came his laboured words, feeling his mouth dry and salty. The bunch of faces shook their heads with incomprehension. "Where mother, father?" asked the boy, using his elementary knowledge of the language he had learned at school. "Where family?"

There was no response to his question. A fisherman brought him some water then lifted his head so that he could drink it. Then he felt light-headed again and fell asleep, muttering in his mother tongue that no one could understand. The days drifted by, as boats came in and out of the harbour. The fishermen looked after him, sharing their lunch with him and giving him a place to rest. When he was well enough, he helped them with their work. But Calex wanted to be alone. He sat on the crag that went the furthest out to sea, perching on the edge and looking out, shedding bitter tears.

After a week, as Calex was learning to gut fish, he saw one of the fishermen talking to a bearded, middle-aged man who was pointing in his direction. Then, the stranger came towards him and Calex prepared himself to talk to him.

"I've had my eye on you, boy," the kind-faced man said. "I wanted to talk to you."

Calex did not understand. "You see my family?" he asked, and the man shook his head with pity.

"How would you like to come and work on my farm?" he asked. The boy gave him a dumbfounded look again. The man scratched his nose and attempted something a little easier. "What is your name?" he asked clearly, to which Calex nodded with comprehension. He stated his name, age and where he came from just like he had learned at school. The man reached out his hand for Calex to shake, a baffling custom that was not practiced in Kinsen. "My name is Hux," he said.

Calex lay dreaming in the dark early hours of the morning. The night was no cooler than it had been for the last few weeks but the sweat on his brow was not from the heat.

He dreamt that his mother was standing in front of him, her face shrouded. She walked towards him and something told him she was smiling.

"You remember me?" Calex asked her softly in his mother tongue. It had been so long and he must have looked so different to when she had last seen him.

"You," she said tenderly, her voice carrying something he recognised from the past. The word she used was 'schlie' which was, in his language, the most familiar and tender of the four forms of 'you'.

"How could I ever forget you?" she said.

Tears streamed from Calex's face and he saw himself as a child again, his face full of the ethereal and innocent beauty of children. It was a quality that still clung onto him even now, although it was fading fast as adulthood approached.

"Mum," he said as he walked towards her, eager to reveal her face from behind the black veil.

"Cal." Her nurturing arms reached out to him. "My darling boy..." He pulled the veil from her face and recoiled in horror. It was indeed his mother's face, as it would always be, engraved forever in his memory. But there were deep, empty black holes where her eyes should have been. They began to bleed, oozing at first then spraying, frantic and unceasing.

Calex awoke feeling hot and cold. He sat up in his bed, trying to grasp onto reality. The dream had been so lucid.

"Mum!" he cried, just in case. "Mum!" No answer came. There was no black veil, no blood. He heard the early morning birds outside, the sounds of the here and now. Pressing his hands to his face, Calex found his eyes warm and wet.

He felt his heart full of blood, tight in his chest, the poison spreading to his shoulders and stomach. There was no chance that he could go back to sleep so he kept his eyes open in the dark, bathing in the sense of loss that clung tenaciously to him. He sank back into his bed and waited for morning.

Haunting images often hung in his mind when he wished they would not. Visions of his family drowning, suffering and petrified. Visions of the last time he saw them, the last words he said. Visions of their lifeless bodies moving with the tide. The wretched feeling of loneliness when he arrived on the shores of Quilemoyena, a small boy way out of his depth. And the terrible slow death of hope that he had now been reduced to a fraction of its original size. The unwelcome visit of these images sometimes plagued his late nights and early mornings. It was something he had accepted as part of his day to day life. Like an illness, there was nothing he could do except let it pass in its own time.

After half an hour or so, Calex felt the urge to get up. His trousers hung over the chair and he pulled out the poem that he had copied onto a piece of paper. It was just about light enough to make out the words:

When the sun sets on one's day
And his soul will fly away

But he stopped reading, quickly losing interest. Out of the window, he saw a man leading a donkey with goods on its back. In the distance, he saw two or three candlelit rooms of the few people who were awake. It was too early to get up but he was wide awake. Thoughts were racing through his mind.

But they were not of his mother, father and brothers. Those thoughts had been replaced by those of that girl, Hero. Calex practised saying her name, whispering it, trying it out on his lips. The drawn-out tension of the first syllable and its satisfying resolution in the round sound of the final 'oh'. Hero... Hero... it felt so thrilling. He thought of her face and her voice and her sweet scent yesterday evening in the dark. It had been so exciting to be with her and talk to her, to show her the starry sky and the fireflies.

And then he had fallen out with her. He had been up-set when he left yesterday. What she said had provoked and annoyed him. And yet these negative feelings had quickly dissolved leaving only positive ones.

Calex had noticed Crimson girls before; he had even briefly talked to them. The rare times when he had found girls attractive was exciting but in a rather qui-et, distant way. With Hero it was not distant at all. The excitement was close: it was loud and obvious. Even saying her name brought about a rather violent reaction whereby he felt insanely happy and sick to his stomach at the same time. It was so unfamiliar to him. He had not even known feelings like that existed. But he was so pleased that they did.

The connection he felt to Hero was unlike how he felt towards anyone else. He had experienced strong affection for Hux and Pentievra, but this feeling was different. The thought of Hero made him smile, his fingers tingle and his heart sing. He wanted to stretch out his arms and run or laugh out loud for no particular reason. This feeling had come to him a few days ago too as he strolled through the city feeling as though he were floating. Calex had never so much as kissed a girl. He had never had an opportunity for anything like that with a Crimson girl. In fact, even exchanging more than a few words with one was a rare occurrence. Rumel, who he knew from the Lusham Locks inn, was the only Crimson woman around his age with whom he had any regular contact. She lived with another woman and, in any case, Calex saw her as a friend. Women were almost as mysterious to him as the realm of the gods.

Suddenly, consumed by these thoughts, Calex decided he had had enough. He had to see her. He owed her an apology for his outburst and for storming off yesterday. That would also be a perfectly legitimate excuse for going to see her again. As well as this, he was still looking for a new plan now that she was starting to outstay her welcome. He did not have any ideas but maybe he and Hero could come up with some together. He decided that had every reason to go and see her. There could not possibly be anything awkward about it.

As he looked out of the window and saw that sunrise had begun, he realised that there was going to be time. Time before work for a quick talk with his new friend.

He hoped she was not sore about his behaviour yesterday and that she would understand. Calex heard Miss Kiberon's loud snores as he walked past her room and into the almost empty street. The still-sleeping buildings were lit with a blue tint and rose ribbons were cast across the sky. Calex caught a lift to Tinklegrove in a cart of onions being pulled by oxen, making conversation with the farmer about the summer and the crop it had produced. The man knew the ground like it was part of himself. In a way, thought Calex, it was.

As they made their way into the countryside, thick rainclouds began to move in fast. By the time they were passing through Tinklegrove it was nearly completely overcast and much darker. Calex hopped off just outside Windberry Farm and felt a cool breeze surround him. There was a buzz in the air; the familiar sensation that it was going to rain. Calex heard intense thunder from over the hills. So, there would be a thunderstorm after weeks of hot and dry weather. It was inevitable, he supposed. It could not stay sunny forever. The tension had to break at some point.

Calex was pleased that Hux had managed to get all the wheat into the barn in time. He remembered the nightmarish harvest of a couple of years ago when it rained all the way through. He and the other farmhands hardly slept for days as they rushed to get all the wheat reaped, dried and ready for threshing.

He knocked on the door, realising he felt ill-at-ease. There was trouble in the air, he could sense it. Seconds went by and nobody answered the door. It was possible that Hux and Pentievra were out: in the village or praying at the temple. Had Hero gone with them? Finally, Hux answered the door, but his face did not blossom into a smile as usual.

"I'm sorry I left without saying goodbye last night,"

Calex said, his voice laced with apprehension. "If it hasn't been done already, I'd be glad to do the washing-up."

He smiled jokingly but Hux's expression did not change. "Hux," Calex breathed with a sense of impending doom. "Is something wrong?"

"There was something wrong until last night," Hux replied sternly, "but there is no problem anymore."

"What do you mean?" Calex asked, feeling his heart tightening. Hux had discovered the truth about the baby, he was sure of it. In that case, where was Hero? Calex knew he was going to be in trouble.

"You know exactly what I'm talking about," Hux said in an unusually stern tone. "How could you put me and Pentievra in danger like that? I expected more from you, Calex."

"I had no other choice," Calex said, defending himself. "I couldn't just leave her."

"When are you going to grow up?" Hux sounded more paternal than ever. "Some people in this world don't deserve your help. I know you, Calex. I know you have a kind heart and good intentions, but don't you realise the danger you put us in? Do you realise what would have happened if anyone had discovered that child here with us? Do you know what they would have done to me and Pentievra?"

"Yes, I do. And I'm sorry. But I truly believe she deserved my help. She's done nothing wrong."

"How do you know?"

"She... told me," Calex said, realising how pathetic this sounded.

"And you believed her?" scoffed Hux. "You're a fool Calex. A complete fool. You'll believe anything from a warm voice and a pretty face."

Calex refused to give in. "Yes, I did believe her," he answered back, "and I still do."

"You could have got me and my wife killed, Calex!" Hux scolded, quickly regretting raising his voice for fear that the farmhands would overhear.

"Calm down! Nobody knows."

Calex caught sight of Pentievra in the kitchen, but she turned away from him. His heart clenched in pain. Pentievra had never been so cold to him before. These were the only people who really cared about him and he could not bear for them to turn against him.

"Don't be angry with me," Calex pleaded, his voice weak with sadness.

Pentievra came towards him. "I've suffered a lot from being blind," she began. "I've been dependent on other people and excluded from many of the experiences that life provides them. But never, ever has somebody taken advantage of my blindness like you have."

Calex was too ashamed to say anything. His head sunk down and he felt Pentievra walking away from him. He felt deeply embarrassed, not to mention horribly guilty, but he could not forget about Hero now.

"Where is she?" he asked desperately.

"We don't know," Hux stated simply.

"But you must have some idea!" Calex spluttered.

"No, we don't, Calex. She left as soon as we asked her to go."

Calex turned his back on him and stormed away from Windberry Farm for the second time in twenty-four hours.

"Give him time and he'll realise his faults," Hux said to his wife. He rubbed his hands together thoughtfully and shook his head, then finished his cup of tea.

Chapter
SIXTEEN

Calex was furious. Heavy drops of rain began to fall and, after flash of lightning and a booming crack of thunder, a heavy shower took their place, which only made him angrier. There were no lifts to be caught on the roads, so he started to make his own way back to the city on foot. Eventually, a cart came along and he jumped on. He told himself he would go to work but he vowed that afterwards that he would do everything he could to find Hero and make sure she was safe. By the time he reached the city gates he was in an extremely bad mood. The rain was falling less heavily but Calex was already soaked to the skin. The cheeky pair of guards were on duty and asked him how his pretty wife was. Calex jumped off the cart and pretended not to hear them. As he passed through the tight, winding streets of Quilemoyena City he expected that he would be late for work but he struggled to care. His head was buzzing with anxiety.

A group of women gathered around a water fountain for their daily dose of gossip. Calex could not help but catch a little of their banter and his heart froze when he heard it:

"They found a Crimson woman with a mixed-blood child."

"A brownborn?!"

"I heard she's made a run for it."

"A Quilemoyenan, is she?"

"They'll find her alright. Bring her back here and rip her to pieces."

Calex could not avoid the gossip. As he listened out for it he found it was everywhere, as if a raging swarm of wasps had been let loose. He imagined where Hero might be at this moment. The possibilities stung him with terror. She might be running away through the forest, begging for sympathy from some shocked Violet or screaming with agony. There was no reason not to fear the worse. Calex could not bear it and decided that he had to find her straight away. His job did not matter. How could he simply leave her and the innocent child that they would parade through the city, its dead body on a stick as an example to others? Calex knew that they would show no mercy to a brownborn and his mother. He had made his decision to turn back, wiping his rain-soaked hair off his face. But a young man's voice stopped him in his tracks.

"Calex!" it called. Calex spun around and saw the face to match it. It was Elidocorc, on his way to work.

Oh, for Heaven's sake, not now! he thought.

"Are you alright, my friend?" asked his jolly colleague. "You look exhausted." Calex nodded and forced a smile. His cheery chum gave him a comradely thump on the back.

"Walk with me and we can be late together!" he said with a laugh. There was no way Calex could turn back now. Elidocorc was keen to complain about his nagging mother and how she was trying to find him a wife. No girl of Elidocorc's choosing would do; she had to be selected by his 'meddling mother' first. He expressed his frustration while Calex politely sympathised with him. His thoughts were elsewhere of course, but he could not let anyone see that. Ever since he met Hero he was having to keep secrets but it was the only way to keep himself out of trouble.

"Her taste in everything totally disagrees with mine," Elidocorc grumbled about his mother's latest find. "Guess what? She likes Kinsen cuisine." Elidocorc chuckled but Calex couldn't find the strength to join in. "What's that fruit you people eat hot?"

"Chanakai" Calex said, hiding his dislike for Elidocorc's patronising use of 'you people'. His mother used to bake this fruit with raisins and honey and his family had eaten it almost every day.

"Well, anyway. She loves it, I find it disgusting. This will never work!" Calex did not smile at this last comment, his patience exasperated. Elidocorc seemed oblivious to this and kept talking incessantly, preventing him from cutting in with an excuse to get away. The two young men soon arrived at the Sacred Heart and proceeded through the empty corridor. Calex knew he had to slip away now before it was too late and he was seen by somebody else, making his escape all the more awkward.

"Honestly, Calex, I don't know why my mother can't just leave me alone," Elidocorc droned on as they stepped into the footbath room. "Anyway, how are things going with your young lady?"

"Couldn't be better," Calex said in a monotone.

"Glad to hear it! I suppose your mother doesn't..."

"I'm sorry Elidocorc," Calex butted in. "I think I dropped a couple of coins in the corridor. I'll be back in a moment." Calex walked out of the room and checked to see if the corridor was clear. It was still empty and he heard the other auxiliaries chanting a prayer in another room. Without another thought, he made a run for it, dashing to the front doors, careful not to thud his feet on the carpeted floor. However, as he reached out for the handle, ready to open the doors and dash past the guard, a figure came and blocked his way.

"Good morning, Calex," Fabian Zora said sternly. Calex was lost for words for a moment. He finally managed to say: "Good morning, sir."

"Where are you off to in such a hurry?"

"I thought I dropped some..."

Zora interrupted him. "I would like to see you in my office, please."

Calex's pulse increased once again, making him feel sick to the stomach. What could Zora possibly want with me? He knows nothing about me at all, Calex reassured himself. How could he know that I know Hero?

He followed his boss to the office and took the seat he was offered. The older man cleared his throat.

"I don't know if you've heard the news that's been spreading throughout the island all morning."

Calex decided to feign ignorance; how would his boss know any better?

"I don't know what you're talking about, sir," he asserted calmly, placing his hands on the armrests of the chair. Fabian spoke again. "Early this morning, four or five hours ago, a woman was seen with a brownborn baby in the countryside. Word has spread like wildfire since then. Have you heard anything about this?"

"Not at all," Calex replied unassumingly.

"Do you know who this woman is?"

"I told you." Calex's grip tightened on the armrests. "I don't know anything!"

Fabian stood up and walked to the door while Calex stayed put in his seat. Calex's stomach somersaulted as he heard a key turning in the lock. A sweat had already started to break out on his forehead. Calmly, Fabian walked back to his chair behind the desk.

"Let's stop playing games, shall we?" he said, sitting down again.

"Mr. Zora... Why did you lock the door?" Calex lowered his hands from the armrests and rubbed them together as anxiety tightened its grip on him, becoming more and more difficult to hide.

"I'm going to ask you again," Fabian told him matter-of-factly. "Do you know who this woman is?"

It was obvious now that he knew. Calex lowered his head and sighed, partly with defeat, partly with embarrassment and partly with fear. "Yes, sir," he said in a little voice. "I know who she is."

Calex's boss smiled. "That's better, isn't it?" he said. "You see, there's no need to lie to me, Calex. I locked the door because you and I have some important things to talk about and I don't want to be disturbed. I know that you know this woman, Calex, because I had you followed, which is something we often do here at the Sacred Heart to check our workers' honesty and integrity. You will have read about this in the Workers' Handbook, no doubt."

Of course, Calex had not been able to read a single word of that document written in the Ekans alphabet.

"At first we followed you to check if you would say anything about the incident the other day. It was your first day in the team and I didn't know if I could trust you. Although I suspected the ring on your finger was Hero's, I thought you may just have found it in the street. To my utter surprise, my spy found that you were actually visiting Hero and he discovered that you had helped her."

"Your spy?"

"Yes. You know Elidocorc, don't you?"

Elidocorc! He had seemed so friendly with his explanations and sociable questions. And just that morning, Calex realised, he had led him into a trap. He would never have guessed before. That two-faced bastard!

Looking down at his lap, Calex feared that he was in serious danger now. If it was not for Elidocorc, he could have run away forever and never had to have this conversation. The reality was, however, that he was trapped in this room, trying to hide his fear from his boss. His job was over, of course, but what truly scared him was the real punishment: prison, deportation, or even worse than that. This day has been like a nightmare, Calex thought, and it's still only morning.

Then Fabian spoke: "I know you think I must be angry with you, but I'm not. In fact, I have to thank you."

"Thank me?" Calex looked up in surprise, barely believing the words. Hero had told him the day before that this man, her husband, had thrown her out on the street and left her for dead. Fabian sensed Calex's confusion and told him that he would explain everything.

"When the baby was born I was convinced that Hero had cheated on me and I wouldn't listen to a word of her protests," Fabian began. "But the more the dust settles, the more I realise how unlikely it is that she would have had an affair with a Violet man. There must be another explanation as to why the baby is a brownborn. I have a feeling I know what it is.

"Almost a year ago an incident similar to the one the other day took place. We were all hoping it was a one-off but now it's happened twice I haven't been able to stop thinking about it. This first sacrifice to protest, Elias String, just a fourteen year old boy, alone and afraid. He begged us not to offer him in sacrifice. Hero wanted to let him go and I felt we couldn't. It was like what happened the other day. I had to make a decision between two terrible options. Well, as I said, I've been thinking about it a lot. And I think that we were punished for our decision by our child being born as he was: the very thing that would destroy our lives."

Calex gave no response for a few, puzzled seconds as he processed the information. Then he spoke: "What are the goddesses trying to tell us by these Violets who don't want to be offered in sacrifice? It must be a sign."

"I don't know," Fabian answered with frustration. "The priests have no answers either."

"And sir," Calex added, "why are you sharing all this with me?"

"Because you're the only one who can save Hero. If anyone finds her she will be killed. Besides, no one can know about these Violets who have tried to escape. It destroys the system, it breaks the rules. Don't you understand, Calex? Quilemoyena would descend into chaos."

Calex felt more important at this moment than he ever had done in his entire life.

"What can I do?" he demanded, feeling the gravity of the situation heavy on his shoulders. His boss – his ally – leaned forward and spoke to him firmly and desperately.

"Calex, I need you to find Hero and the child. I need you to help them escape without the truth being discovered. I need you to take them somewhere they can be safe. If you find out something that would help us understand what's going on, you must let me know. Of course I won't ask you to do this for nothing."

Fabian opened the draw of his desk and took out a wad of banknotes. Calex felt a surge of hope. The possible future came into focus in an instant. This money meant freedom - it was enough to get away from the island for good. It was enough for them all to start a new life far away from here. Fabian told him there was no less than one thousand demarit sitting on the desk.

"Thank you, Mr. Zora," Calex gasped, as Fabian placed the notes in a little draw-string bag.

"I know that it's over between Hero and me," Fabian said wistfully as he stood up and unlocked the door. "But I just want to know that she's safe."

"I'll start searching for her right away," Calex announced, putting the bag of money deep into his pocket. "And if I fail, I'll die doing it."

"If you find out anything about these rogue sacrifices or the brownborn child, anything that could help us get to the bottom of this mystery, you will keep me informed, won't you? Write to me at 214 Carrowbean Boulevard, my home address. I want to be sure that nobody else will get that information before I do."

"Of course, sir. 240...?"

"214 Carrowbean Boulevard," he repeated, and then a shadow of sadness came over his face as he said quietly: "Hero will remind you, when you find her."

Smiling with gratitude, Fabian stretched out his hand to shake Calex's. Their hands joined together briefly. Then, without a second to lose, Calex headed towards the front doors of the Sacred Heart.

"If you ever come back," Fabian called down the corridor, as the opening doors revealed the light of day, "I'll make you an officer!"

Calex pretended to not hear this last comment. Thanks but no thanks, he thought as the doors shut behind him. It was startlingly clear now that his destiny was to be far away from the shores of Quilemoyena and the walls of the Sacred Heart.

Fabian took a deep breath, feeling strangely better than

he had done in weeks. A feeling he had forgotten existed seemed to glow throughout his body, right down into his fingertips. It was hope. It was the life-giving feeling that things were going to work out. Two other officers were in charge of making the selection for the ceremony today so Fabian sat back down at his desk to go through his mail. There was a bill from the water authority for fountain maintenance, a notice about taxes and... an invitation to a dinner party. The latter was from Esroh Tiger, the probable future Presidential candidate.

"Persistent, isn't he?" Fabian said to himself with a smile.

The Chief Officer of the Sacred Heart picked up his quill pen, dipped it into some ink and wrote that he would indeed be able to attend.

Chapter
SEVENTEEN

*I*t was even busier than usual outside Miss Kiber-on's boarding house. A cart led by a donkey had toppled over on the paving stones, the eggs it was carrying smashed into a gooey soup of yolk, white and shell. Passers-by gathered around nosily to survey the damage and watch the heated argument that was taking place. The cart-owner was quarrelling with a man who had walked in front of his vehicle moments before it fell on its side. They argued about whose fault it was while a dog barked excitedly at them, aggravating the donkey who protested noisily.

At the same time, two people took a seat on a bench opposite the boarding house. They were brother and sister, grown-up but only just. In their hands were triangular pastry parcels filled with lamb meat that they had bought from a nearby vendor. They enjoyed watching the egg-cart spectacle while they relished their breakfast. Soon, the man they were waiting for arrived, wearing a hooded cloak.

"He'll be here any minute," the newcomer muttered,

taking a seat beside them on the bench. The conversation between the three of them was to continue in hushed tones.

"What's with the hood?" asked younger man.

"I don't want him to recognise me, stupid," answered the hooded figure.

"Looks more like you're trying to draw attention to yourself. Anyway, was it easy to get out of the Sacred Heart without anyone noticing?"

"Easy as pie."

"You realise you're going to be in big trouble when you go back," said the girl.

"My dear sister," came the retort. "I'm not going back. It's finished for me now, being an auxiliary and Zora's little spy. And you, Rotagilla, you'll be able to stop working for that tailor, and Gorf you'll be able to stop... well..."

Gorf didn't have a job. He liked sleeping too much and his parents who they all lived with would never let him go hungry.

"In a couple of days we're going to be stinking rich." Elidocorc announced.

"I hope you're right, Elly," his sister mumbled.

She rolled his eyes at the way he always seemed to think he was on a stage, gazing out into the middle distance and waving his hands around with exaggerated gestures. Even his wide stance suggested he was always on the brink of performing a grand soliloquy. His theatrical manner, coupled with the hooded cloak, were not going to help him blend into a crowd.

"I suppose if it doesn't work you could try your hand at theatre." she scoffed.

"What on earth do you mean?" Elidocorc asked, as if there were a crowd of people watching. He held out his hand as if he were expecting someone to put something in it.

"Well, sometimes, Elly, it seems you were made for the stage," Rotagilla said. "You know, like an actor or something."

"An actor?" Gorf said with a snort. "He's nowhere near handsome enough."

Elidorcorc didn't appreciate his brother's joke. Gorf was delighted to have wound him up so much and guffawed.

"You two are infuriating," growled Elidocorc.

"Me?" shrieked Rotagilla, "what did I do?"

The eldest brother sighed dramatically and insisted they get back on track.

"Focus!" he ordered. "And have you both forgotten that we're supposed to be blending in and not drawing attention to ourselves?"

"Ha! Coming from you," laughed Rotagilla.

Elidocorc put his face in his hands and asked himself if he needed these two. He came to the conclusion he needed to put up with them, his chances of success being better if they worked as a team.

"This is a great plan," he told them. "How can we fail? Hardly anybody knows that woman everybody is looking for is Zora's wife. I suppose her family and Fabian Zora know but they're not going to give her away, are they? The only other person who knows is me as I was sent to spy on Calex. When I followed him to that farm he went to speak with a woman working in the field. I recognised her as one of the officers at the Sacred Heart. Not just any officer, but the Chief Officer's wife who had stopped working months before. I went back and reported to Fabian Zora and we are the only ones who know about Calex's connection to his wife. Don't you see? This is an opportunity that's too good to miss."

"So you think we'll make a lot of money?" Elidocorc's

younger brother asked.

"We'll make a fortune," Elidocorc said confidently, "and we'll be famous." And I'll be able to finally get away from you lot and our nagging mother, he thought.

"But Calex Maro and Fabian Zora," the sister said, taking a big bite out of her pastry parcel. "What will happen to them?"

"They will burn in the marketplace while everyone watches."

"Really?"

"Oh for goodness sake, Rotagilla. Are you in this or not? You're not having second thoughts are you? That woman has committed a terrible crime and she will be made an example of. And Calex and Fabian Zora must be punished to for trying to help her."

"You're right," his sister spat. "There's nothing more disgusting than bringing a brownborn baby into the world."

"What's the plan, Elly?" their brother asked.

"Calex has been given the mission to find Zora's wife." Elidocorc had heard everything, eavesdropping on their conversation that morning. "We will follow him and he will lead us straight to her. Then, when the time is right, take them back to the city."

"Then…?

"Then glory will be ours," Elidocorc quipped. "Did you bring everything we need?"

"I packed a bag with things to keep us going for a few days: water, some money, a blanket," came his sister's response. "And the horses are ready to go, of course." They had borrowed three horses from a neighbour in exchange for a few demerit. None of them were particularly confident on horseback but riding out into the countryside to follow someone would not be possible without.

"I said we were going on a little trip to the coast and back," Rotagilla said. "He said he didn't need the horses for a few days and he was certainly happy to take my money in exchange. He knows we live next door, anyway."

Elidocorc nodded in approval.

"I've got the bow and tranquillising arrows," Gorf said, showing his contribution.

"So you managed to get hold of them? Good work," said Elidocorc.

The arrows were made to be used on horses and Gorf had stolen them, as well as the bow and quiver, from a veterinarian who lived in their building. In peaceful Quilemoyena City, it wasn't easy to acquire weapons. Either you were from the upper class and enjoyed the pastime of hunting in the woods close to the city walls, or you had a specialist job that gave you access to tools that could be used as weapons. The local butcher had a variety of knives to steal, but Gorf didn't want to harm the people they were after. Bringing them back to the city alive would be much better than killing them.

"Be careful with those tranquillising arrows, Gorf," Elidocorc warned him. "You have to shoot them into muscle. The thigh, for example."

"I know that,' Gorf retorted. "Wouldn't be much use shooting it into their eyes, would it?"

"Certainly not." Elidocorc winced at the thought. "You mustn't seriously injure them or kill them. They'll be worth much less if they're dead," he said.

"You talk like I don't know what I'm doing," Gorf complained.

"Well, do you?"

His brother hesitated, saying nothing.

"Have you ever even shot an arrow before?" Elidocorc asked with a sigh.

172

"No. Have you?"

"No."

"Well, how hard can it be? Just pull back the bow, aim and let go."

Elidocorc sighed, a grand gesture of despair. The tranquillising arrows could be perfect for their purpose, but none of them had the faintest clue about archery. Elidocorc's brother and sister considered this point and they finished their breakfast, wiping their greasy fingers on their tunics. Their older brother kept an eye out for Calex Maro, grateful that the fallen cart was attracting everyone's attention, making them much less conspicuous. When Calex finally arrived, out of breath from running, he noticed the cart-owner arguing noisily about the eggs but not the three nondescript people sitting quietly on the bench secretly waiting for him.

Calex entered the boarding house for what he presumed would be the very last time. After collecting his few possessions he would leave for good. Miss Kiberon followed his form with her eyes as he dashed past her open-doored office and up the staircase. The weighty woman sneered as she sorted her paperwork. She did not trust that boy. There were many dark characters in Quilemoyena City and she had always tried not to let any of them in her boarding house. Some years ago, Miss Kiberon had rented a room to a man who seemed to be rather odd: always rushing about, always rather sneaky and secretive. He turned out to be on the run from the law over some dodgy business involving smuggling pearls. Miss Kiberon nearly lost her licence to run her business and ever since she had been more careful. But maybe she had made a mistake with Calex Maro. He was constantly running in and out, often in a hurry and he never paid the rent on time. Around one year ago, that room on the top floor had been empty and nobody else was interested so she had let him have it, not wanting to lose money. With hindsight, she regretted that she hadn't been more sceptical when she let in a mysterious foreigner, who was much too young to be living alone in the first place. He had begun to remind her of the man who nearly destroyed her livelihood. She did not like Calex Maro and she felt that she had every reason to feel that way.

Miss Kiberon carried on with her work, checking her payment records as she did every week. Nearly all present and correct, she was pleased to see. Quite a few people had been asking about rooms to rent here recently. She considered that now might be a good time to raise the rent. Calex Maro interrupted her thoughts. What does he want? she thought. He had an overly friendly smile plastered on his face and she wished he wouldn't bother.

"Miss Kiberon, I arrived at my room and found that I've received a letter."

"Ah! I've received one of those before," she jeered. What an idiot, she thought as she looked down to study her records again.

"Well, as you may know, I haven't yet got to grips with the Ekans alphabet. Could you please read it out to me? I'd be most grateful."

Miss Kiberon seemed impressed. So this Calex had contacts who wrote letters in the Ekans alphabet? She never thought that he would know people that sophisticated. Still, she made a point of seeming to be put out by having to read the letter. It would not take much time and effort to oblige the fool.

"Oh, go on then," she sighed.

She reached out over her desk and Calex passed her the scroll. It was poorly presented, on a dirty scrap of paper, with no sign of a wax seal. Miss Kiberon sneered at it like it was covered in cow dung. It was another easy excuse to look down on Calex.

"And there was me thinking you had friends in high places for a moment there," she said. "I guess not."

Dirty letter, no wax seal, poor presentation… that must just be the way they live in Kinsen, she thought. If these foreigners really must live here, they should at least make an effort to conform to the Quilemoyenan way of life.

"Pour me some water, will you?" Miss Kiberon asked him as she rolled out the damned thing. As she began to read out the letter, Calex's heart began to beat fast as he realised who it was from.

Dear Calex,

I know I haven't known you for very long but I don't have anyone else to turn to. You're my last hope, the only person on my side.

Realising it was from Hero, Calex asked Miss Kiberon to stop and reached for the piece of paper that should have never made its way into her hands. She kept reading aloud nonetheless, turning away from him, and raising her voice as she continued.

We are in the area the Sacred Heart refers to as Sector 375. I will stay in a barn there until sunset. If you don't come I will move on, I don't know to where. I know it's selfish to put you in more danger, but it's a question of life and death now.

"Miss Kiberon, please stop! This is private!" insisted Calex, but he knew it was too late. She kept on reading, as if to taunt him.

I understand if you choose not to come, if you've had enough

and don't want anything more to do with me.
It's up to you. Whatever you decide, I want to thank you for
helping me and my baby.
Your ever grateful friend, Hero.

Miss Kiberon placed the letter down on the desk and
sneered at the boy it was addressed to. He handed her
the glass of water but she knocked it violently aside,
breaking the glass into small pieces and splashing its
contents over the floor and wall.

"I had a feeling you were mixed up in something," she
seethed, "but this is beyond what I could ever dream
of." Calex took an alarmed step back as he realised that
not even she had escaped the morning's gossip.

"It's not what you think," he offered, being all he could
come up with. His skill for making up stories had let
him down. There was no way out of this one.

"I've never trusted you," Miss Kiberon sneered, standing up.

"I know, but if you let me explain…"

"Get out!" the landlady shouted, finally losing her patience. "I want you out! Now! This is not a place for
criminals."

Calex grabbed the letter from her hand and raced up the
stairs to collect his things. Making him stay there to de-
nounce him would not be in her best interests. It would
be terrible for the reputation of her boarding house.
She would eject him from her residence as quickly and
calmly as possible and never speak of him again. The
boy swiftly emerged with his few possessions in a leather shoulder bag that was probably worth more than its
contents.

"There'd better not be a trace of you left in there, Maro."
He tossed her the key.

"There isn't," he replied. Calex could not bear to meet

her fiery eyes before he left.

"Oh and before you go," she seethed, "you can clean up that broken glass on the floor."

Calex finally met her gaze. That really was too much. "Oh, get lost!" he huffed and left the building.

Miss Kiberon was furious and for a while she paced up and down the room. She needed to get outdoors for a while. She needed some ale. Trying to cool her nerves, she grabbed the ceramic jug of water and drank straight from it. It was warm and stale. She slammed it back down, lucky that it didn't smash. From now on, no foreigners, she thought to herself. Quilemoyenan born and bred only.

Then, she saw the silhouette of a couple form in the doorway.

"Can I help you?" she asked cautiously.

A humble-looking man appeared with a visibly pregnant woman on his arm. He cleared his throat and asked in a quiet voice: "Are you Epoletna Kiberon?"

"Indeed I am. And what can I do for you?"

"We were wondering if you had any rooms available."

Miss Kiberon was happy not to decline. "Yes, I have something that would be just right for the two of you."

The woman rolled her hands across her belly. "I mean, three," she added, cocking her head.

"We're glad to hear it," exclaimed the man, exchanging nods with his wife. It would be horribly cramped in that room but Kiberon knew that they would not find a better deal within the city walls. This impoverished pair were obviously looking for the cheapest room possible and she had it. Perhaps she should have been more suspicious: were this couple on the run? Had they eloped together when she ended up pregnant? As usual, Kiberon's sheer greed pushed aside any concerns. It appeared that the people looking for the cheapest rooms were always the dodgiest but Kiberon simply thought of her purse getting fatter and fatter.

"There's everything you need here," she announced. "The bathroom and dining room are on this floor and dinner is provided every night. There's no cot in that room but I'm sure we can get one before the little one arrives. When's he due?"

"I don't know," said the woman shyly. "A few weeks perhaps."

"Plenty of time for you to settle in then," Miss Kiberon beamed. "Should we do the paperwork right away?"

"You haven't told us about the rent" the man said nervously. "Someone told me it's fifty demarit a week here."

Miss Kiberon was pleased to introduce her new rates. "Fifty five," she announced with a yellow-toothed grin.

*I*n the wet streets of Quilemoyena City, Calex destroyed the dangerous scroll immediately, tearing it into little pieces and leaving them in different piles of rubbish along his way. He felt so angry with himself. How could he have been so foolish as not to realise the letter might be from Hero? Who else did he know who was well-bred and educated enough to use the Ekans alphabet in a casual letter? He was bewildered that Hero had managed to get that note to his address. She had perhaps given it to a carefree Violet child to deliver in exchange for the only money she had left.

And now, Calex realised, he was homeless and possibly in grave danger too. Calex stood outside the closest city gate and soon managed to hitch a lift with a farmer heading out in a northerly direction towards a village called Willowkey. Calex had never heard of it and asked the farmer if he knew the sector number of his destination. The farmer laughed at his question; of course he didn't know. The sector numbers were used by Crimsons at the Sacred Heart. Violets, on the other hand, knew the names of towns and roads and didn't pay any attention to the Sacred Heart's system. Thanks to working there and casually observing the Table of Choice, Calex had learned a little about sector numbers. He figured from the farmer's description that this place must be between 360 and 390 in Sacred Heart terms.

He soon found out he had figured incorrectly. After an annoyingly slow journey on wet muddy paths, Calex was dropped off in a village square, disappointed that he was only about halfway to his destination of Sector 375. A wooden signpost told him it was 223. The farmer was not going as far as he had hoped.

He would see about getting to the barn by finding another lift. It would be harder to find someone now that he was out in the countryside. The road was empty and he needed a drink. The need to quench his thirst had started to take over his thoughts, replacing those of Hero. He could no longer ignore this thirst.

There was what seemed to be a tavern in the village square. As Calex approached, he saw the words Willowkey Arms painted above the door. Stones crunched under his feet as he walked past the butcher's, blacksmith's and tailor's, and he averted his eyes from the gaze of the few Violet villagers who saw him. He was filled with the paranoid assumption that they could read his thoughts. It felt as if they could tell that he was an ally of the most wanted criminal on the island of Quilemoyena. The reality was in fact worse: he was her only ally and she was desperately waiting for him to come and meet her. This thought made him hurry his pace and he strode into the tavern, whose walls were decorated with antlers of every type, and swiftly perched himself at the bar. The few eyes in that gloomy establishment inspected him then got back to their own business.

"What can I get you, my Crimson friend?" asked the innkeeper, who had been mopping the floor.

"A Herringbone, please." Although he would have preferred a large glass of water, he knew better. The water that ran in streams and rivers was usually safe to drink, but Calex had often got stomach upsets by drinking water from just anywhere, not knowing if it had been stagnant in a barrel for days on end. Ale was always a safer bet. As money was no longer a problem, Calex decided to treat himself to a good one. A large mug of Herringbone appeared, Calex passed over a silver coin in payment and then quickly proceeded to drain the mug. Despite expecting a fishy aroma, the ale had notes of hibiscus and carrowbean – floral and a little nutty with a bitter aftertaste. It was a flavoursome and robust brew. Calex ordered another one.

"So what brings you to Willowkey?" the innkeeper asked, placing a second mug in front of him.

"I'm heading to the coast," Calex said, which was, of course, the truth.

"Running away from something, are you?" The innkeeper's tone was jokey.

"No," Calex exclaimed, more defensively than was necessary.

"Running to something, then."

Calex shrugged and gave a little hiccup in response to the ale. He was in no mood for making conversation; not in these circumstances. While he lapped up the contents of the mug, the innkeeper wandered over to where two other customers were drinking.

Calex listened to their exchange: "I wouldn't mind that reward they're offering."

"How do you know there's a reward?"

"There must be! Ask that Crimson, there. He'll know."

They turned to Calex, who they rightly assumed had

come from the city and would have fresh news about the gossip. But the Crimson lad was no longer there. On hearing the subject of their conversation, he had taken to his feet and left the murky darkness of the tavern.

Out of pure desperation, Calex took the reins of one of the tallest horses tied up in the tavern's stable. Protesting about this unfamiliar rider, the dusty-coloured horse seemed to ignore Calex's efforts to lead him out of the tavern's stable. Just as Calex was about to give up, the horse started to co-operate. Calex mounted him and rode into the village square, then before anyone had a chance to suspect him of stealing a horse, made him gallop away on the road heading north out of the village. Calex hardly had a Violet's mastery of horse-riding, but he was certainly better at it than most Crimsons thanks to those years spent in the countryside. He headed northwards, much faster than an oxen-pulled cart could take him. The road was drenched from the rain, and mud soon coated the horse's legs, splashing up to its rider's shoes and trousers. The thick soup of cloud disappeared and some patches of blue emerged in the sky as Calex approached his destination.

Eventually, he caught sight of the little wooden signpost labelled 375 and saw signs of a sparsely populated village. Among a few cottages he noticed a barn, the only one in sight, and made his way to it. He was now so close and the fiery urge to find Hero was stronger than ever. Calex got the horse to slow down to a trot, looking out for a trap and paranoid that someone might be watching or following him. A couple of Violets working in the cornfields had turned their heads at an outsider entering their realm.

A black terrier appeared from what seemed like nowhere and started yapping at the horse and running around its legs. Startled, the horse snorted and flared its nostrils. "Steady, boy," Calex said, but the horse threw him off anyway. Calex landed on his side in the grass with a thud. He regained his senses and was relieved that he was not hurt. As he pulled himself to his feet, he saw the horse galloping away into the distance, back in the direction of Willowkey. Calex hoped he would soon be reunited with his owner.

The fierce little dog had wandered off and there was not a single person in sight. Calex anxiously stepped into the dark barn, his breathing slowing down. The barn was a huge wooden structure and the sound of his footsteps was amplified. Several hens clucked as they roamed around and an abundance of hay was piled up at the far end. One or two slats in the wooden roof were missing and sunlight poured through onto the floor below in bright stripes. No one would ever be able to tell there had been a thunderstorm a short time earlier. Calex heard the hay crunching beneath his feet as he surreptitiously walked farther in.

"Hero?" he called in a loud whisper. "Are you here? It's me, Calex."

An intense sense of relief flooded him as he saw her emerge from behind a hay bale. And it was her. Her small frame, her sweet and freckled face. She managed an exhausted smile.

"Calex," was all she said as she walked towards him.

"What happened to your hair?" Calex gasped. Her rich ginger locks had gone, leaving unevenly cut hair, much shorter than his.

"I sold it and used the money to get that note to you," Hero told him. "Does it look so bad?" Calex ran his fingers through it, shook his head and smiled at her tenderly. Lit by the sun, it was almost the colour of butterscotch.

"Thank you for coming," she whispered. She clamped

her arms around him and pulled him close. Calex was nervous, but let himself hold her. They embraced for a while, each with plenty to say to one another, but feeling no need to say it. Eventually, Calex told her of how his landlady evicted him when she read the letter.

"I'm sorry. It never even occurred to me that you wouldn't be able to read the Ekans alphabet," Hero apologised. "It all happened so fast. It was a huge risk to send it to you and I almost didn't do it."

"I'm glad you did," Calex said. "But I was going to look for you anyway." He looked her straight in the eyes, running his hand through her boyish haircut.

"I just can't shake you off, can I?" she joked.

Calex chuckled and shook his head. "No way," he said fondly. "Listen, I'm sorry about yesterday..."

"No, I'm sorry," she jumped in. "I felt really bad after you'd left. I thought that maybe you'd never want to speak to me again."

Calex smiled. "I'm the one who should be apologising, losing my temper like that," he said.

"Let's forget about it," she concluded, hugging him again. Her ear was pressed against his chest where she could feel the beat of his heart. Calex felt self-conscious thinking of how loud it must have been beating; embarrassed that Hero might realise just how much he liked her.

They stood in the area of the barn where the sun shone down, like two actors on a stage in a spotlight. A feeling of giddiness embraced them both, dizzy from one another's beauty.

"I spoke with Fabian," Calex said, knowing this news would be important to her. "He gave me a thousand demarit to take you and the baby away." Calex gave Hero a concise version of what Fabian had said. She listened closely to his every word, wide-eyed with attention.

"So at last he believes me," Hero sighed. "Oh, there's so much to ask you. How did he know that you knew me?"

"He had me followed."

"Ah, yes. Fabian always seems to have someone he can call on to spy for him. But anyway, Calex. We need to leave. I'm a fugitive, remember?"

Calex ignored her last comments and slipped his hands around her waist, surprising the both of them.

"Are they spying on us now?" he dared to say, looking her straight in the eyes. She could not find her words, left absolutely speechless by this comment.

Maybe this could be a good time to kiss her. But damn! How was he supposed to know when? He remembered one of the farmhands in an idle conversation saying something about 'the right time' but how was he supposed to know what that meant exactly? The farmhand had not said anything about that. Calex wished he had asked.

The magical moment was quickly interrupted as the sound of footsteps approached. Calex and Hero remembered that they were trespassing and they let each other go.

"Who are you?" It was a Violet farmer, her dirty face bewildered at the sight of these Crimsons. "And what are you doing on my land?" she demanded.

Calex acted quickly. "I'm an officer of the Sacred Heart," he announced confidently. It might have sounded more natural coming from Hero – she'd had far more practice after all.

"Has my time come?" The woman's little voice trembled as she fell to her knees.

"Not today, my friend," came Calex's apologetic response. The woman's look of enchantment disappeared. "Oh," she grumbled, standing up. "Then what are you doing on my land?"

"We're just doing a random check for stolen livestock in this area," Calex told her, as calmly and professionally as he could manage. "There's no need for you to ask us questions. Continue with your work."

The farmer frowned. "That's all very well, sir, but what has stolen livestock got to do with the Sacred Heart?"

Good question, thought Calex. He considered her point but no clever and convincing story came to him.

"Well," he began sheepishly, "it has more to do with the Sacred Heart than you think." The woman's face looked alarmed and she took a step closer to Calex as if to divulge a secret.

"Listen. I'm just borrowing these hens from the farm next door, I swear," she confessed. "I promise you I had no intention to keep them forever. I…"

A little whimper had broken out into a scream. The tiny child had awoken in the hay. Hero rushed over to tend to him.

"What are you doing with a baby in my barn?" demanded the woman, creasing her forehead. Hero picked the infant up and tried to comfort him. The woman looked closer and her suspicions were confirmed. The puzzle was solved as she realised exactly who these people were. She had heard the gossip from the milkman an hour before.

"Why, you!" she shrieked. "Adnap! Come quickly! Adnap!"

"We need to run," Calex whispered to Hero as the farmer called for her husband. "Come on, let's go!"

He threw their bags onto his back while she clung to the baby. She had a long piece of cotton with her, to wrap him up and then tie around herself, but there was no time to sort that out now.

They ran out into a cornfield. Though not as sharp as

wheat, Hero's bare calves would be scraped nonetheless, her trousers ending at the knee. Both of them lost their balance on the uneven ground many times and nearly fell. They kept on running nevertheless, although their legs were desperate to stop. The field gave way to a patch of woods. The baby cried louder, uncomfortable from being shaken about so much, and he had a way of soaking up the anxiety around him.

When the trees surrounded them sufficiently, they slowed down their pace.

"I hate running," Hero said, gasping. "Shh, little one. Settle down."

She rocked him, desperately trying to soothe him.

"Could you take him for a second?" she asked Calex, who nervously held the baby as Hero wrapped the fabric around her body, creating a secure pocket. When she was ready she wrapped him up in the fabric, Calex helping as best he could.

"He seems to like that," Calex said, and then: "I think we're alright. No one seems to be following us."

"But for how long?" Asked Hero, hopelessly.

"Come on, don't think like that," said Calex. "Let's just get our breathe back."

They both sat down on the mossy ground, exhausted.

"We should probably make our way to Evah-Schir," Calex suggested. "It has a large harbour and I know the town well. It's where I arrived on the island, where I met Hux. We could take a ferry tonight."

"To where?"

"I don't know," Calex said. "But does it matter?"

"I don't suppose it does, really," she said with a shrug. She looked down at the baby in the wrap.

"He's sleeping," she marvelled, amazed by the fact that he was oblivious to everything going on around him. Her heartbeat could be felt strongly now that he was close to her chest, and he had felt instantly soothed.

Calex too reflected on the baby's unawareness of everything besides its own basic needs. "It's incredible, you know, when you think about all the trouble he's caused."

He instantly realised that this sounded rude and Hero told him off for it.

"It's not his fault," she tutted.

"You're right," Calex said by way of apology. "Of course it isn't." He hesitated before he said what was on his mind. "It's funny though..." he continued, "how he is... the way he is. The... mixed blood thing."

"You want to know about that?" Hero asked, turning her head to look straight at him.

"Well, if you want to tell me."

"Honestly? I haven't been with anyone besides Fabian. That's the truth." Her voice sounded defensive, as if Calex had accused her of something she had not done.

Calex, meanwhile, blushed a shade of red brighter than Hero's hair. He gave a little grunt in response and gulped. "That's not what I was asking," he mumbled. He brushed his hair back awkwardly in a futile attempt to hide his beetroot face.

"What were you asking then?" Hero asked, a little amused.

"I don't know exactly," Calex admitted with an awkward shrug.

"Listen, Calex," Hero continued. "This might come as a surprise to you but there's nothing to tell. It's a mystery to you as it's a mystery to me." Hero looked down at the child's face and smiled. He was as pure and innocent as any other baby. None of this was his fault and he deserved to be treated with love just like every infant in the world.

Hero gazed unerringly at the child's face but Calex's

eyes were regarding her, the short locks of hair stuck to her face with sweat. He focused on this and the sound of her breathing which was so captivating. Once again, he inhaled her earthly scent carried by the light breeze. He could tell how much she needed rest and a place not to be scared anymore. Then he sensed something else coming from nearby. There was a crackle of dried leaves on the forest floor and a rustle of the living ones on the trees. There is someone here, thought Calex anxiously. He noticed Hero tense up too, and the light hairs on her arms rose. He expected a group of burly men with weapons to appear imminently from the dark of the forest, but he was wrong.

In front of them came just one person: a Violet boy in his mid-teens. Both the Crimsons looked at him, but Hero was far more shocked than Calex. Was he really who she thought he was? Could it be? She looked at the palm of his right hand to confirm her suspicions and saw the long, thick and ugly scar that travelled all the way up to his elbow. Now there was no mistaking it. She was sure it was him.

With sheer surprise she muttered his name: "Elias String."

Chapter NINETEEN

"What is it?" whispered Calex to Hero, startled by her reaction. "Who is he?"

"His name is Elias String," she said. Calex recognised the name but at first he could not remember why. Then he recalled his conversation with Fabian Zora that morning. The first Violet sacrifice to protest his fate. However, Zora had never mentioned that the boy was still alive.

"That is indeed my name," said Elias. "But tell me, have we met?"

Hero was confused. The boy must have been pretending not to remember her. After all that had happened, how could he forget?

"You were a sacrifice at the Sacred Heart about a year ago," Hero said.

Elias nodded calmly. "I was."

"Yes, Fabian Zora told me about that," Calex said. "But, if you were a sacrifice, what are you doing here? Did you escape?"

"Yes, I escaped the Sacred Heart. But I must ask, how do

you know this?"

"You don't remember me?" Hero asked, starting to feel annoyed. "I suppose you're someone who goes round attacking people all the time then."

"I attacked you?"

"Yes, in the Temple of Emo in the city." Elias looked confused. His eyes narrowed as he thought hard. Then he shook his head with bewilderment. Calex observed the scene in confusion, watching it play out with a lost expression on his face.

"That time is mostly a blur to me."

Elias String's eyes squinted as he focused earnestly on regaining his memories.

"I remember sleeping for many days and finally waking up. My mother and my neighbours all thought I was nearing death but by some miracle, I survived. I had been drugged with carrowbean root essence and it made me very ill for several days. Could you tell me who are you, exactly?"

"I'm Hero Zora. I was an officer of the Sacred Heart."

"Ah yes." Elias was remembering something. "You were the one who came for me that morning. You were with another man... the Chief Officer."

"That's right."

Elias looked Calex up and down. "It was not this man."

"You smothered me with your own blood," Hero reminded him.

"I did what?" Elias gasped. "I'm sorry. I don't recall."

"Alright then, let's try another question: why did you run away from the Sacred Heart?"

"That's an easy question. I didn't want to be sacrificed. Would you?"

"Well no, but that's different," Hero replied. "We're Crimsons. And anyway, It's the goddesses who choose who gets sacrificed, not you. You caused us a lot of trouble, you know. We were worried that the goddesses would punish us for letting you go."

"And did they?"

"We were worried about all sorts of things. A plague, drought, famine. But none of those things ever came to pass, at least not yet."

Elias made his own conclusion: "So they must have been on my side," he said.

"But why did they choose you?" Calex intervened.

Elias's eyes glazed over and he suddenly seemed troubled. "I have a feeling I know," he said. "But I think it will take some time to explain."

"I don't know if we have time for this," Calex said, shaking his head.

"Of course we do!" Hero said firmly. "This is really important, Calex."

"What's the hurry?" Elias said to Calex.

Calex sighed. "Just take my word for it," he said.

Elias String didn't seem satisfied by that answer.

"We are on the run, Elias," Hero said, trusting her instinct that it was safe to open up to him. "My baby was born with mixed-blood and everyone on this island seems to have found out about it."

"I hadn't," Elias said, trying to take a look at the baby. Out of habit, Hero had hidden his face from view. "Anyway, what does that mean? Mixed-blood?"

"What do you think?" Calex said, rolling his eyes. "Half Crimson, half Violet."

Elias's eyes opened wide. "A real, living brownborn."

"I don't like that word," Hero said.

"Can I see?" Elias asked, leaning forward.

"No," said Hero, stepping back. "He's not a freak show attraction."

"I mean no harm," Elias reassured her. "He is surely as precious as every other living thing."

Hero was very touched. "You'd be the only person in this world to think that, apart from me," she said with sadness.

"And me," Calex added, which made Hero's eyes swell with tears.

They were surrounded by nothing but trees and vegetation, and the nearest road was well out of earshot. The only sounds were those of the birds. Yet, both Calex and Hero felt ill-at-ease.

"We shouldn't talk about all this out here in the open," Hero said cautiously, lowering her voice. "I don't feel safe."

"My house is just over there," Elias said, pointing. Calex gave Hero a subtly wary look. Could this be a trap?

"That sounds good to me," Hero said, before Calex could object. She had already decided that Elias was harmless.

Elias led the way and they arrived at his house, which was well isolated on the outskirts of a village. It was an old house made of stone, riddled with lichen at its base and with ivy at its sloping roof. If it could, it would speak of the dozens of Violet people who had lived within its walls. The dark blue paint on its door was peeling away to reveal a green layer of paint, which itself was peeling away to show the ancient but sturdy wood beneath. Elias pushed his whole body weight onto it and let everyone in.

"You're safe here," Elias said. It was not quite enough to reassure Calex. After Hux and Pentievra's reaction that morning, it did not seem wise to trust anyone anymore. Still, the inside of the house was cosy and inviting. Pots and pans sat on shelves and hung decoratively from the walls. Glass jars of many sizes covered the windowsill, filled with peppercorns, sea salt, dried herbs, preserved vegetables and honey. There was a large stone fireplace where a few tired embers were glowing and a large sheepskin lay on the floor before it.

Calex and Hero took a seat at the kitchen table, taking in their surroundings. Elias, meanwhile, set a log on the fireplace and was using the bellows to reawaken the flames.

"Cup of tea?" he asked and they accepted gratefully. Although they had not realised before, they were both very thirsty. Elias poured some water from a bucket into a pot and set it over the fire, which had sprang back to life.

"Where are your parents?" asked Hero.

"Dad was taken for sacrifice a couple of years ago, and mum's out working in the fields," Elias replied. "I'm normally out there too of course but the farmer's given me the day off today. It's my birthday!"

"Happy birthday!" chorused Calex and Hero in unison.

"I'm fifteen today," Elias said proudly. "I made it."

He remembered, with some distress, his close shave with death. Hero struggled to believe she was now sitting in the boy's house, about to share a cup of tea with him. She had never thought she would see him again. Elias was taller now than that day at the Sacred Heart. He was lanky with corn-coloured hair that looked like it could use a wash. Most remarkably of all, he was still alive.

"I decided shortly after I escaped the Sacred Heart that I wanted to dedicate my lives to the gods, even more than is normal for a Violet. This world they created for us. It never ceases to amaze me. Since my escape, every sound I hear, every smell, every taste, fascinates me. The gratitude I feel for the gods. I can't stop feeling it and I wouldn't want to."

"That sounds amazing," Calex said. "I wish I could feel like that all the time."

Hero agreed. It sounded like Elias String had made a paradise of his own mind and it was a wonderful place to be, better than any physical palace.

While the water heated up, the three continued to chat, although it was mainly Elias enthusing about a caterpillar he had found on a leaf that morning, as if he had never seen one before.

"Its movements, the way it moved itself along. It made me laugh! I thanked the gods for that creation. It brought me so much joy!"

What happened to him? Calex wondered. As admirable as his appreciation for life was, his were unusual ramblings. Yet in true Quilemoyenan rural tradition, nothing of importance would be said before the tea was served. Elias noticed that Calex's eyes was wandering around the room.

"Make yourself at home," he invited. "Have a look around if you wish."

Calex's eyes fixed on the bookshelf whose shelves were packed high with well-used books. Except for a few, all the books were written in the Kreen alphabet. Calex slipped one out of the bookshelf. From its spine he could see that it was the classic telling of the Allirog Redips tale by Suma, although it had lost its cover a long time ago. Calex took it to the window where there was more light and turned to the yellowing first page. He read aloud:

Sing, goddess, of the Quilemoyenan, Redips, who discovered many an island, the folk who lived there and their strange ways. Come tell me, O Emo, of he who set sail on the Barromedian Sea to never return to his homeland. Tell me, from whatsoever source you may know, how he...

Suddenly, Calex looked up. Carefully, he surveyed the

view out of the window. He could have sworn he had seen something moving in the bushes. Perhaps it was just a wild animal, or his imagination.

"That was beautiful," Elias said. "I loved that. Thank you for reading it aloud."

"Sure, no problem," Calex said.

"Keep it if you like," called Elias's voice as he poured the boiling water into the teapot.

"Sorry?"

"The book. Keep it. I can't read."

Calex smiled. "Thank you but we're travelling light."

"I would love to enter the priesthood one day," Elias said wistfully. "But the fact I can't read would make that impossible."

"Well, it's certainly never too late to learn," Calex said, thinking of his own inability to read the Ekans alphabet. "You just need to find yourself a teacher."

"Easier said than done," Elias said with a shrug. Everyone he knew was illiterate too.

"Tell me about it," said Calex, smiling. Calex hadn't managed to find himself a teacher before but now Hero was around she could hopefully teach him to read the Ekans alphabet. He would get round to asking her soon enough, when they were out of harm's way.

Elias served the tea and took in the aroma. "Smell delicious, doesn't it?" Before he took a sip, he started admiring the shape of teapot, marvelling at the craftsmanship. "Look at the curve of it and that lovely handle," he enthused. "It's so beautifully made."

Hero found this endearing and smiled, but she couldn't match Elias's enthusiasm. In her house had been much more impressive examples of fine craftsmanship, most of them she'd never properly observed. The teapot brought Elias a joy and wonder usually reserved for those who had tried their own hand at pottery and understood the struggles of creating such a well-made object.

"It's about time we heard your story," Hero prompted before another distraction came along, as she blew on her cup.

Chapter
TWENTY

*E*lias String began.
"It all started when somebody told us about this house. The last owners had been taken for sacrifice a few days before and the house was abandoned. My mum decided to move in before anyone else got here."
"It was so terribly cold," he continued, remembering the details vividly as he retold the story. He recalled how he and his mother had trudged through the fields with sheepskins on their backs, battling against the raging wind and snow that was quickly gathering beneath their feet. Huddled together, they arrived at last and were relieved that the house was exactly where it had been described to them. There would surely be plenty of work on offer in the surrounding fields; just what impoverished folk like themselves needed. They both looked up at the stony structure whose sloping roof was carpeted with snow. A crow hopped across, leaving a string of marks with its feet. The first snowfall of the season had started the night before and not stopped since. Winter had fallen suddenly and earlier than ex-

pected in these parts.

"The house was much more comfortable than we were used to so it was definitely worth the effort to get here," Elias said. "We managed to get a fire going and we were soon nice and toasty, thanks to the house being in good condition, with glass panes in the windows, no less. So much better from where we'd come from. We searched in all the cupboards but the last people hadn't left any food. There were no pickles or grains, only some salt and herbs. The problem was, with it being so cold for the season, was that the whole island seemed to have shut down and there wasn't a single shop that was open."

Elias recalled the wrinkling carrot the last people had left on the otherwise empty table. His stomach growled. He shared it with his mother, knowing that in its half rotten state it was probably doing them more harm than good. Out of the window, the ground was frozen solid and nothing good could come of it. A hungry little bird searched for food but flew away without a worm in its beak. Beyond were evergreen trees standing together through the mist of snow. Where the trees stood was the edge of the forest and Elias had the idea to look there for food.

Elias continued: "So I went into the forest with a basket and a knife. I remember it now - my fingers and toes were killing me, I was so cold. I could see smoke rising from the chimneys of the houses in our new village and I wished that I could be all wrapped up, safe and indoors, as well. Soon, I told myself, as soon as I find some food to bring back."

Elias recalled how he had wrapped the old sheepskin tighter around him. He lucidly remembered wearing it whilst snuggled up in his father's arms by the fire, long before he had been taken for sacrifice, the smell of roasting meat making its way through the house. The hail was pounding deliciously hard on the windows and his father's hold made him feel safe and secure. It was a sweet memory but, as all Violet country folk knew, fortunes could change. One year could be kind to them while the next was cruel. If work dried up in one village, you moved to another. Which is exactly what Elias and his mother had done.

The boy went on with his tale: "I came across a dead squirrel, all frozen in the snow. I put it in my basket even though I've never had squirrel before but maybe my mum could have managed to make something nice out of it. Eventually, I found some blackberries and put them in my basket till the bush was empty. Then I decided to go back to the house. It wasn't very much food but if I'd stayed out there any longer I think my nose would have dropped off. But then I stopped, because in front of me was a deer. A graceful young deer with delicate legs. It was the only animal I'd seen alive in that forest. What happened next was beyond my wildest dreams."

"Did you manage to kill it? That would have kept you fed for a few days," Calex interjected.

Elias didn't answer his question. "Before I go any further I want to tell you about something that happened to me a few years ago, so that you'll understand the end of the story.

I was swimming in a lake with some other kids and that's when I made a discovery that's been on my mind ever since. I've never told anyone about it before."

Elias stopped speaking and poured more tea and for a moment, Calex and Hero were worried that he had changed his mind and would not go on with the story. But after a sip of tea and a deep breath, Elias continued. He remembered a bully with the face of a bulldog – aggressive but gormless – who had come towards him in the lake. With his enormous size and intimidating manner, it was no surprise that many of the village children were scared of him. The boy splashed him and Elias, not quite knowing how to interpret this gesture, splashed back to join in the game and be friendly. But he had not read the signs correctly. For the older boy, Elias's actions meant starting a fight.

The bully pushed Elias under the water, forcing his weight over him. Down there, Elias saw fleshy weeds and the murky shadows of fish. Despite the bully's intentions, Elias was not scared. His skinny form moved swiftly underwater so as to escape a second attack. When he came up for air, he saw his predator looking around for him in confusion. A smile floated up onto his face as he saw that he had baffled the other boy, who looked annoyed that his victim had managed to get the better of him.

Elias felt much more comfortable over here, away from the others. He let himself sink beneath the surface again. He liked the free, weightless feeling of swimming underwater. It was as if, for those few seconds, he could experience being a fish, an entirely different being. He soon found he was close enough to the edge of the lake to touch its sandy, stony floor with his feet. Elias took a deep breath then descended all the way to the bottom. He looked around then closed his eyes, gradually letting bubbles of air escape from his lungs. When they were empty, he did not move a muscle and concentrated on what there was to listen to. It did not take long for him to realise that he could hear two people talking – a man and a woman – although the water muffled the words to the point of being incomprehensible. Why talk under water? Elias thought. And how did they have enough air to continue doing so? He opened his eyes to locate the two people, turning himself around but seeing that there was nobody.

On coming up for air, he saw that the other children were all across the lake. Elias went down once more to find out if he was just imagining things. But no – he heard the conversation continue and the voices become a little clearer. He possibly heard the word 'Quilemoyena' but apart from that he could not identify a single word.

When Elias came up again, he felt uneasy. He could not see these people and they may well have just been figments of his imagination. Elias was scaring himself. He wanted to ask someone else if they could hear the voices too, but who could he trust? Who would not laugh at him? There was one girl swimming in the lake that day who he might consider something of a friend. Elias finally managed to get her attention and separate her from the rest of the group. He described what he had heard and the girl's eyes widened with anticipation. On the count of three, they both disappeared under the water. Elias heard the voices straight away. He rose to the surface and waited for the girl to appear. Surely she heard it too, he thought, she must have done.

"Well?" he said when she emerged.

"It's all in your head, Elias," she concluded. "I can't hear anything down there except... water."

She turned to make her way back to the other children.

"Wait!" Elias called anxiously. "Don't say anything to the others, okay?"

"Sure," she said. She swam away, leaving Elias String alone and somewhat shaken. Fascinated but disturbed by his discovery, he never mentioned what he had heard to anyone else again.

Calex and Hero wondered what this story, interesting though it was, had to do with the incident in the forest. Elias got back to the story in question: "So there was the deer standing in front of me and I reached for the knife in my trouser pocket. I didn't have much hope. The deer would surely not let me get close enough to kill it, but I couldn't let this chance for food pass me by. I thought about using the berries I'd collected earlier as bait. Then I noticed: it was no longer snowing and the vicious wind had stopped. It was not even that cold. The grey sky was giving way to rays of sunlight and a little blue. Then suddenly, there was an incredible flash of white light. I fell to the ground and the berries flew everywhere. I thought the light had burned my eyes out. I thought I was blind! But no, my vision was coming back, and the light was cooling. But in front of me, the deer had gone. In its place was something entirely different."

Elias recollected how he stood there transfixed for a few seconds before it came to him that he should be bowed down on the floor. Before him was a towering woman, Violet-blooded like himself, but more than twice as tall. Her skin appeared the same shade of creamy, pale blue. She seemed to be wearing a long white robe but the white light that emanated from her was so intense that he could not tell. The boy knew from pictures in books and statues in public places that this was Emo of the three holy sisters, the divine protectors of the island of Quilemoyena on which he lived. He had heard stories of gods revealing themselves to people in legends. But why him? An ordinary Violet boy?

"Lift your head," she said. Her voice was soft and kind. "Do not be afraid."

Elias's sudden realisation made him gasp: hers was one of the voices he had heard in the lake that day. He knew it without a shadow of a doubt. It was clear now. The voices he had heard were those of the gods.

As the memories came back to him, Elias was glassy-eyed and his hands, held together on the table, were shaking. He was finding it difficult to speak.

"I don't remember what she said. I was so awe-struck. I just passed out."

Chapter TWENTY ONE

*T*wo days had gone by before another human being stepped foot in that corner of the forest. For the Violet miller Axel Noil, hunting was a hobby that both amused him and provided dinner for him and his wife. Since he started hunting here about five years ago, he always thought of this area as his little secret. There never seemed to be anybody else around; he had it all for himself. That was why he was so surprised to come across the body of an adolescent boy lying amongst fallen autumn leaves in the melting snow.

At first he thought the boy was dead, most probably killed by wild animals. On closer inspection, however, he found that there was not a mark on him. When Axel checked his pulse, he realised that the boy was as alive as himself. Sure enough, his chest was slowly rising and falling. Axel tried to revive the boy, shaking him and calling in his ear, but to no avail.

With his bow and quiver over one shoulder, Axel Noil managed to lift the tall, skinny boy over his other. He carried him back to his windmill which was thankfully not so far away. When his wife, Eva, saw him approaching with a human body over his shoulder she feared that her husband had accidentally hit him with one of his arrows. She was relieved when he explained everything to her.

While the upper floor contained the windmill's internal mechanism and the source of their livelihood, the Noils lived on the ground floor. They put the boy in the bed of their eldest son who had moved away years before. Eva brought a glass of water to his lips and he eventually opened his mouth and accepted a little. Regaining a little strength, he blinked and looked around him. Eva asked him a few questions but he seemed too confused to answer. He soon sank back into a deep sleep.

The next morning, the Noils found the boy sitting up in bed with his eyes open. He seemed disorientated and distant, only responding to their questions in monosyllables. Axel and Eva managed to find out that his name was Elias String and that he had been out looking for food in the woods. When Axel asked him why he fell and was unconscious he did not answer, staring vacantly out of the window. Either he had received a blow to his head that had made him forget or he was hiding a secret, they concluded. The Noils went about their business of grinding and selling flour while the boy stayed in bed. Although still dazed from his experience, he managed to make sense of the world around him. Looking out into the field, he saw that the snow had disappeared altogether. The weather, though autumnally chilly and windy, had vastly improved.

"The next day," Elias recalled, "I was feeling in much better shape. Also, I was worried about my mum. Of course, she didn't know where I had got to. I hoped she wasn't starving. The miller and his wife gave me some bread and soup in the kitchen. Just as they were seeing me off, we started to hear the bells... "

Elias's voice trailed of as he vividly recalled the sound. "In the name of the gods, it was horrible!" he shrieked. "Mr and Mrs Noil were overjoyed as you'd expect them to be, and I know I should have been too but... that meeting with the goddess changed something. I just wasn't the same anymore. And then you came in" – he looked at Hero.

For Fabian and Hero, it had started out as a completely normal day. There were seven Violets already in the carriage and Fabian and Hero made their final stop at a windmill. The middle-aged couple inside had heard the bells. Everyone knew what those bells meant; the bells that sounded to the trotting of horses an hour or so before midday. The couple in the windmill always wondered if the day would ever come when they would hear the ringing right up close, having come for themselves.

"It's time!" came Eva Noil's excited whisper. She took her kitchen apron off and hung it on its peg for the last time. Both she and her husband went into the bedroom and hastily changed into their best clothes which they had been saving for this very day. Axel wore an elegant velvet tunic of dark blue and Eva wore a rose pink linen dress that touched the floor. She picked up her hairbrush but her hand was trembling. Sympathetically, her husband took the brush from her hand and arranged her hair, then took her in his arms.

"I can't believe this is it," Eva whispered against Axel's shoulder.

"I know, sweetheart" Axel replied, tightening his grip around her. "You imagine it so many times but nothing can prepare you for the real thing."

The couple headed to the kitchen to share their joy with

their guest, the boy whom Axel had found in the forest a couple of days before. They could have found something smart for him to wear too, despite there not being much time. He was, however, frozen in his seat, a look of terror upon his teenaged face. The day the Sacred Heart had come for his father was one of celebration. Elias felt a tinge of sadness that he would never see him again, but the knowledge that his leaving was for the greater good more than made up for it. Yet now, Elias felt nothing similar to what he felt that day. He simply felt petrified.

"What is the matter, child?" Eva's tone was incredulous. "It is that special day. We are truly blessed."

Elias looked as if he wanted to escape, waiting for his moment to run, but stunned like a small animal under the gaze of a predator.

Then Fabian and Hero came through the front door.

Their Crimson blood gave their skin a different appearance from the others in the room. The man was around thirty; strong-looking with a broad chest and muscular arms. He wore a silvery-blue tunic that came down to the floor and a heavy medallion that hung around his neck. His square face was adorned with a neatly-trimmed beard. This man had a presence that demanded respect and attention.

The woman at his side was a great deal younger and smaller than him with almost translucent skin which was lightly freckled. Her hair was long and shiny, a rich shade of ginger-brown. Despite her size, she held herself with authority. She too was dressed in elegant robes; hers were a regal dark green.

The Crimson man spoke. He spoke with the refined style of someone from a privileged family with an important job.

"We've come from the Sacred Heart." It was the standard greeting. "Are you ready to come with us?"

"Oh yes!" Eva cried, struggling to contain her excitement. They both stepped forward and shook hands with the officers. The Noils' overjoyed reaction to their arrival was exactly what the officers expected.

"Come then, my friends," the man announced. "The carriage is waiting for you."

Axel and Eva Noil headed to the door, hand in hand. The officers proceeded to follow them.

"We've got theatre tickets for tonight, Hero," Fabian said under his breath. "I hope you haven't forgotten."

"Oh, what play is it again?" Hero asked.

"I don't remember, Hero," said Fabian, amused. "I think you must be the only person I know who goes to the theatre for the play and not just to be seen."

"Fabian, wait."

"What is it?"

"There's a boy under the table!"

They both looked at him. He was obviously trying not to be seen and the expression on his face was one of terror. The officers frowned with confusion at his unusual attitude to their presence. They waited for the boy to speak, but he said nothing.

"We've come from the Sacred Heart," Hero said, repeating the standard greeting. "Are you ready to..."

"No," came the boy's answer.

There was nothing but stunned silence from the officers. Finally, Hero asked the boy to come out from under the kitchen table.

The boy did so of his own volition - it would have been better than being dragged out - and then he pinned himself to the back wall of the kitchen.

"What's...going on?" Fabian asked him.

The boy struggled to find his words. "I don't want to go," he muttered. Nobody knew how to respond. What kind of person was this? A Crimson painted Violet? There did not seem to be another reasonable explanation.

"Why?" came Hero's perplexed response.

"I'm scared," he told the officers. A string of words flowed urgently from his mouth: "I don't want to come with you. I want to go home. I want to be with my mum. I want to live."

He was suddenly hit with a grave feeling of concern for his mother, realising that he cared for her more than anything else in the world. He imagined her at this moment, sick with worry. She could be out searching for him this very instant in the forest. If he let himself be taken away, she would never know what had happened to him. Nobody knew he was here in this windmill. No, he could not let this happen! He could not let himself go with them! Panic started to rise in his chest.

"Well, what do we do now?" Hero asked Fabian in a low, urgent voice.

"We can't just leave him behind. Rules are rules," Fabian said matter-of-factly.

"But something's not right," Hero retorted. "He's speaking like a Crimson."

The Violet couple were still at the front door. "I found him in the forest a couple of days ago," Axel intervened, hoping to shed some light on the situation. "He was unconscious so I brought him here. He's barely said a word and stares into space most of the time. I thought maybe he'd hit his head or something."

"Maybe he doesn't want to come with us because of something that happened out there," Hero suggested, her brow furrowed in thought.

"Like what?" Fabian scoffed impatiently. He was concerned that the ceremony was due to start at noon and they had no time to waste. Surely the rules were clear and indisputable. Collect the sacrifices and bring them back to the Sacred Heart. They had to behave in a dignified and refined way but the procedures the officers had to carry out were straightforward and repetitive. Or at least they had been until now.

Hero turned to the terrified Violet boy who had been watching them anxiously.

"What's your name?" she asked gently.

"Elias," he whispered. "Elias String."

"Elias, tell us what happened to you. Out there in the forest."

"Before, I would have come with you happily," Elias said.

"Before what?" Fabian snapped, eager to get out of there.

"Before I met Emo."

The goddess Emo! Divine protector of the island of Quilemoyena! Could this be true? Hero didn't know what to think. It would certainly explain why a Violet did not want to be taken. There were no records of this kind of behaviour.

Fabian was more stubborn and would not even consider changing his mind. The Noils were undecided, but what they thought had no importance in deciding the boy's fate. Truth be told, they were a little annoyed their glorious day was on the brink of being ruined by this commotion.

"I'll do anything you ask," Elias begged. "Just leave me here. Choose someone else. No one will ever know."

"The goddesses will know," Fabian told him sternly. "They know everything. And they will punish us for not doing our duty."

"If you take me they will punish you," Elias argued, "Emo will punish you."

"How do you know that?" There was a hint of mockery

in Fabian's voice.

"You may laugh at me now but you won't later," Elias said with grave seriousness. Hero felt threatened by his words but Fabian remained unshaken.

"This is nonsense," he snapped, wanting to end the farce once and for all. "We're going to be late for the ceremony. Let's get going."

"Don't be so hasty," Hero warned him. "Maybe he's not lying. Why else would he be disobeying us? Have you thought about that?"

"There are no two ways about it," Fabian retorted. "I understand that the way he's acting is extremely odd but his story is impossible. Why would a goddess reveal herself to a Violet peasant boy? Do you have any physical proof of this... divine encounter?"

Elias shook his head helplessly.

"Our duty is to collect the ten first people we come across in this area," Fabian told him. "You, Elias String, are one of them."

"No! Please! I don't want to die. My mum is waiting for me" Elias had been trying to keep himself together, to be calm and reasonable. This is how his mother told him to behave in difficult situations but sheer stress was overwhelming him. The boy grabbed Fabian's tunic, saying "please, please." Fabian frowned and pushed him away.

"Your mother will be happy for you, child," said Eva Noil from the front door.

"This is not negotiable," Fabian told then all. "I don't want to hear another word."

Hero sighed, resigning her suspicions that they were not doing the right thing. Fabian was the Chief Officer after all.

She turned to the Noils. "Go ahead to the others," she told them, ushering them out of the front door. Axel and Eva nodded then ran over to the carriage, trying to forget about the boy and enjoy their special day again. They threw their arms around their neighbours who had already been collected and were waiting there. As congratulations were shared, the couple took a seat in the carriage beside the others and joined hands with them.

"Was there a problem back there?" asked one of the sacrifices. "You took your time. We thought maybe you were out at the shops."

"That would have been bad timing!" said Eva and they all laughed.

Friends and family members who had not been selected gathered around, looking happy for their loved ones.

"Mum! Dad!"

The Noils turned to see their eldest son Libreg running across the grass to meet them. "I just heard," he called, catching his breath.

They exchanged hugs and spoke hurriedly to one another. "Send your siblings our love, won't you darling?" Eva said. By the time their other children heard the news, Axel and Eva would be gone.

"Of course, mum." Libreg brought his hand to her cheek. "Of course I will." Tears began to brim in his eyes and his parents could not help themselves from welling up too. They knew that there would be tears; it was just a question of when.

"I'm so proud of you today," Libreg exclaimed as the tears escaped down his cheeks.

"And we're proud of you, sweetheart," Eva sighed.

"The windmill is yours now if you want it, or give it to someone who needs it," Axel said, taking his son's hands firmly in his.

"I'll take care of everything," Libreg reassured them, hugging them both tightly.

Chapter TWENTY TWO

*B*ack in the windmill, Fabian was looking through his bag.

"I'm sure I've got some in here," he said, mainly to himself. "I need to be quick, damn it."

Then he pulled out what he was looking for. Carrowbean root essence. He used it when he had trouble sleeping. It was hard to come by as it had proven very easy to overdose on. Several people who took it had never woken up, the apothecary later finding they had a fight on their hands, or with wealthier customers, a lawsuit. Fabian had an expensive bottle of the stuff though and could measure it out in drops, thanks to the pipette in the screw top lid. Sometimes he would find himself wide awake at four in the morning with anxiety, made worse by knowing he would have to get up in only a couple of hours. He was so grateful for carrowbean root essence on those nights and always kept it close-by.

Fabian took a cup and filled it with the freshly boiled water from the stove. He discreetly put a couple of drops of the essence into it.

"Here," he said to the boy. "Drink this."

"Why?"

"It will make you feel better, that's all."

Elias String didn't take the cup, his scared eyes looking into the Chief Officer's.

Fabian didn't avert his glance.

"I said. Drink. This," he repeated, with more menace.

Afraid of getting hurt, Elias drank the contents of the cup. It tasted fine, maybe it was just water. He knew it was naive to think it might be, but he was terrified.

"You won't hurt me, will you?" asked Elias. Fabian didn't take his eyes off the boy and he said nothing at all.

"Tell me you won't hurt me."

"I can't," said Fabian, quietly, but Elias didn't hear him. He was already crumpling onto the floor, unconscious.

"He's sleeping," Fabian said to Hero. "Help me carry him to the cart."

"No wonder you never let me try that stuff," said Hero. "It's lethal."

"It's not lethal unless you don't know what you're do-ing. This boy is sleeping. I've given him just enough. We need to make sure he doesn't make a fuss on the journey back to the city. He will sit between you and me. Now come on, we need to hurry."

Hero shook her head with disapproval.

"This doesn't seem right," she said.

"Stop complaining and do as I say!" growled Fabian, almost at the end of his tether.

The officers sat the boy between them at the front of the carriage and they set off, leaving the waving loved ones and neighbours behind them. Far from a leisurely-paced trip back to the city, Fabian asked the driver to make the horses go almost twice as fast as they usually did. The other sacrifices did wonder what had been going on and why the boy was unconscious, but they didn't let it distract them from the moment they had been waiting their whole lives for. They trusted the officers of the Sacred Heart to know what they were doing. Some of the quietly reflected on their time in this world and some of them were chatting and reminiscing. Half an hour later, they were applauded by passers-by as they entered through the city gates. The sacrifices smiled with satisfaction, some waving at the Crimson crowds. Occasionally they had been the outsiders, gazing at those in the carriage with respect as it passed nearby. Now they were the ones inside and their heads were held high with pride. A Crimson woman lifted her young daughter onto her shoulders so she could get a better view of the carriage passing.

"Are they the sacrifices, mummy?" the child asked.

"Yes, that's right darling," replied her mother. "You can tell them thank you."

The little girl did so and the sacrifices waved to her.

"What a sweet gesture," cried Eva Noil from the cart, "Bless her."

They proceeded through the gates of the Sacred Heart and the sacrifices were awestruck by the sight of the magnificent courtyard and the towering volcano. They saw a little smoke rising tantalisingly from the top and they could smell the gas like rotten eggs that emerged from it too.

The horses leading the carriage came to a stop and one by one the sacrifices got out and lined up for their final walk. Fabian and Hero, joined by the ten auxiliaries, shook hands and kissed cheeks.

Axel turned to his wife. Smiling with jubilation he had never found her more beautiful. They exchanged private words of love and gratitude to one another.

This was just as good as they had imagined it. A priest

led the way and each of the sacrifices were escorted up the volcano by an auxiliary.

One auxiliary was left behind however, the one who would be accompanying Elias String. He seemed hesitant.

"Mr Zora, sir," he said. He wanted to ask why the boy was unconscious but it seemed cheeky to ask his boss that. "I'm not sure if I can carry him by myself."

"I'll carry him over my shoulder," Fabian told him. "You walk alongside me."

The procession began and they headed up the slope. Fabian was a strong man but he began sweating and struggling quickly. It was exhausting to walk up such an incline in the hot sun with a sacrifice over his back. The boy seemed to be stirring from his sleep. If Fabian had timed it right, they should be at the summit before he came to.

Hero stood in the courtyard, watching them go and wondering if they would ever come to regret this. Three more officers came out of the building, asking her what was going on. After all, this ceremony was usually very predictable.

It took ten minutes to get from the courtyard to the summit. At the top, the sacrifice and auxiliary pairs stood around the crater, spaced equally apart. Fabian put Elias String down on the rocky ground and breathed a sigh of relief. The Chief Officer hardly ever came up here, usually staying down in the courtyard, and it seemed to him to be a strange, eerie place. It was smelly and the heat from the crater felt like standing near a bonfire. Far from being a barren place, it seemed to have a spiritual presence, like all the gods themselves were there, at least in part.

Elias started to wake up but he had no recollection of the Crimson man before him or the words that had passed between them.

"Where am I?" he asked groggily. "I'm so tired."

"And you will get to sleep soon," Fabian said.

The sun was now directly overhead and the priest stepped back. He had said the final prayer and there was now nothing between the sacrifices and oblivion.

Elias looked across the crater of the volcano, still too sleepy to stand up.

The miller Axel Noil smiled at his wife Eva for the very last time. She, then he, jumped into void and was gone. Axel felt a split second of fear, a sudden flash of hesitation, but it only lasted an instant. He found himself falling now, falling fast and gaining momentum. His Violet destiny to be sacrificed was fulfilled at last. He was completely at peace, intoxicated with joy. He saw his wife disappear into the lava and then he too was swallowed up. The delirium of this long-awaited moment. When the molten rock seared the surface of his body, absorbing the precious blood from his severed vessels, he was too enraptured to even notice. Not a trace of his existence remained, his blood absorbed into the earth, his purpose fulfilled.

The boy's heart somersaulted in his chest as he realised what was happening, adrenaline waking him up fast. He got to his feet and trembled uncontrollably as he peered into the vast hole of rocky blackness. Sulphurous steam emerged from the cracks inside, filling the air with its stench and turning the rocks yellow. A terrifying drop gave way to a scorching hot pool of molten rock.

"Where am I?" cried Elias, more urgently. Nobody answered but he didn't need them to. He knew this was the summit of the volcano of the Sacred Heart, famous throughout the world.

"Why am I here?" Elias asked to anyone who would answer him, although nobody did. Again, he already knew the answer. He had been brought here for one reason alone: to die.

Elias watched in horror as the other sacrifices jumped, their bodies falling away from the edge of the crater. He was weeping now, his heart breaking. Finally his eyes met the Chief Officer's.

"Do you know?" asked Elias. He was the only sacrifice left now, the others having all jumped. "Do you know why I'm here?"

"Yes," Fabian answered, nodding. "You were chosen for sacrifice today."

Elias screamed. The scream had upset the auxiliaries and the priest, who stood nervously, looking awkwardly to the ground.

"Don't make me do this," Elias pleaded. He fell to his knees and grabbed the bottom of Fabian's tunic.

Fabian signalled for the nearest auxiliaries to restrain the Violet boy down. Time was running out. The sacrifice need to be completed. The two auxiliaries were filled with pity and guilt in the face of duty, grabbing an arm each, pulling the boy back up to his feet.

"I'm begging you," Elias tried again, resisting.

"It'll all be over in seconds," stammered one of the auxiliaries in a weak attempt to offer some consolation.

"I can't," Elias sobbed. "I can't do it."

The two auxiliaries eyed each other, silently sharing the fear that they might have to end up pushing him themselves.

This is your destiny," the priest called from across the crater. "To honour the gods." Then to Fabian he said: "It's past midday. We don't have any time to lose."

Elias squeezed his eyes shut and took a deep breath to slow down his thudding heart.

"I have to do this, don't I?" he said to the auxiliaries. "And there's nothing you can do to help me?"

The auxiliaries both shook their heads with genuine regret.

"All right," Elias whispered. "Just give me a second." The auxiliaries looked at one another, both wondering if the boy was finally accepting his face, but not daring to unclamp their hold on his arms. He began to step towards the end of the crater, wiping away his tears to see clearly where he was going.

Silence chilled the air as everyone waited for Elias String to jump. When he did so, their day's work would be done and they could allow themselves to put this whole nightmare behind them. But the boy still didn't shift an inch.

"We haven't got all day!" came the priest's booming voice. Elias looked up and saw him - a balding, heavy-set man named Lemac - making his way hastily around the edge of the crater towards him.

"Push him," he commanded Fabian. "In the name of the gods! Push him!"

"You heard what he said," said Fabian, putting the responsibility on the auxiliaries instead. "Push him,"

The auxiliary to Elias's right stepped forward hesitantly but the one on his left pulled him back. "That would be murder!" he protested.

"Push him!" the priest roared, losing his patience. His round head had gone from pink to lobster red.

"I didn't sign up for this job to kill people," the auxiliary objected and his fellow worker joined him with a "me neither".

The priest did not answer back. He would take the task into his own hands. Seeing what was coming, Elias tried to flee but the priest wrapped his arms around his skinny belly as he kicked and tried to break free. He was no match for Lemac. With a great cry of force, the heavily-built priest hurled him over the edge as the boy let out a terrible shriek. The auxiliaries squeezed their eyes shut in horror. The cries of protest were replaced by a grim, hollow silence.

"Show's over," called Lemac. None of the ten auxiliaries moved nor looked at one another. Lemac started making his way down from the crater back to the courtyard and they all followed suit. The auxiliaries who had held Elias by the arms looked particularly shaken.

"That was your job I did back there," Lemac seethed to Fabian. "It's about time we had someone as Chief Officer who was worthy of the job."

"I beg your pardon?" Fabian answered angrily. "Are you trying to get yourself sacked, Lemac?"

"Sack me if you want, I don't care," huffed Lemac, "I'm due for retirement soon anyway. I might as well just say what I think."

Chapter
TWENTY THREE

When the sacrifices hit the magma a sound is produced, quickly joined by the fizzing of water turning to steam. Although this sound occurs around one hundred metres from the lip of the volcano, it is still possible to hear it if you listen closely enough. If someone had been focusing on the task of listening for this sound, they would have heard it nine times that afternoon, not ten.

Elias String had not hit the magma. As he fell, he had managed to grab hold of a rock in the vent about two metres from the crater. The rock crumbled a little on impact and some small pieces headed down into the depths, but not him. He made the mistake of looking down, which scared him so much that he almost lost his grip. It was as if death itself had opened its mouth for him and he saw right to the very back of it. Crying out in fear and panic was his natural reaction but Elias managed to suppress it, so as not to attract attention.

Concentrating hard and trying to stay calm, Elias pulled himself up onto the rock. That was the hardest part.

Then he used both his arms and legs to pull himself out of the volcano. Triumph came over him like a wave as he took a few breaths on his hands and knees. But the battle was not over yet.

It would have undoubtably been wise to wait out the rest of the day at the top of the volcano and then escape at night, but Elias hated that place and was desperate to get away.

On the count of three, he got up to his feet and started to head down the rocky slope. The far side of the volcano was much too treacherous to attempt running down so Elias had no other choice but to run down the slope that everyone used and probably get himself spotted in the process.

In the courtyard at the foot of the volcano, Fabian Zora was discussing the events with his wife and two other officers. The auxiliaries and a couple of the officers had already left the grounds. They had seemed in a hurry to leave. The priests were also huddled together, lost in the mystery of the situation.

"This has never happened before," came Fabian's troubled voice, "in the whole history of this island." It was he who noticed the boy first. "Look!" he cried and the other officers and priests turned their eyes towards the slope. Sure enough, the boy was making his way down as fast as his bare feet could carry him. Then the figure disappeared from their view as he made his way around the other side of the volcano, away from them. The priests and officers stood without moving, struggling to believe what they were seeing. Fabian barked out orders: "Get him!" he cried. "Don't let him get away!"

Fabian, Hero and the two other officers started to run. They were, of course, bare-footed which slowed them down considerably and caused them a significant amount of pain. After all, the rocky grounds of the Sacred Heart were certainly not designed for running.

Elias knew they were coming after him and although dizzy and disorientated from fear, he did not slow his pace. He may have ended up facing the terrifying abyss once more, but escape was still worth a chance.

Somehow, Elias found his running skills enhanced, perhaps by the goddess or perhaps simply by his own hellbent compulsion to escape. He came to the stone wall of around three metres, which he tackled easily, finding places for his hands to grab hold of. The wall hadn't been designed to trap people in with barbed wire or anything similar, so he was able to make it all the way to the top and swing one leg over. Fire shot through his heart as he saw the officers coming closer towards him, nearly at the wall themselves. In a state of panic, he dropped down the other side of the wall and his bones and muscles cried out in protest. With all the strength he had left in him, he picked himself up and ventured through the city streets which were busy with the typically-bustling midday crowd. He barged his way through, ignoring gripes of "oi!" and "watch it!" Elias had never seen such a busy place in his entire life.

Behind his back, the officers had gained on him, but it would be hard to catch him surrounded by all these people. He heard the Chief Officer's voice through the roar of the crowd: "Stand aside! Stop that man!" But Elias was quick and nimble, enjoying a burst of adrenaline-fuelled energy after narrowly escaping death, and managed to make his way through without anyone stopping him. The narrow streets gave way to a square which led to the Temple of Emo.

Elias smiled. He had been subconsciously led to the temple of his protector. She would surely grant him sanctuary.

He slipped in through the heavy wooden doors and

gave a deep sigh of relief that echoed against the stone walls. It was a modest temple, quiet and peaceful and – most importantly – empty. This was typical of the Quilemoyena City's temples as few Crimsons were concerned with religion and spiritual matters. A priest or priestess was on duty during the daytime for tradition's sake more than anything else. So as not to anger the gods, the city's temples were taken care of and maintained by a Violet priest or priestess. You could occasionally spot foreign tourists in them, enjoy a little sightseeing and bringing some extra wealth to the island, but today this one had no visitors.

Elias looked around for potential places to hide. He nearly jumped out of his skin when the priestess emerged. She had been mopping the floor but came over when she heard the doors open. She was alarmed by his appearance; his feet were bare and his clothes tattered and torn. More importantly, he was a Violet inside a temple within the city walls: an unusual sight indeed. While Violets could be found in the city in the form of merchants and farmers, they were there to do business and wouldn't commonly end up in a temple.

"I've come here to pray to the goddess Emo," Elias told her before she had the time to ask what he was doing there. "Can you direct me to the chapel?"

"Of course, follow me," she said, one eyebrow raised. "What brings you here, young Violet?"

"Long story," Elias answered.

The priestess led the way up a set of steps inside the temple that led to the chapel. "Your business," she shrugged. "It's right in there." She opened the door for him and left him in peace. She scurried off to continue mopping the floor, still wondering what he was doing there.

Now that he was by himself, Elias sat down on the single wooden pew and let himself rest. They must have lost track of me by now, he thought. He got his breath back and massaged his sore feet with his hands while considering what he was going to do next. He decided to wait in the chapel until sunset, which meant he would have to do nothing for a good few hours. With any luck, nobody else would come in. When it was getting dark, he would make his way to the city gates and try and find his way home. He had no idea how to do this, but his priority at the moment was to stay alive and keep away from the wretched Sacred Heart.

Then his heart sank as he heard the creak of the temple›s main door followed by footsteps. He heard a female voice exchange words with the priestess although it was too far away to make out what they were saying. It might have had nothing to do with him but Elias thought it probably did. He leapt up, searching the chapel for a place to hide. Yet there was little choice. He would easily be seen if he hid between the pews and the altar's high, bare table was not much of a hiding place either. He couldn't escape as the windows were high up and made of glass. They would surely end up cornering him.

Swallowing hard, he put his back to the wall nearest the door. When it opened he would be hidden from view. Soon enough he heard footsteps coming up the steps to the chapel. Somebody came in and walked forward. From the back, Elias could tell it was the petite female officer with red hair. The memory of her finding her in the windmill that very morning came back to him. The priestess must have told the officer of the his presence. If not, she may have quickly inspected the room and left empty-handed, but as she already knew he had to be there, he knew his chances of escape were almost non-existent. Elias waited for the inevitable.

Emo, prayed Elias inside his head, please tell me what to do. He looked up at the female officer and their eyes met, his watery blue and hers hazelnut brown.

"Come with me." The woman reached out her hand. "It's not too late to die an honourable death."

She was trying hard to conceal her nervousness at having to deal with this situation alone. The officers had all split up as they lost sight of each other in the crowd. She was the one who had found the runaway sacrifice but she wished the others were here now.

"My day to die is not today," Elias told her with quiet rage. "I have the strength of the goddess Emo within me. I can do whatever I like. And none of you Crimsons can touch me."

"My duty is to take you to the Sacred Heart. They are the Chief Officer's orders. Come with me."

Elias was not intimidated. Hero did not really know how to order people about. They usually followed her like sheep, based on her high social status. Her command was not at all convincing and Elias almost laughed in her face. She was not so much older than he was and she was physically smaller. And she was not, of course, carrying a weapon. After all, the officers of the Sacred Heart had no need for weapons. Hero knew herself that Elias was more powerful than she was. Her calm, confident façade was betrayed by fear and Elias could see through her like glass.

"You should be the one to die today," he taunted, spitting out the words. "You should be punished for doubting me, for doubting the power of the goddess herself." Elias was edging his way towards the exit.

"There are two other officers waiting for you at the door," Hero tried. "There's no point trying to escape."

"Is that so?" Elias said with a smirk. He did not believe her for a second. The hesitation in her voice gave it away.

Within a split-second, Elias had disappeared from the chapel, his feet zipping down the stone steps. He was moments away from becoming just another person in the midday crowd. Yet a thin metal pole appeared in front of him as he reached the lower steps. The priestess was pushing out a long candlestick from around the corner. Her timing was excellent. Elias did not have the time to react and tripped over it. He fell hard and cried out when he hit the floor with a loud smack. As the shock subsided, he began to feel a sharp pain in his shins.

Hero was at the top of the steps looking down, watching Elias on the floor, struggling to get up. She headed down the steps to deal with Elias herself, feeling that victory was almost in her hands. She now had the perfect opportunity to get the boy under her control with the help of the priestess. That is, if she too had not fallen down the stairs. In her haste, she tripped, unaided by any tool. She tumbled down and banged her head at the bottom. The priestess cried out in surprise as Hero appeared next to the boy. Elias had had time to recover from his fall, yet instead of making a run for it while his hunter lay dazed and possibly injured on the floor, he did something that nobody – including himself – had expected.

As if he had been taken over by some incredible force, Elias grabbed Hero and pushed her onto her back, pinning her down firmly between his legs.

"What are you doing?" shrieked the priestess. "Get off of her!"

Hero was still disorientated from the fall. Blood had started to escape from her nose and she could taste a little in her mouth. The priestess was telling Elias to leave Hero alone, pulling on Elias's arm. He pushed her aside with as much energy as it takes to waft away a fly, except that she fell to the ground. What was the source of this strength that had possessed him? Hero's eyes looked up at him, showing signs of both confusion and fear. In turn, he looked down and spoke to her with a frightening intensity, his eyes fuming.

"My life isn't going to end today," he told her. "It's going to begin."

He took the candlestick beside him which he had tripped over moments earlier. At the bottom of it, the metal separated into three parts which served as a tripod. At the top, there was a large disk in which to set the candle, with a sharp spike to hold it in place. Without even a hint of fear, Elias plunged his left wrist into the spike then opened the wound by drawing it downwards. The priestess cried out with disgust, frightened and confused.

Violet liquid escaped from the boy's arm as he smiled triumphantly. Had he finally lost his mind? He smeared the blood over both his hands and then looked at Hero, whose nose was still bleeding.

Without warning, he clamped his hands over her face. She squealed and struggled but she could not escape the force of his body weight, her wriggling form staying put between the legs that trapped her.

He's trying to strangle her! thought the priestess desperately. He's going to kill her! She took the candlestick as the struggle continued, attacking him with the bottom end, the three metal prongs serving as an effective weapon. Elias took the blows from the candlestick until he could take no more. In any case, something told him his job was done. He released Hero, stood up and raced out of the temple as quickly as an animal of the forest.

The priestess did not pursue him. Instead, she rushed to Hero's side.

"Are you alright?" she asked, as Hero felt the kind touch

of hands on her shoulders. "He's gone."

"Are you going to catch him? Bring him back to the Sacred Heart?" Hero mumbled, still in a daze. Her face and neck were covered in Violet blood.

"Do you want me to try, I…"

"No, I think it's best we leave him," said Hero with clarity. "We've spent all day trying to fight him but his will is too strong for even the entire Sacred Heart to stop."

"It's too late now anyway. He could be anywhere," fumed the priestess. "He smothered you, the scoundrel. He tried to kill you."

"No, no, I don't think so." Hero's voice did not reflect the priestess's anger. She touched her face. The blood just below her nose was a mixture of Crimson and Violet. "Why did he do that?" Hero whispered to herself. "I don't understand."

"Did he hurt you?"

"No, he didn't. I just felt powerless; he was so strong but he didn't hurt me at all."

"I'm going to get a cloth and some water to clean you up. I'll be back in a moment, my dear."

As the priestess left her side, Hero looked up to the stone ceiling which seemed to break up and move around. Her head was swimming. She did not have the strength to sit up. Wearily, she let her eyes close.

Chapter

TWENTY FOUR

$\mathcal{E}$ lias concluded the story. He finally made it back home in the middle of the night and his mother was overjoyed to see him. He told her nothing about where he had been, kept it to himself. The wound on his left wrist healed and left a scar that he made an effort to keep concealed from her.

There were parts of the story he couldn't remember, but Hero filled him in. He had no recollection of being found and drugged at the windmill but Hero had witnessed it all. He was even more surprised to hear about what had happened in the chapel but was glad he hadn't hurt Hero.

"I just can't believe you're sitting here now, drinking tea with me!" Elias exclaimed, wiping away his tears.

"Me neither," Hero said with a chuckle. She put her hand gently over his. "Thanks for sharing all that with us," she said. "It seems like the goddess really was on your side. But the reason why is as much a mystery as ever."

They quietly drained their cups of tea, which had gone

cold by now.

"We have to go," Hero said eventually. "We've got to get to Evah-Schir before sunset."

"Why?" Elias said, wiping his tears on his sleeve.

"We're leaving the island," Calex said. "It's too dangerous here."

"Do you need some food for the journey?" Elias offered, and uncovered a piece of cheese and loaf of bread from under some fabric on the sideboard. Calex and Hero's mouths started watering as soon as they saw the food heading their way. Several minutes later, there was nothing left except a few crumbs.

"You were really hungry, weren't you?" Elias said. Calex took out a coin out of his bag and handed it to him. "What!?" Elias cried. "I could buy ten loaves for this much."

"Well, it is your birthday," Calex pointed out and both he and Hero had the same thought at the same moment. They suddenly burst into song, chanting a Crimson ditty reserved for birthdays:

It's your birthday, happy birthday!
It's a joyful day today.
May your days be long and merry,
May the sun shine on your face.
It's your birthday, happy birthday!
It's a joyful day today.

The end of the song gave way to raucous laughter.

"Well, I hadn't heard that one before," Elias remarked. "I liked it though."

"Now it really is time for us to go," Hero said, getting to her feet and picking up the baby. Calex slung their two bags over his back. Elias walked them to the door and opened it wide. Calex and Hero thanked Elias again for the tea and food, and most importantly, the story. They exchanged goodbyes and left with a smile. Elias watched them from the door, as they headed back into the forest. Their eyes caught sight of a deer feeding off a dead rabbit. The deer looked up at them, startled by their movement.

Then all of them were almost blinded by a white light. When they opened their eyes, a female figure stood in front of them, glowing and towering above them.

"It is her," whispered Elias. "My goddess, my angel, my protector."

He remembered the first time this happened, recalling how his heart swelled then as it did now. He recalled her sudden appearance in the snow in the place of a wandering deer. How she placed her enormous hand on his head and spoke in a voice he recognised from years before at the bottom of a lake. Silence filled the air for a few seconds, even the breeze stopped. It was as if time itself had slowed down at her whim.

"Thank you for coming back to me!" Elias whispered, tears filling his eyes anew. "Did I do well?"

"You did," she said. "You served me well, Elias String." Her voice sent shivers down his neck, as if it could cut through a diamond.

"Greetings Calex Maro, Hero Zora," she continued, turning to face them. They were too stunned to utter a sound. "My visit is for you too. Listen carefully. I don't have long."

Emo drew closer to Hero and knelt down so they were almost the same height. The goddess's creamy blue face was huge before hers.

"Can I see him?" She asked.

Hero realised she meant the baby and she showed the goddess his face.

"Blessed child," Emo said. "Even more beautiful in the

flesh. May I touch him?"

Hero nodded silently, still unable to speak.

The goddess placed a single finger on the child's forehead and the baby gazed back into her eyes, fascinated. Emo then began to tell them what had happened a little over a year ago, far away from the island of Quilemoyena: in the palace of the gods.

Chapter TWENTY FIVE

"Grapes, grapes, always grapes," complained Lush-am, frowning at the bowl of fruit in front of him. He lazily stretched out on his chaise-longue and let his eyes close. Lusham was the sole protector of the island of the Geshtin Fields, which was around the same size as Quilemoyena. The Geshtin Fields was the largest of a group of three islands known together as the Geshtin archipelago – the others being Little Geshtin and Prince-upon-Sea. These three islands were isolated in the ocean, four hundred kilometres south of Quilemoyena.

Lusham's room in the palace was as grand, elegant and indeed fit for a god. The floor and walls were made of marble and two golden-plated open doors led out onto a terrace overlooking the splendid garden.

The god's eyes opened as he heard a knock on his door. "Come in," he called, not needing to raise his voice as the marble amplified it sufficiently.

When he sat up he saw the three holy sisters – Quil, Emo and Yena – who were otherwise known as the pro-tectors of Quilemoyena. Whatever could they want with him? They often casually exchanged words at dinner-time but they never sought him out deliberately.

"Good morning Lusham. We have some important business to discuss with you," Quil said. Her voice certainly sounded very serious. Lusham got to his feet. He had a head of glossy, bright red hair that flowed down his back. Like the three sisters, his face was youthful with a flawless complexion, and he wore long white robes that touched the floor.

"Take a seat, ladies," Lusham ushered them. There were a few chairs around the room and he took three of them and placed them opposite his chaise-longue. The sisters thanked him and sat down.

"So, what can I do for you?" Lusham asked.

Emo took the lead. "You are the first god we are going to share this with," she told him.

"And I suppose I should be flattered," the red-haired god joked. The sisters did not smile.

"It's nothing personal," Quil cut in. "Most of the other gods are out playing croquet on the lawn. In any case, we need an opinion before holding a meeting with everyone."

"Tell me," Lusham invited, gesturing with his open hands. "I'm all ears."

Emo took a deep breath. "Lusham, we have had enough of our Violet citizens being used to fuel the planet. After all, the sacrifices are for the benefit of the Geshtin Field's citizens too."

"Well," Lusham said with a smile and a shrug, "Quile-moyena has the fortune, or perhaps misfortune, of having that volcano. What are you suggesting exactly?"

"We want to stop the sacrifices," Emo said, matter-of-factly.

"What?!" Lusham was almost laughing. "You know very well that the planet would collapse within days.

No more rain, no more nutrition in the soil, no more leaves on the trees. That would be a death sentence for every Crimson and Violet on the planet."

"We have a solution," Emo told him.

"And what might that be?"

Lusham listened in shock as Emo explained the details of the new system the sisters had designed. A cupful of blood from every living Violet on the globe would be collected every day. The blood would then be delivered to Quilemoyena by boat then transported inland to the volcano. True, the blood would not be fresh and some of the essential substances would already have disappeared. This is why it would take so much blood to make up the required amount to fuel the planet.

At the end of the explanation, Lusham burst out laughing. He stood up and began to pace the room. "I admire the…diplomacy of your solution," he said. "But…"

"But what?" said Emo.

"I've never heard anything as ridiculous in the entire history of time!" Lusham snorted.

Emo was becoming angry and got to her feet. She and Lusham were around the same height – over three metres – and they looked at each other straight in the eye.

"Why shouldn't our inhabitants be able to live full, natural lives like yours?" Emo prompted.

"Their lives are natural," Lusham retorted. "They've been living like this for hundreds of years."

"That doesn't make it natural. Generation after generation, they've been brought up to believe that's the order of things. It's their culture."

"They've been brainwashed," Yena intervened, "and nobody has ever challenged them to think in a different way."

"And they don't complain," said Lusham. "Everybody's happy. Why change the system that works perfectly well. Why cause a problem? In any case, your idea is far too complicated. It would never work."

"We can see that you are very much opposed to our ideas," hissed Quil, "but we will be holding a meeting with the other gods. Perhaps some will be on our side." All the sisters were on their feet and facing him.

"I doubt that," Lusham spat with increasing frustration. "I will be keeping an eye on you. If you go to Quilemoyena to put this absurd plan into action, I will destroy the whole island with storms." The sisters had forgotten that Lusham had the power to do this. All the gods had their specific abilities and Lusham's was to conjure up hurricanes with a click of his fingers. The sisters all shared the same gift: they were able to physically enter the human realm by replacing any living deer on the planet at any given time.

They considered Lusham's horrible threat. Furious and without a word of goodbye, they turned away from the red-haired god and let the door slam loudly behind them. In the corridor, walking back to their part of the palace, they could not hide their anger.

"We should have known it wouldn't go down well," Emo fumed. "But we don't care what the others think. We believe firmly in this new system and nobody will change our minds."

The others expressed their agreement and Emo speculated. "If we go there and do the job ourselves it will attract too much attention. We need to get it done subtly."

"Yes," agreed Yena, "otherwise Lusham could wipe the whole island out."

Quil wondered if the other gods would threaten them too. "I don't think the others will support our ideas either," she said sadly. "They're as opposed to change as Lusham is."

"I've got a plan." Emo stopped her sisters and whispered to them, her excited head brimming with ideas. They would appoint someone on the island to do the job for them. Who better than someone born for this task, someone neither Crimson nor Violet and therefore completely without bias.

The three sisters spent the rest of the day deciding how they were going to put the plan into action. It would involve seeking out a Violet with a connection to the spiritual world closer than most, someone who could be subconsciously guided by their will. On studying the goings-on on the island from a distance in the Great Observatory, a certain boy of fourteen seemed like an appropriate candidate. One of them would have to make a quick trip to the island and hope that the gods would be too busy playing croquet to notice.

Chapter TWENTY SIX

*H*ero, Calex and Elias listened to the goddess with fascination as she spoke to them of the strange other world in which she and her fellow deities resided, obscure and unreachable to mortals.

"So now you understand," Emo concluded. "This baby was no accident. He was born to carry out the will of the gods. When your blood mixed with Elias's, the baby that was already inside you was transformed. You were already three weeks pregnant, my dear."

Hero's head was spinning with the goddess's words. "What exactly do you need him to do?"

"When the time comes, he will know what to do. He has, of course, inherited Elias's innate spiritual sixth sense. My sisters and I will guide him."

"You want him alone to change a system that has been in place for hundreds of years?" Elias butted in. "It seems impossible and for a brownborn it is even more than impossible!"

"I cannot deny that this is a difficult task," admitted Emo. "This is all in the future but it is a time that you must prepare for now. Look after the child, educate him, teach him how to fight. Tell him of both Crimson and Violet ways. Give him the skills he will need to make the people in power listen. I must go. If other gods notice I am here I will be in grave danger. You remember what Lusham threatened to do."

"Will you come back?" asked Hero hopefully. "We will need your guidance."

"I will try," Emo told her. "Don't be afraid. The wheels are already in motion. Calex, you noticed the second Violet who did not want to be sacrificed. She could feel that times are changing. She is one of a rare kind of Violet with a stronger connection to the spiritual world than most." She looked at the boy standing at the door and smiled at him. "Like you, Elias."

They watched unerringly as Emo's form began to fade. She became less and less visible until she disappeared altogether. The world around them was left inanimate. They felt the strange afterglow of the goddess's presence. There was an unfamiliar buzz in the air and all around was an eerie light as if there was a solar eclipse. Birds were making more noise than usual, some flying around the treetops as if troubled. In the place where the goddess had been there lay a lifeless deer.

"Come on," Calex encouraged Hero. "We don't have any time to lose." They waved goodbye once more to Elias String who still stood in the doorway. Elias waved back, still entranced as they were, and watched them walk away across the meadows.

It would take many hours to get to Evah-Schir on the north coast, the largest settlement outside of Quilemoyena City. There was a major road that ran between the city and the harbour town and Calex and Hero needed to locate it. Calex asked directions to the road from various farmers who vaguely pointed the way. Once they reached the road they didn't dare walk on it directly; that would be too risky. Instead, they walked parallel to it, through fields of wheat, barley and corn. The land was more or less flat and there were not many people around. The only problem was the distance. With their feet and legs tired and aching, and knowing that there was much further to go, Calex suggested standing on the road itself and hitching a lift. At first, Hero was totally against the idea but then she realised it might not be so bad after all. People knew of a woman with a baby on the run, but the sight of a couple and a baby was completely normal. True, they were Crimson, which made them stand out more than Violets in the countryside, but it was not a suspicious sight.

The road to Evah-Schir was smooth and evenly covered in small stones, and one of Quilemoyena's best. They waited patiently for somebody to pass northbound. It took a number of minutes before a cart came into view. This one was fairly large and carried straw.

"Evah-Schir?" Calex called to its driver, who did not slow down his pace.

"All the way," the driver confirmed. "Hop on the back."

Calex helped Hero to jump on and then lifted himself up. They were comfortable within the straw and the ride was not too bumpy. They could rest their feet at last.

"You don't think we're being followed, do you?" asked Hero.

"No," said Calex. "Well, I don't know for sure but I don't think so."

The cart took them the last fifteen or so kilometres to the coastal town, and they were pleased with their decision to hitch a lift. They arrived in Evah-Schir just before sunset. It was a port not especially of beauty but of intense character, from the roar of the market to the lively harbour. This was Calex's first impression of the island and in six years it had not changed. It was perpetually busy with cattle and human traffic, from fresh-faced foreigners who came to find work to young pickpockets with muddy faces, both Crimson and Violet.

How strange it felt for Calex to be here again! After he had left Evah-Schir with his new guardian Hux, he came back every so often to find out if anyone else from the shipwreck had come to shore. He asked fishermen and sailors in the harbour and shopkeepers and passers-by in the street. Much to his dismay, these interrogations always came to nothing and as time went by his visits became less and less frequent. During the first year, Calex insisted that Hux take him back every week and he was willing to oblige. His guardian could not deny the poor boy this weekly favour. Then, Calex went back every month, then every three months, then twice a year. The expectation that there might be some news always lingered. Calex always came away disappointed and one day he decided he had had enough and stopped coming altogether. That was two years ago now. He wondered if any of the fishermen at the harbour would recognise him.

The market was closing down for the evening, its cobbled ground littered with dirty lettuce leaves and squashed vegetables. The locals had come to search for last-minute bargains and beggars were there for scraps of food that could not be sold the next day. Calex and Hero walked through the slippery-floored food market and came to the area where other goods were sold. Here, a glamorous lady folded the exotic silks she had been selling of almost every colour in existence. In the stall next to her, a scruffy young man with little marble statues was selling off a couple of his creations for half price now that the day was coming to a close. Just opposite, an elderly gentleman selling pipes was optimistically waiting for business even though there were few people around.

Calex's eyes caught sight of a jeweller who was putting his silver necklaces and bracelets into a black box to keep them safe until the following morning. He lifted out an identical case from underneath the market stall and opened the lid. Seeing that it was full of rings, an idea floated into Calex's head. He looked down at his finger and when he looked into Hero's eyes he knew that she was thinking the same thing as him.

"Would you be interested in buying this ring, sir?" Calex asked the jeweller, approaching him.

"I'm here to sell, not buy," came the retort. He dismissed him matter-of-factly, not even taking a look at the shiny object the stranger held out to him. Calex shrugged as if to say 'never mind' but Hero did not give up as easily.

"It's solid gold encrusted with three rubies," she persuaded. The jeweller finally looked up to examine the item. He took a magnifying glass from his bag and inspected it, holding it up to the sunlight.

"It's quite a beauty," he remarked as his eyebrows moved slowly up his wrinkled forehead.

"One hundred demarit and it's yours," Hero announced before he could ask.

"Eighty," the jeweller tried.

"It's a deal." The money and ring were exchanged quickly and Calex and Hero were soon walking away from the jeweller who was absolutely delighted with his new acquisition.

"He got a bargain," Hero said under her breath. "We sold it at a fraction of its true price." Calex turned to her wondering if they had made a mistake. "But everybody's happy," she reassured him. "I'm just glad to get rid of the thing."

The pair reached the livestock end of the market where two calves were being swapped for five lambs. The farmers were struggling to get the animals to cooperate in getting them onto their carts and the air was filled with shouting, bleating and mooing. As chickens pecked around at their feet, Calex and Hero headed to the seafront where the smell of fish became stronger and stronger.

The harbour was situated in a semicircular bay. Alcoves had been built into the the cliff face. These went back several metres into the cliff and allowed fishermen to prepare and organise their equipment. The harbour was sealed off by cliffs at either side and there were wooden steps leading down to sea level in three places. On the left-hand side of the harbour stood an impressive lighthouse.

Calex and Hero walked down the steps down to the seafront. They went to where Calex knew the ferryboats came and went, knowing that they must board one as soon as possible. The news of Hero and the baby had spread like a plague and by now it had probably reached every last corner of the island. They didn't know if people had a description of Hero, and if they did they would be in even greater danger of being caught. They would not be safe until they had left the shores of Quilemoyena. As they walked, they kept up her guard, always wary of the glances of passers-by.

The broad wooden jetty where the ferries docked was currently empty and Calex caught the attention of a man who was perched on a mooring bollard. The daydreaming fisherman looked up as Calex spoke to him, his weathered face a reddy-brown under the hot sun.

"You want to leave the island, do you?" said the fisherman. "Well, there's only one ferry due to leave this evening. I believe it's going to Prince-upon-Sea."

"Prince-upon-Sea," Calex repeated. He looked at Hero, whose face was blank.

"What's it like?" Calex asked the man, who frowned at him in response to this seemingly silly question.

"How would I know?" he shrugged. "Do I look like a traveller to you?"

"What's this?" called another man, who was gutting fish from big wicker baskets close-by.

"This fellow here wants to know what Prince-upon-Sea is like," called the fisherman.

"Well...er...it's alright, y'know." The fisherman struggled to find a description as he took his eyes away from the sliced-open cod in his hand. "Mild weather, smallish. I'm not too sure myself actually. Famous for its rock formations or something."

"Prince-upon-Sea it is then," Calex decided with an air of finality.

"Wait, Calex," Hero stopped him. "I have a funny feeling about this island. Something tells me it could be dangerous."

"Why would you think that?"

"I don't know. Maybe it's something Emo said."

"She didn't even mention Prince-upon-Sea. In any case, we have to leave tonight and this is our only choice." Calex turned to the fisherman seated on the bollard. "It leaves tonight, you said?"

"That's right," he replied. "Nine o'clock sharp."

Calex and Hero wandered back into the marketplace, both of them starting to realise how hungry they were. The strong scent of herbs flooded their noses as a market seller was putting the dried plants onto his cart. Others sellers were bantering about the day's business. Gypsy women bombarded Calex and Hero, asking for money in every sort of accent they had ever heard, and their children ran about, collecting scraps of meat and vege-

tables from the cobbled ground. Calex and Hero managed to find a food stall that was late finishing up. They
bought some bread and cooked fish that they relished
on the steps of a nearby temple. Neither one spoke as
they satiated their hunger, already feeling their energy
coming back to them as they wolfed it down. As they
picked the remaining fish from around the bones, they
noticed how Evah-Schir was much poorer than Quilemoyena City. They surveyed the scene in front of them:
housing tightly packed in the narrow streets and clothes
hung on lines between the buildings. The inhabitants
were not as well dressed as the city folk and the way
they talked was less refined. The town itself was dirtier
and full of bad smells in every corner. Evah-Schir was
indeed rough around the edges.

Stray cats meandered on the temple steps, eager for
leftovers. Calex and Hero eventually gave in to their
miaowing and the skinny creatures jumped on the fish
bones. As Calex flicked the breadcrumbs off of his lap,
his attention was caught by the temple.

"I'd like to see inside," he said, looking up at its tall red
brick façade. He could see that some of the roof was
missing, and a family of birds had made their home
there.

"Go in if you like," Hero encouraged him, wanting to
feed the baby in peace.

"I wouldn't stay out here alone," Calex said.

"It's okay," she said, getting to her feet. "I'll go round
the side of the temple. There's nobody there."

"Fair enough," Calex said uneasily as he headed towards the entrance. "I won't be long."

Calex put his hand on the great doors but stepped back
when he realised they were worth looking at. They were
cast in steel and featured a relief. Calex noticed on the
left door, there was shown a man sailing out to sea. On

the right door was the same man, bearded and young, arriving at a shore. No other details of this land were depicted. Calex was reminded of this old legend once more and a voice behind him confirmed his suspicions. "It's the temple of Allirog Redips," pointed out the woman who swept the steps.

Calex frowned. "I didn't know that he was worshipped as a deity," he said. "Is it open?" The old woman nodded.

Calex let himself in, pulling back the heavy door with all his strength. Inside, he was faced with a dark, cool space, with a passage leading up to the altar where incense was slowly burning. He was glad to be alone. Calex walked up the passage and past the chairs either side, hearing his footsteps echo up to the rafters. There was a little sunlight entering the room in stripes through the incomplete roof which reminded him of the barn earlier.

To Calex, this temple seemed more holy than the Sacred Heart itself. It was a place of simplicity and poverty, but Calex could feel a beauty in the stillness. He did not feel clean enough to be in such a place. He wanted to feel fresh water washing away the salt on his arms. His curls had wound themselves up tight in sweat and his yellow shirt was sticking to his body. The day had been so hot, after the brief and strange thunderstorm that morning. Yet here in this stone temple it was refreshingly cool. Calex loved the bareness of this place. The white walls and plain stone floor. He felt like he could stay here forever. Pigeons cooed and fluttered above him, their mouths full of scraps from the market. Calex came up to the altar and stopped, wondering if he should be doing something there, kneeling or praying.

His eyes widened with surprise as he saw a man had appeared in front of him. Calex did not quite know what to say. He was aware of the man looking at him, probably disapproving of him bringing his scruffiness and dirty face into a temple.

"I'm sorry," Calex mumbled nervously. "I thought it would be alright to come inside."

"It is," replied the man. He looked about thirty years old, and wore a short beard flecked with blond hairs and a bronze tan.

"Are you in charge here?" asked Calex.

The other man chuckled. "You could say that. I am Allirog Redips." Calex brushed the notion aside through its implausibility. But then he saw that the man was a little transparent, and his outline seemed to be lined with a thin layer of gold.

"You're a ghost!" Calex exclaimed, instinctively heading for the door in fright.

"What are you afraid of?" the man asked, causing him to turn around. "I'm not going to hurt you, Calex."

"How do you know my name?" Calex gasped: the great legend of Quilemoyena knew who he was!

"I know a whole lot more about you than just your name."

"Surely I'm dreaming," Calex muttered.

"I'm real," the man reassured him. "I come here now and again. It's my temple isn't it?"

"Of course. You have every right to come here." Calex shook his head. This has been a day like no other, he thought.

"Why are you so surprised to see a ghost? You came face to face with the goddess Emo just this afternoon, did you not?"

"That's true," confirmed Calex. "But I still don't understand. You're... dead."

The man nodded. "Well, I'm not exactly a simple human. I am semi-divine."

Calex made a guess: "The goddesses rewarded you for your travels?"

"They rewarded me for being the first mortal to reach the other side."

"So you did make it! I always believed you did!" Calex chuckled, remembering the countless debates he had engaged in over the years. He looked at the older man with a sense of childish fascination. Laying awake at night as a young boy, staring at the ceiling, he had pictured Redips's adventures.

"What did you find?" he asked fervently. Calex was so close to finding out what he had fantasised about for so long. He walked towards Redips so that he could see the entire altar through his head. His eyes shone like sapphires, almost too bright to look into. Redips spoke to him in a soft voice, and with a fresh smile of wonder. "I found the realm of the gods," he revealed simply.

Calex's expression did not change. He tried to grasp hold of the idea. "It's here? Just across the Barromedian Sea?" Calex pressed, anxious to know but almost unable to speak.

"Yes. I tried to come back to tell people but my boat was capsized in a massive storm."

"How unfortunate."

"Fortune doesn't come into this, my friend. A certain god – Lusham – sent a hurricane. He was angry that a human had stepped foot in the realm of the gods."

"And then you were made into a demi-god?"

"When I was drowning, seconds away from death, a goddess lifted me up into her arms and out of the water. When I woke up I was back there, in an enormous white bed, surrounded by several gods."

"Not Lusham?"

Redips smiled. "Not Lusham."

"Tell me what it's like."

Redips paced the altar as he spoke. "When the storm began to rage and I knew I was done for I tried to carve something about my experiences into the side of the boat, desperate to share at least something of my travels with other people, but I didn't have enough time to write more than a few words.

The palace of the gods itself is quite magnificent: a white-stoned castle with marble interiors with halls and corridors so large that your voice echoes for seconds if you speak. Then there are the grounds surrounding it: the lavish rose garden and the vegetable patch; the sculpture garden featuring a statue of every god; and the lush green lawns that stretch out until they give way to sandy beaches. At the very centre of the castle is the Soup of Souls."

"The Soup of Souls?" Calex said.

"The Soup of Souls is a huge bowl where souls – bright blue balls of light – wait for new humans to be born. There is always a god or goddess on duty to guard and stir the soup. The souls must be kept moving or they shrivel up and die definitively. When it's time for a baby to be born, the god or goddess will reach down and pick a soul from the soup. Then that new life will begin. When a person dies, his soul will find its way back to the Soup of Souls."

"Aren't Crimson and Violet souls separated in the Soup of Souls?" Calex asked.

"There are no such thing as a Crimson or Violet souls, my boy, only Crimson and Violet bodies." Redips said. "In your next life you could be Crimson or Violet."

"And there is also the Great Observatory," Redips continued, evidently enjoying sharing this information with a mortal. "It's a sort of circular pool where the gods can see whatever they want in the humans' realm. They might even be watching us now," he said with a chuckle.

Calex did not smile; something was evidently troubling him. "Please let me know one last thing," he pleaded, his heart beating fast and tears welling up in his eyes though he wished they would not. He tried to keep calm as he posed his question but emotion was causing his voice to break. "What happened to my family? You must know."

Redips shrugged. "I don't have access to the Soup of Souls and the Great Observatory. I'm just a demi-god. There's no way I could know about that."

Calex felt himself fill with panic. He could not let his chance slip away now. "I need to know," he stated firmly.

"I'm sorry about what happened to you, Calex. Really, I am. But I can't help you."

"You can't just leave me here like that!" Calex begged, as desperation made him lose his manners. He blinked away the tears that were blurring his sight. Perhaps Redips knew something but he simply did not want to share it. Calex reached out to the ghost knowing full well that his hands could not touch him. He felt the urge to grab the bottom of Redips's tunic while he knew, however, that like trying to touch a ray of sunshine his hands would just pass through it.

"Please tell me. Are they there? Please answer me, I'll do anything!"

"Calex..."

"I have been searching for the answer for so long. If I knew the truth I could finally put my mind at rest."

Allirog Redips looked into the longing eyes of this young man, suddenly reminded of himself. He remembered his hell-bent desire, from his mortal life, to reach the other side. A yearning more powerful than anything. Calex's desperate breathing was amplified by the stone walls and high ceiling. "Please," his lips whispered as he knelt at the ghost's feet, his pleading hands together and reaching up to him. Calex's lips trembled and he squeezed his eyes shut, forcing the tears inside them to run down his face.

"Calex? Can you hear me?" It was Hero kneeling down in front of him. "What's wrong?" she asked softly, touching his cheek with the back of her hand. "Were you... praying?"

"I was...daydreaming," Calex mumbled distantly, not looking her in the eyes. How long had he been there? He had lost track of the time. Calex looked around to see Allirog Redips, but he had gone as abruptly as he had arrived. Calex stood up. His eyes scanned every corner of the temple, but the ghost had left not a trace of his presence.

"Redips!" he called, dashing about, his voice echoing against all four walls. "Allirog Redips!"

"You saw Allirog Redips?" Hero looked baffled and also a little scared.

Calex came to meet her, beads of sweat visible on his brow. "Yes, I saw Allirog Redips. Would that seem so strange after this crazy day?"

"I don't think anything would," Hero admitted with a smile.

"I asked him about my family," Calex told her hesitantly, "but he said he didn't know anything."

"What do you think happened to them, Calex?" Hero said gently.

"I think they died on the night of the storm. That's what I think. But I just want the proof. I thought I finally had it."

Hero left him alone with his thoughts in the temple. He sat before the altar for what seemed like a long time, sitting as still as the furniture. It was only his eyelids that moved. The sun's light became dimmer as the sky morphed into orange. Without realising anything had been changing, Calex found himself barely able to see the altar anymore. He remembered what he was doing here in Evah-Schir. There was a boat waiting for them half a kilometre away, due to leave the island in twenty minutes.

Chapter

TWENTY SEVEN

*B*ack at the harbour, the queue for the ferryboat was not hard to find. There were about thirty peo-ple in front of them, going all the way to the end of the jetty where the biggest boat in the harbour was docked. Calex and Hero joined the queue behind a man with a little dog on a rope. There were both families and lone travellers, young and old, Crimson and Violet. Calex noticed a young man with scruffy clothes, unkempt hair and a twinkle in his eye: a fellow with a bag of little but a head full of dreams.

At the front of the queue, two people were taking mon-ey from the passengers and letting them board the boat. The queue was moving fast and Calex and Hero could see people walking across a plank of wood to get onto the deck of the boat. They looked up at the enormous white sails that would carry them to Prince-Upon-Sea. Below the decks there would be hammocks for sleeping. As the queue moved steadily, Calex and Hero came increasingly closer to the water. Calex could not hide his nervousness. His body tensed up as if it itself had a memory and not his brain, because he had not even thought about the shipwreck. When the memories came into his mind, he realised why he felt so ill at ease. He told himself that hundreds of people travelled in boats every day. The weather was glorious and had been for weeks. There was no need to fear a storm. But wait – there had been a thunderstorm just earlier, completely unexpected. Who could say that there would not be another? Come on Calex, he told himself, don't panic, just take it easy.

Before he knew it, the man and his yapping pet were passing over the plank. Calex and Hero suddenly found themselves at the front of the queue.

"How many passengers?"

"Two," Hero told the Violet woman taking the money. "Well, three. We've got a baby."

"It's free for the baby," chirped the woman, not even bothering to look. "That's forty demarit, please."

Calex looked discretely through the little sack of money and pulled out two twenty demarit coins which he handed to the woman.

"Thank you. Now, if I could just have a look at your identity papers. Just one of yours is enough."

"That's just as well because I don't have mine," Hero said, remembering when she had been asked to show her identity papers at the city gates.

"Just a second," said Calex, rummaging through the bag. There was his other shirt, trousers, the Allirog Redips book, a bruised apple, a stale hunk of bread...

"Oi! What's the hold up?" called somebody behind them in the queue.

"I can't find them," Calex said with a restrained sense of panic.

"What?" came the surprised voice of his companion.

"I can't find my papers." Calex brought his hand to his

forehead where beads of sweat were emerging. "They're gone."

"Are you sure?"

"Absolutely sure." Calex felt his pockets, which were empty except for the now-disintegrating piece of paper onto which he had copied a poem. Hero proceeded to look through her own bag, just in case.

"I can't let you on board without seeing your papers," the woman stated bluntly.

"I swear I had them this morning," came Calex's retort. He sighed with exasperation when he saw that Hero's search had come to nothing.

"Here's your money back." The woman held out the two coins but Calex was not at all interested in taking them.

"Perhaps we can make a deal," Calex uttered, stepping towards the woman. "How much do you want?"

"You can't bribe me. I'm not going to risk losing my job."

"For goodness sake!" cried the old fellow behind them, "I haven't got all day."

"Could you leave the queue, please? Sir, madam?"

Defeated, Calex took the money back and left the queue without a word. Hero followed him and they went over to the harbour wall, by one of the arches.

"I swear I had them this morning," Calex said, feeling utterly desperate.

"I believe you. I just don't understand," Hero sighed. "Is there a hole in your bag?"

"No, there isn't," Calex replied. "Maybe they fell out of the bag on the way from the temple."

"It's unlikely."

"I know, but we should look."

They walked back to the temple, following their tracks and scrutinising the ground. But their search came to nothing and hope was draining fast. It was getting dark and there were no more ferryboats due to leave that evening. They could not bear to turn around and watch the one bound for Prince-Upon-Sea leave the harbour. They sat on the steps of the temple, relieving themselves of their bags. Hero lay the baby down next to her. Both she and Calex sat with their elbows on their knees, too worried and upset to say anything. The setting sun cast a long shadow behind each of them, stretching out further and further towards the temple door as the minutes passed.

"We'll find a solution in the morning," Calex said eventually, feeling the air cooling around them. "There's nothing we can do now."

"I'm sure we'll be able to bribe someone to let us onto a boat without papers," Hero offered, "and we don't even care where it's going."

"We're going to be alright." Calex attempted to reassure Hero, and himself, with a forced, closed-mouth smile. He wished that she would say the same thing to him too. It was bewildering that the papers had gone missing. Calex's bag was secure and it had not left his side all day. Thinking about it did not bring any answers. It was a mystery.

Before all light had disappeared, they stood up and went in search of a cheap inn in which to spend the night. It did not take them long to find what they were looking for in the streets of Evah-Schir. Walking in, asking for a double room, paying for it and receiving the key took only a matter of seconds. They were soon walking up the stairs to the second floor, where there were four rooms, while the staircase continued up to a third floor. The bedroom was good value for money and the smell of lavender in a pot on the bedside table covered up the fact that the inn was old and in desperate need of refurbishment. They unloaded the bags and Hero slumped down on one of the beds. Calex lit the candles on each of the bedside tables by using the already-lit candles in the hall. He looked out of the window that overlooked the street. It seemed to be quiet and safe here and it was certainly not very noisy.

Calex sat down on the other bed and realised how tired he was. It was as if fatigue was the liquid in his veins. He could have let his eyes shut there and then but he did not. He got up to go to the washroom on the ground floor before going to bed. There were two buckets of water that the innkeeper had prepared for them. Calex washed himself using a sponge and all the water in one of the buckets. It was cold and refreshing – a welcome relief. As the water drained away, Calex cleaned his teeth by chewing a stick from a specific tree that had antiseptic properties. An old mirror with rusty cracks leant against one of the walls, its edges lined with black mould. Calex found himself looking at his face and chest. The thought that he was to sleep in the same room as Hero had entered his mind a few hours earlier. He longed to feel grown-up but he was not sat-isfied by his reflection. He still had a childish loveliness about him, which was indeed fading as adulthood ap-proached. Lovely though it was to others to whom it had already fled, Calex wanted to be through with it. To look at himself in a mirror and see a man looking back. The soft angles of his face would harden with time. The fluff on his chin would turn to a real beard. Calex was not sentimental about it. He wanted the transformation to take place right now. He wished also that it would be a mental transformation as well. That he would feel confident and proud. Instead, he felt the weight of his inexperience and the sheer nervousness of entering the realm of adults. As a man, or a member of the male sex at least, he knew he should take the lead. But he wished she would make the first move and relieve him of the responsibility. He was thinking too much. His heart was thumping, his palms were clammy. It was an uncomfortable sensation. Dried off and back inside his clothes he felt less exposed and much safer. The unfamiliar bedroom was calling him and he could no longer ignore it. When he arrived, he found Hero fast asleep with her arm around the baby on one of the beds. She was asleep and there was nothing to do but sleep himself. He instantly felt relieved. Calex looked out of the window at the dusty, empty street and sighed deeply. This is not what he had hoped for tonight. He wanted to be leaving the island, every second farther away from its shores. Bending down, he kissed Hero's sticky forehead, hoping that tomorrow night they would be together as well, but in happier, safer circumstances.

It was time to get some sleep. He blew out the two candles, removed his shirt and slipped into the other bed as the waxy smell filled the room. Tomorrow would present new challenges and danger would be just as imminent as it had been today. If he thought too much about it he would never be able to sleep so he imagined he was in his room at Miss Kiberon's like many a night before. It was not easy. Even with his eyes closed, Calex found it difficult to relax but eventually weariness overcame him. Tasting the salt from Hero's forehead, he slipped into the profound sleep that comes after a long, action-packed day.

Some hours later, he found himself staring at the bedroom wall. He did not understand why as his sleep had been so relaxing and well-deserved. Nevertheless, there was something stressing him and at first he could not think what it was. Then he remembered, as his heart sank, where he was and what had brought him there. He willed himself to go back to sleep. After all, the peaceful world of dreams was so superior to this one. Yet he suddenly had the sensation that Hero was awake too. Not that he could see or hear her, but he just perceived it, like a sixth sense. He rolled over and met her eyes, which were wide open and glossy in the moonlight.

"I can't sleep," she whispered. Calex did not know how to respond and simply held her gaze. "I'm scared, Calex," she said. His heart melted when she said his name.

"Everything's going to work out," he breathed. "It always does." Calex had borrowed this phrase from somewhere and used it without giving it any thought. But as soon as he said it, he felt comforted too. He saw a tear making its way down Hero's face and onto the pillow, instantly absorbed. Without a moment's reflection, he got up and knelt by her bed. More silent tears fell as he stroked her head, running his hand through her cropped ginger hair that had been much longer a few days before. They were both wide awake. After a while, he spoke:

"Do you know about soap?"

"Soap?" she asked, sitting up. "Is it like a candle?"

Calex explained what soap was, telling her how effective it was for washing yourself.

"My parents were soap-makers," he began to tell her. "There was one room in the house where my brothers and I weren't allowed to play and that was the workshop. My parents wore rubber gloves and overalls while they worked, to protect them from the lye, you see. There were all these measuring jugs and bottles of oil and dye on the shelves. One part of the workshop was used for preparing the batches and another for curing them which took a few weeks. There was purple soap with violet petals inside, pink with rose petals, even black with seaweed. My parents always smelled of some fragrance or other, even when they took the overalls and gloves off and left the workshop.

"When I was ten my parents started teaching me the trade. And then they wanted to come to Quilemoyena, two days' journey by boat, to bring back something that only grew on this island: carrowbeans. They wanted to make a new kind of soap, something that no other soap-maker in Kinsen had ever tried before. My parents always talked about faraway lands, getting on a boat and visiting somewhere else. They had a sense of adventure, you see. They wanted to leave me and my brothers with a neighbour but I insisted on them taking us with them. If we'd stayed behind I would still have Malfex and Irendex. We could have kept the workshop going, put our skills to work, even though our parents were gone. Instead I insisted over and over that they take us to Quilemoyena with them... and I lost them all."

Hero put her arms around him. "It wasn't your fault," she said softly. "You mustn't blame yourself." It seemed like an eternity before they broke their embrace. How easy it was to hold and be held by her, how easy it was to talk about anything and everything.

"I'm going to take care of you," he whispered, both her hands in his.

She smiled. "We're going to take care of each other," she said.

"We should get some sleep," Calex said, although he didn't move away to the other bed. Somehow her arms were around him again, and his around her. He was afraid. This is what he wanted, wasn't it? And yet his heart beat furiously, almost painfully, and he found himself thinking about the simpler option of walking away and being alone. The familiarity of that would at least be comforting and safe. Why did he feel like this? Why must his heart tear him in two directions? Towards her and away from her. And then her lips were on his, and only the magnetic force pulling him towards her remained. It was unclear whether she had started kissing him or if he had started kissing her, but one thing was clear: it was happening. He wasn't sure what to do but quickly worked it out, and when he finally pulled away his smile was reflected in hers. "You're so pretty," he said very softly. She kissed him again, like some magnificent fruit had been brought to his lips. "You're beautiful," she sighed, her hands in his dark brown curls, freshly washed. "You're all I ever dreamed of." He was in a frenzy – they both were – and thoughts of sleep and danger were forgotten. He had found intimacy with this girl and nothing else mattered in the entire world. He found himself using the Kinsen word schlie that he had not uttered for many many years: the most affectionate and tender of the four forms of you that existed in his native tongue. "Schlie trie es," he whispered between kisses, and repeated it as he kissed her from brow to neck.

"What are you saying?" she asked, almost laughing, giddy from his touch.

"I love you," he said. "You're mine."

Chapter TWENTY EIGHT

e could not bear to leave her side and felt she didn't want him too. They drifted off on the same bed, the baby with them too. Sleep did not come deep and restful. Calex couldn't take his mind away from the awareness of the girl beside him. The rapport between them had irrevocably changed and his stomach still felt full of butterflies. No matter how much he needed rest he would not get it. When he finally dipped into slumber he relived her kisses and her touch. He kept waking up, convinced it had all been a dream. But every time there she was, asleep with her hand on his chest. Hours later, his dreams were filled with the sound of soft but persistent knocking on the door. In a sleepy daze, Calex thought that the knocking might be a figment of his paranoid imagination. But this too was no dream. When he looked at Hero and saw that she was awake and had heard it too, he knew it was real. There was undoubtedly somebody at the door.

"What's that?" Hero whispered, frozen in the bed.

Calex got to his feet and went to the door, but he did

not dare open it. "Who's there?" came his nervous voice. "It's Elias String. Let me in! Please – I need to talk to you!"

"Elias?!" His eyes wide open with astonishment, Calex opened the door. The boy slipped in and shut it firmly behind them.

"What's going on?" Hero whispered urgently, getting out of the bed. "What's the matter?"

"I'm sorry, I'm sorry about this. I... I just needed to tell you both before it was too late." Elias's disorganised words tumbled out of his mouth.

"Tell us what?" Calex demanded.

"You're being followed," Elias informed them. "There's a group of three people – Crimsons – who know you're here and they're planning to attack during the night. I think they're siblings: two young men and their sister. They don't want to kill you. They want to take all of you back to Quilemoyena City in the daylight and have the glory of having found you."

Both Calex and Hero began to panic, their sleepiness evaporated.

"What are we going to do?" Calex asked, trying to keep his cool.

"Calm down. Let me explain," Elias said, not so calm himself. "I went to the part of the harbour where they load up the cargo ships. I found a captain and his crew heading out to Eggon at first light."

"Eggon. The nearest island." Calex said, reminding himself and the others.

"From there they'll take you to wherever you want to go, in exchange for a generous price," Elias went on.

"We'll be able to pay them. Money isn't going to be a problem," Calex said, realising it was the first time he had been able to say that.

"They said they'll send one of their crew out in the rowing boat to pick you up from the harbour just before daybreak. If you're not there waiting they'll leave without you."

"Well, we're not safe here," Hero broke in. "We should leave this inn right away and hide out at the harbour until morning."

"My thoughts exactly," said Elias.

"Well, let's go." Calex slipped on his shirt and reached for his bag while Hero got her belongings together and took the baby into her arms.

"We can't leave by the stairs," Elias told them as they got ready. "The people who are after you are staying in this very inn."

"How in heaven's name do you know all of this?" Calex finally asked what had been on his mind since Elias had burst into the room.

"That's not important right now." The Violet boy continued to take the lead, improvising a plan. "We need to tie the bed sheets together to make a rope. Then we can leave by the window."

"This is madness!" Hero muttered although she was unable to think of a better idea. Calex and Elias had already begun to strip the beds, tying the end of one sheet with the next. Before long, their makeshift rope was long enough to reach the street from their second-floor window. Meanwhile Hero blocked the door handle with the candlestick, making it difficult for anybody to open the door from the outside. As she turned around, the boys were pushing one of the beds to the window as it scraped across the floor. They tied the end of their rope around the bedpost. "I'll go first," said Elias bravely. He tested the sturdiness of the rope and felt satisfied, but as he lifted himself out of the window he quickly lost his confidence. If he fell, he realised, he would break every bone in his body. Throwing caution to the wind, he started to descend, abseiling down the sandy outside wall of the inn, focusing on the task in hand and not once looking below him. He made it down to the empty street in one piece and was relieved to feel solid ground under his feet.

Calex was next to go. He offered to take the weight of the baby to make Hero's descent easier, but she refused to leave him that responsibility. Instead, he slung their bags over his back. "What are you waiting for?" whispered Elias impatiently from the street. He saw no lit candles in the windows of the inn or surrounding buildings, but this did not allow him feel at ease. The clock was ticking and there was no time to talk. Calex had appeared and he was slowly making his way down the wall. He made the mistake of looking down and felt so frightened he nearly froze. He too breathed a sigh of relief as he reached the ground, and Elias gave him a comradely thump on the back.

Both of them looked up to the second-floor window. Hero met their gaze with a look of terror. She had seen how Elias and Calex had struggled to get down. The task required strong arms, a good sense of balance and, most of all, two hands. With the baby, it would be impossible. What is she doing?" wondered Calex as her face disappeared from the window. Hero was on her hands and knees, looking underneath the door. Although it was dark, she could see there was nobody standing behind it waiting for her.

Realising that leaving by the door was the only way, she slipped out into the corridor. The wooden floor creaked as she walked to the staircase. There was no way to prevent the noise, no matter how gently she crept, so she hurried her pace. As she reached the bottom of the first flight of stairs, her heart started to thud even faster; there was a woman sitting on a chair in front of one of the bedroom doors. Then Hero realised that the woman's chin was slumped on her chest: she was fast asleep. She passed by the woman, staying close to the banister so as not to brush her legs, and headed down the final set of stairs down to the ground floor.

She caught sight of the front door but then everything went black. Hero realised that there was a hand covering her eyes and the sharp blade of a knife at her neck. She felt hot breath on her ear and a female voice started to speak to her:

"Don't say a single word or I'll slit your throat. Listen to my instructions. You're going to come back up the stairs and into my room. Any screaming, any struggling, and you're done for."

"Hero!"

It was Calex's voice.

"Ah! It's the pathetic, lovesick fool who brought her here. You could be a rich man by now, you know. Instead you chose to become her only friend. How touching, how sweet. I admire you, I really do. Sadly I'm now completely sure that you'll soon be regretting your decision, when you go back to Quilemoyena City as our prisoner!"

Hero was too petrified to speak. The knife's blade was cold and sharp on her skin. She felt somebody sweeping past her, heading up the stairs. The woman, in reflex, tried to stop him, and Hero managed to get away from her, able to see at last what was going on. The woman tried to take hold of Elias's ankle to make him trip but she missed. The knife in her other hand fell and Calex grabbed it.

"You're really not very good at this, are you?" said Calex, mocking her. "I've never seen a more amateur crook in my entire life! Elias, get the sheets!"

The woman made raced up the stairs to alert her brothers but Elias had appeared there, the bed sheets in his hands. She froze, trapped between Elias and Calex who had her precious weapon.

"Sit down," Calex ordered.

"What?"

"Sit back on that chair. Elias, make sure she stays there." She did as she was told and Elias tied her hands, then her legs, to the chair. She did not dare to call her brothers. Calex looked pleased, even amused. She frowned at him, her lips tight. Finally, Elias made her open her mouth, stuffed a pillow case inside, and then tied another sheet around her head to keep it in place.

"Mmmmmmmmmmmm!" came the woman's voice.

"Good job, Elias. Let's go."

The woman heard their footsteps running in the street and knew they were gone for good. She started to make noise to wake up her brothers and get their help, but she knew she would be in big trouble. Soon enough, the door behind her opened and the two of them came out. Rather than looking concerned, they looked very, very angry.

"Rotagilla? What happened?" came Gorf's quiet but furious voice.

"You had one thing to do, Rotagilla!" Elidocorc snapped, struggling to keep his voice down. "Just one thing: keep an eye out for the girl, put a knife at her throat if she appears and come and get us."

"Mmm! Mmm!" Rotagilla was trying to say something. Her brothers untied the sheet wrapped around her face, then pulled the now-wet pillow case out of her mouth.

"I was doing exactly what you told me to!" Rotagilla splurged at last. "Until the Kinsener came along to help her."

"I should have known you'd mess everything up, you stupid girl!" Gorf spat.

"I've had it!" Rotagilla could no longer control her temper, hating her brothers more than ever before. "Why do you two always get me to do your dirty work for you? How did you expect me to stay awake all night, after all the running around we've been doing, without falling asleep?"

"You did what?" Gorf gasped. "You fell asleep?"

"No, I didn't" Rotagilla lied to prevent more trouble. "Of course I didn't!"

"She fell asleep! Incredible!"

"Shut up! Both of you; stop your bickering!" Elidocorc stormed, thinking of the precious time they were wasting by arguing. "Do you have any idea which way they went?"

"Ha! Of course she doesn't know."

"Shut your mouth, Gorf!" Elidocorc interrupted in exasperation. "We need to try and find them. Come on. There's still time..."

Calex, Hero and Elias raced towards the seafront through the empty streets with little light to guide them, past the Temple of Allirog Redips and the vast, empty marketplace. Far from exhausted in the early hours of the morning, the adrenaline that shot through their veins made them feel more alert than ever before. The baby in Hero's arms began to cry as she thought he might. The sounds of waves soon became apparent, along with the cooler air. They headed down the steps to the harbour which faced nothing but the sea.

Calex heard the sound of running behind them, or was it just his imagination playing games with him? Perhaps the footsteps he heard were his own and those of his companions. Without formulating a plan, Calex headed to the lighthouse and the others, not having another suggestion, followed him. They watched their footing on the treacherous rocks and disappeared behind the lighthouse. The sea was so close here that they could feel its spray on their faces. The wind was harsh and the rocks sharp and slippery.

"This was a mistake," sighed Calex.

Although the sound of the waves did a good job of concealing it, the baby was wailing. "Hero, you have to make him stop," Calex said edgily. "He's drawing attention to us."

"I'm doing my best!" Hero exclaimed.

Calex left her to it and inspected their surroundings. The lighthouse's beam flashed around as it did every few seconds. Calex's eyes looked from the top to the bottom of the tall, round structure and saw the door at its base. Hoping they could find refuge there, he ran up and banged on the door, hoping he could be heard over the sound of the waves. There was no answer. Calex tried the handle just in case but it was locked shut.

So where would they go?

"The arches," Elias suggested. The fishermen's alcoves built into the wall of the harbour were dark and deserted; full of barrels, nets and spare boat parts. During the day they were full of freshly-caught fish but in the middle of the night there would be plenty of space to hide out in.

Calex agreed with Elias's reasoning but he was curious as to what they were up against. "These people looking for us," he said to the Violet boy. "How many of them are there again?"

"Three Crimsons," Elias replied, sure of himself. "That woman on the chair and her two brothers."

"Do they have weapons?" asked Calex.

"One of the brothers has a bow and arrows."

"But how do you know all this?" Calex asked again, a question Elias had avoided answering the first time it was asked.

"I followed you to make sure you'd be alright," Elias said with thinly veiled heroicness. "I was worried that you'd get into trouble so I thought to keep an eye on you."

"Elias, you can't possibly know how grateful we are," Hero gushed. Calex looked away, not sure if he wanted to be included in Hero's 'we'. He did not know if he believed Elias's words: was the boy really on their side? Was he just being paranoid? Whatever the answer, there was a more pressing issue to deal with right now. Calex's thoughts switched back to their escape to the fishing arches. He peeked around the back of the lighthouse and inspected the harbour and seafront. The lamplights from the street that lined the coast revealed that no one was there. The fishing boats, especially the small ones, were bobbing gently on the water. Apart from that, all was still.

"Perhaps they're looking in the marketplace or something," Elias said.

"Maybe" Calex said anxiously. "But they could be waiting for us among the boats or above the arches. Just because you can't see them moving doesn't mean... "

But Elias had already made up his mind and Hero followed him as he fled. Calex, however, did not move a muscle. "Wait!" he called after them in an anxious whisper, but it was too late. Feeling instinctively that it was unsafe to go, he stayed where he was and anxiously watched the other two sprinting the short distance to the harbour's stone wall.

Despite having made a run for it after Elias and with a newborn in her arms, Hero was the first to dive into the nearest arch. She pinned herself to the wall, slumping to the ground as her heartbeat slowed down. She had made it. She was safe.

But where was Elias String?

He soon appeared, stumbling into the alcove.

"Elias!" shrieked Hero, louder than was it wise to. "What's happened?"

"I've been hit," Elias muttered, falling down. Now she saw it. There was an arrow going all the way into his side.

"They're here," Elias warned her. "You need to hide."

Chapter TWENTY NINE

Calex, still at the lighthouse, saw what was going on. His worst fears had materialised when he saw that Elias had been injured. Their hunters were here. His eyes darted about, looking for the person who had shot the arrow. He saw a figure leaning over the seafront balustrade, second arrow poised, waiting for his victim to reappear. Calex sank away into his hiding place. He knew it would be far too dangerous to join Hero and Elias in the fishing arch. There was nothing he could do now to help them. He could only sit and watch in anguish from the obscurity of the lighthouse's base.

Terrified and in a state of shock, Hero's first move was to put the baby, now quiet, at the back of the alcove where there was no light at all. She then put her shaking hands under Elias's shoulders and heaved him back there too. The Violet boy's breathing was laboured and although Hero could not see it well in the darkness, she could tell his wound was deep and bloody. Violet liquid was seeping out in a steady flow. The arrow had perhaps pierced a lung through his ribs. Hero recoiled at the sight of Violet blood.

"I'm sorry," the boy said, his voice shaking due to the injury and to tears that were coming fast.

"Why? What reason do you have to be sorry?" Hero whispered, emotion choking her voice too. "You've saved us, Elias."

"No," Elias sobbed, his voice full of regret. "I... I stole Calex's identity papers. I'm so sorry."

"But why? Why did you do that?" Hero's whisper was sorrowful.

Elias took a deep, painful breath. "Because I wanted to be the one to take you and the baby away," he began. "I followed you and I was planning to talk to you and tell you... tell you that I thought this mission was made for me. The goddesses made me a part of this. They never appeared to Calex in the woods. He never heard their voices speaking to him in the lake."

He took a breath, Hero was speechless.

"I took Calex's papers at my house so he wouldn't be able to leave the island. I meant to take his place. But then when I followed you to Evah-Schir, I realised there were others following you too... and they wanted to have you killed. Then I realised that the mission the goddesses had given me was to help you, by saving you from these people. Can you forgive me?"

Hero did not know what to say. If Elias had not stolen Calex's papers, they would be far away from here by now and out of danger. She was deeply annoyed by Elias's dishonesty, but felt the greatest pity for him as well.

"The papers are in my trouser pocket," Elias whispered laboriously. "Take them." Sure enough, Hero found them and she put them into her bag.

"And now this is it," Elias continued, sobbing again. "This is my time to die."

"No," Hero insisted. "You're not going to die. You're going to live. You're going to live." For after all, she had always wanted him to live, right from that day at the windmill when he was a pale, scared Violet boy who clung onto life like a Crimson. When he was forced up the volcano she had found herself giving him the benefit of the doubt and pleading for his life. How funny that history repeated itself. It was as if the gods were laughing cruelly in their faces.

"A pointless death…" Elias mumbled.

"Don't talk like that," Hero told him. She took Elias's hand and held it firmly. A puddle of Violet blood had collected around the wound and much of it had been soaked up by his tunic. At least the bleeding had stopped and when Hero noticed this she felt there was still a good chance Elias could be saved. Yet, the boy himself seemed to have lost all hope. He felt his strength draining away and the taste of blood in his mouth. The physical pain he felt had faded as Elias's mind slipped into fatigue and delirium.

"A pointless death," he repeated weakly. "A meaningless death…" Dying at the Sacred Heart would have been better than this. Here his blood was wasted, his death for nothing. Nothing could disappoint a Quilemoyenan Violet more than a death that wasn't anything to do with sacrifice.

"I'm going to help you, Elias. Just stay calm and keep breathing." Then, silently, Hero put her finger to her lips and nobody said another word. They saw the silhouette of a man with a bow and arrow ready in his hands. He walked around slowly, having lost sight of his prey.

"I don't think they're down here," he called to his fellow hunters. "I couldn't see very well and I'm pretty sure my arrow missed. I tried to shoot it at that boy who was with them."

"You didn't use a tranquillising arrow, did you?" his brother said, his form too appearing to their quarry.

"Of course I didn't! I used a real arrow."

A third hunter joined them; the girl who they had left tied up to a chair. "Good," she said. "That bastard deserves it. Who'd have thought they had an ally? I reckon they're heading along the coast now."

"Really? I reckon they've gone back to the marketplace," the archer said.

"Damn it, Gorf!" yelled the other man, losing his temper. "We had them in the palm of our hands!"

Gorf hung his head. Victory had almost been theirs and now it was slipping away fast.

"We should keep searching for them in the town," he said, disheartened.

"No. It would be better to look along the coast," said the sister.

"We're done for!" snapped Elidocorc. "We can't see anything in this light."

The siblings disappeared from Hero's view, continuing their argument, and she allowed herself to move, looking down at the boy's face. His eyes were closed, his lips parted, and he did not appear to be breathing. Elias's hand was still in Hero's and she squeezed it, hoping with all her heart that he would squeeze back. But Elias String's hand did not react.

"Oh no... Elias, please...!"

She urgently shook his shoulders but it was no use. That which was there seconds before had now gone forever.

From the side of the lighthouse, Calex had watched the scene, straining his eyes in the darkness. He had seen how Elias had been hit with an arrow and he saw Hero drag him to the back of the arch. It was too dark to see what was going on there now. He had watched in near-agony as their enemies came and went. Now, there were no signs of movement and he did not know what to do next. Should he wait longer or should he go to the arch straight away? Hero's form appeared at the front of the arch. She was waving to him, trying to get his attention. Calex waved back to show her he had noticed. He saw her sad, weeping face. No words were necessary; Calex realised what had happened. There was no other possibility: Elias was dead.

Calex too could not stop tears escaping from his own eyes, a pain in his forehead forcing him to cry whether it was convenient in these circumstances or not. Then Calex noticed a figure descending the steps down to the harbour. He disappeared from Hero's view, and as he did so, she realised someone was coming and slipped back into the darkness of the alcove.

Calex took another peek to make sure and his fears were confirmed: the figure was making his way towards him. From the street, he must have seen Calex come out and exchange glances with Hero. If it was any consolation, the man was alone. He and his siblings must have decided to separate in their search. Another stupid idea, thought Calex, as only one of them had a bow and arrows. Calex realised, however, that he was not doing much better, as he had become separated from Hero, and their one and only ally was dead.

Knowing that time was running out, Calex quickly ran through his possibilities. He reached into his pocket and felt for the knife that he had taken from the woman on the stairs, realising the man coming for him must have been one of her brothers. He could have just stayed still and waited, but what if the man had a knife too? Calex had always run away from fights, never retaliating as his opponent would wish. But in this grave situation, where it could well be a question of life or death, did he really have a choice?

Calex decided to try the door of the lighthouse again. Nobody had answered the first time but perhaps it was worth a second chance. He raced up the steps and banged furiously on the door.

"Come on, come on! Open up!"

To his relief, he heard a key turning in the lock. Aware of how little time he had, Calex pushed open the door and let himself in.

"What the...?" The Violet lighthouse keeper was angry and confused. "What do you want? There's nothing valuable here."

"I'm not here to burgle you," Calex silenced him, taking it upon himself to turn the key in the lock. "There's a man who's following me."

Calex had chosen the right moment to come to the door. The lighthouse keeper was usually at the top, tending to the light and doing maintenance work. The first time Calex had knocked, he had not heard anything. Fortunately for Calex, he had come downstairs a few minutes earlier to get some pig lard – the fuel for the flame – from the bottom of the lighthouse.

The whole door suddenly began to shake again, followed by the rattling of the handle.

"It's him!" Calex shrieked. "Please don't let him in!"

He raced up the spiralling staircase, leaving the lighthouse keeper speechless.

"If you don't unlock the door I'll break it down!" growled the voice from outside. The old man hesitated, his hand hovering over the keys. The voice continued: "and then I'll make sure you regret not opening it."

The lighthouse keeper was accustomed to the occasional disturbance in the middle of the night when there was a boat in danger during a storm or an accident in the harbour, but he had never had to deal with this kind of trouble. Frightened by the aggressive tone of the man behind the door, he unlocked it and stood aside. The second intruder raced past him and bolted up the stairs like a wild rabbit, the sheer force blowing out the candle in his hand. Calex's pursuer did not stop running until he got to the gallery, at the top of the lighthouse.

The lantern room just above them and the light it created was intense against the blackness of the night. The flame was surrounded by the glass lens and windows to block wind that could blow it out. Nevertheless, its heat was like a miniature version of the sun. Calex was cornered; there was nowhere he could go. Sweat sprang from his pores, from the heat and from fear, covering his face with a shiny film.

"Got you," said the man as soon as he appeared.

Calex looked at his face and was startled to discover that he recognised him. He could barely believe it: he knew his attacker. His lips formed a word – the name Elidocorc – but no sound came out. Interestingly, the man did not look at all surprised to see him. Calex quickly realised how it all made sense. The Sacred Heart auxiliary and spy Elidocorc had taken advantage of the knowledge he acquired doing his job. He had seen a golden opportunity to achieve fame and fortune as the one who had found and captured Quilemoyena's most wanted criminal. That deceitful, manipulative creature! Elidocorc had made Calex believe he was his friend. Fabian had revealed the truth about Elidocorc being a spy just before Calex left the city, but he had no idea that Elidocorc had even grander ambitions. Far from being a friend of Calex, he was now his worst enemy. He killed Elias String, thought Calex, and now he's here to kill me too.

Elidocorc walked towards him. The flame of the beacon, brightly burning to signal land to sailors at sea, made his dark eyes glisten.

"Where's the girl and the baby?" Elidocorc asked. So he doesn't know, Calex realised. He recalled the first time they had met, in a sauna at the Riverside Bathhouse in Quilemoyena City. Calex had thought him kind, honest, and open. How he had enjoyed the apparent coincidence that they both had the same job at the same place. "You deceived me," Calex said.

"Everyone's got to make a living," Elidocorc quipped.

"I'm not talking about the spying, that was your job." Calex retorted. "I mean what you're doing now. Don't tell me Fabian Zora put you up to it. I'd know you were lying. He's on my side."

"Knowledge is power," Elidocorc said with a smirk. "What I know is going to make me rich. In the morning, your dear Hero and her brownborn baby will be back in Quilemoyena City. And me? I will be moving out of my parents' house at last and getting myself a nice little villa in the east of the city. Brownborn baby? Goldborn, more like." Elidocorc laughed at his own little joke. "But there's only one thing in my way."

"Your stupid brother and sister?"

Elidocorc rolled his eyes. "They've disappointed me, that's true. But that's not what I'm talking about. I mean you, Calex."

"You think I'm scared of you but I'm not," Calex said, his voice quivering.

"Ha!" Elidocorc laughed. "It's just as well you're not going to take Hero away. You're a coward. There's no way someone as spineless as you could replace Fabian Zora as her husband. It would just be too pathetic."

Calex peered down at his feet, aware that he had had the same kind of doubts himself. Could Elidocorc possibly be right? No, he realised. There was something more powerful happening between him and Hero, something that Elidocorc could not see.

THE CRIMSONS AND THE VIOLETS

"I love her," Calex declared. "And she loves me. And that's something that someone like you could never understand."

"I think it's time I got rid of you once and for all," Elidocorc snarled and headed towards Calex to punch him in the face. Calex dodged his aim by ducking. Elidocorc punched him in the stomach instead and Calex fell down, feeling dreadfully dizzy and sick.

"Not even putting up a fight, coward?"

"I don't want to hurt you," Calex said weakly. "I just want you to leave us alone and let me go."

"No way," Elidocorc growled, starting to kick Calex on the floor and calling him all manner of offensive names. Shielding himself in a tight ball, Calex's whimpers could barely be heard through the roar of the fire. He used all his force in getting up to his feet, while trying to move away from his attacker. There was little space up here on the gallery; the only way out was down the lighthouse steps. Elidocorc, still with all his strength, then clamped Calex's neck under his strong hands and pushed him against the base of the lighthouse's red-hot beacon. Calex heard the tips of his hair singe, and smelt it too. His face was already dripping with sweat in the heat and Elidocorc's grip around his neck was cutting off the oxygen supply to his head. Hurt and frail, and dangerously close to being burnt alive, an image suddenly came into Calex's mind. It was Hero, waiting for him in the fishing alcove. She needed him and as soon as Calex pictured her, his hand reached for the knife in his trouser pocket. Using only his survival instinct, he thrust it into his attacker's back.

Elidocorc yelped and stepped back, releasing his hand from Calex's neck.

"My sister's knife!" he remarked. Calex looked down at the knife still in his hand. It was covered in Crimson blood. Calex had got more used to the idea and sight of Violet blood in the past couple of weeks, but Crimson blood made him flinch. The injury would not be serious. It could act as a warning, making Elidocorc reconsider and let Calex go. He could go back to the city, get on with his life and job at the Sacred Heart, and nobody would ever need to know about this. Calex was about to say as much, but Elidocorc was heading towards him again looking more menacing than ever.

Elidocorc took his own knife out of his pocket, similar to his sister's, and swiped in the direction of Calex, lightly cutting the back of his hand and making him drop his own knife to the ground. Elidocorc pinned Calex back at the edge of the beacon, but this time with a knife at his throat instead of a hand. Was this it? Was he really going to be murdered at the top of the lighthouse in Evah-Schir? The situation had a sweet irony about it: this is where he had arrived on the island and this is where he would leave. It had a neat circularity to it, he had to admit. But wouldn't he rather be leaving on a boat with the girl he loved?

Of course he would. With a final burst of energy, Calex grabbed Elidocorc's arm and held it aside, pushing him back against the stone barrier. He didn't realise his own strength. Without warning, the barrier crumbled. Stones and pieces of cement from the wall crashed down onto the rocks below. Calex stopped walking towards the wall in the nick of time, but Elidocorc lost his balance. He tried to grab Calex as he fell, to drag him with, but Calex took a step back. Elidocorc, with a high-pitched cry, disappeared from his view. Calex put his shaking hand over his mouth. He was alone now, and he could only hear the sound of the waves lashing against the rocks, and the gentle crackling of pig lard that kept the flame of the beacon burning.

Knowing it would be unwise to waste another second, Calex headed down the spiral staircase of the light-house. He headed over the rocks, looking away from the broken body of Elidocorc that lay there, and went towards the fishing arch. He saw Hero standing at its entrance waiting for him and he quickened his pace.

At last, he desperately took her into his arms and the grip she responded with was even stronger.

Hero finally found the ability to speak. "Your face, Calex. You're hurt. What happened up there? I saw the wall break and I saw something fall. My god, I thought it was you!"

"It was him, Hero. It was Elidocorc. I knew him from the Sacred Heart."

"Elidocorc... from the Sacred Heart? The auxiliary. It can't be true!"

"I know. It's crazy but it makes sense."

"I didn't know if you would come back," Hero sobbed.

"He nearly killed me," Calex told her, beginning to weep on her shoulder. "But, I thought of you and you saved me. You saved me, Hero." His hands ran over her back, desperately wanting to touch her. Desperately wanting to disappear with her to a warm, dark place where his body no longer ached with exhaustion and bruises. The knowledge that he could have her, all of her, in due time, dawned on him and gave him strength. The smell of her hair, just behind her ear, and the comforting warmth of her touch, melted away the tension in his body. They stayed that way, locked in the embrace, their hearts filled with a dizzy mix of relief and sadness unfamiliar to them. Minutes passed and they did not move from where they were.

Eventually, Calex found himself leaning against one of the barrels with Hero resting her head on his lap. Both of them were too shaken to sleep. It would have been impossible, anyway, in the presence of the Violet boy's dead body nearby. Earlier, Hero had untied her fur-trimmed black cloak from around her neck. She had then covered Elias String's corpse from head to toe, draping the arrow that was still lodged in his side. It did not seem right to leave the body uncovered.

Calex and Hero were so tired and upset that they did not know if they had been there for one hour or two. They did not even notice that the light was changing and everything had become bathed in blue. Just as he succumbed to fatigue and his eyes finally began to close, Calex noticed that another silhouette had appeared at the mouth of the arch. He stiffened with panic, hoping that they had not been seen. But the figure was moving farther into the alcove, taking small, steady steps. Calex felt the Violet woman's eyes looking at him. He got to his feet.

"Who are you?" Calex asked, exasperated. "What are you doing here?"

"Calex Maro?" the woman said. Her Evah-Schir accent was strong, her voice husky. "That's you, isn't it?"

"Yes," Calex confirmed, walking forward and realising that the sun was rising. They saw each other clearly now. The woman was middle-aged with greying, un-kempt hair, and she wore men's trousers. She inspected Calex too, seeing that his face looked tired, his eyes red and heavy. A large bruise was forming around his right eye, reaching up to his forehead where a lump had appeared.

"I've been sent to take you to our ship," the woman said.

"Thank you," Calex said solemnly.

"You are serious about this, aren't you? The lad said you'd be willing to pay a generous price."

That lad was lying dead at the back of the alcove, Calex recalled with horror. "Yes, I'm serious," he confirmed.

"I suppose we can talk about the money later," the woman said. "But the crew is waiting for us. We're due in Eggon in two days' time."

"Can you just give us a minute?" Calex asked, stepping back into the alcove.

"Yes, but be quick," she replied. She pointed out the rowing boat at the end of the nearest jetty and told Calex that she would be waiting there.

"It's time to leave," Calex whispered to Hero. "Are you ready?"

"Definitely," Hero said. They both looked at where Elias String's body lay.

"He stole your identity papers in the forest," Hero told Calex.

"So that's why...?"

"They're in my bag now. I'll explain everything later, okay?"

Calex made a deep sigh and shook his head, then said softly: "Goodbye Elias." The body would surely be discovered, probably later in the day, but they would be long gone by then.

"Goodbye Elias," Hero echoed.

Chapter
THIRTY

The harbour was by no means safe. A good few fishermen had already appeared and although Gorf and Rotagilla seemed to be off their trail, Calex and Hero had no way to be sure. They were soon in the rowing boat on their way to the cargo ship. Fortunately, an early morning mist was hovering over the sea which helped to obscure them from view. They did not say a word and kept their eyes on the horizon, where the black of the night sky was becoming blue. Nobody felt any need to speak and add to the existing noise. The rhythmic swishing of water under the oars seemed sufficient. Morning was arriving at last and they were leaving Quilemoyena. It was indeed a moment of relief – victory even – although a sense of loss loomed over them. Both Elias and Elidocorc had been harbouring secret plans, and now both were dead.

Hero looked back to the direction where they had come from and could no longer see the harbour or the shore for all the mist.

At last, she spoke: "I've decided a name for him," she

said to Calex, looking down at the baby. "I'm going to call him Allirog. It's so fitting for a child with such great things ahead of him."

Calex's smile widened and he nodded with satisfaction at her choice. "It's perfect," he told her. "Just perfect."

Calex looked back out to sea. He was not entirely fearless but almost, now. The feel of the bobbing floor made him feel a little uneasy, but the pleasure of the sea breeze on his face was enough to make him want to stay.

He would write as soon as he could to Hux and Pentievra back in Tinklegrove. His fatigue brought a strange clarity to his thoughts. He began to write the letter in his head:

Dearest Hux and Pentievra,
I am ashamed about what I did and it hurts so much that you are upset with me. But I hope you can see why I did it. I had to help Hero at any cost. Maybe I'm crazy but I'm in love. I am going away with her, it doesn't matter where. I need to get away and start my own life, to find my way in the world. I feel very different from how I did a few weeks ago. Something has changed, I am sure of it. I have taken charge of my own life.
I do not know when we will meet again but you will be in my heart wherever I go. Can you find it in your hearts to forgive me? Please do not be angry with me. Please do not forget me.
All my love, Calex.

Tears came to Calex's eyes once again when he thought about the letter he would write. He cared deeply for Hux and Pentievra and he knew they cared for him. This was unconditional. But he needed to say sorry for causing them trouble and betraying their trust. He hoped they would understand and accept his apologies. In fact, he had no doubt in his heart that they would. It occurred to him that he might never see them again. They were both getting old, that was true, and it would be terrible if they died simply from a disease or from old age. If they were going to leave this world, he hoped it would be at midday in a pool of molten rock, after a joyful entrance into Quilemoyena City on a cart whose bells jingled in time to the trotting of horses. There was indeed a possibility that their paths would not cross in the future, but he accepted it stoically. That's the way it has to be, Calex said to himself.

He would write to Fabian Zora as well to tell him that Hero was safe, not disclosing where they were in case the letter fell into the wrong hands. When they reached the other side they would have so much to do. Calex would be involved in bringing up the child, on whom so much importance was resting. It would be far from a simple life.

But now, these thoughts of the future seemed trivial and irrelevant. There was only this moment. The rising sun lit up the surface of the ocean, its light bouncing off the rippling water in glittering silver. Rosy-fingered dawn brought with it peace and freedom. The sunlight seemed to illuminate Calex's own heart too, melting away the weight caused by the life-changing events of the last few weeks. Calex let the morning breeze brush past his open hands and over his face. His heart was swelling with hope, and soothing light. Looking back towards the coast, he saw the burning beacon at the top of the lighthouse go out. It was morning.

An object came into view through the mist. It was a two-masted cargo ship: the kind that could stay for days out at sea. The furled sails were bound to the spars, and the boat stood stationary in the placid ocean. As their little vessel approached, Calex noticed two Violet men on its deck waiting for their arrival. The sailors waved to them then tossed a rope ladder down the side of the ship.

Even in these calm waters, the woman had a tricky task to bring the rowing boat to a stand-still at the larger boat's side. "You go first, young man," she said. Cautious of the waves which could make him lose his balance, he got to his feet. He took a firm hold of the ladder with his hands and carefully made his way up to the top. The two sailors helped him onto the deck then one of them made his way down to help Hero.

"Welcome on board," said the other, reaching out his hand. "I'm Yeknod. You've already met my wife, Tac. This is our ship." The Violet man's leathery skin was heavily tanned from a summer spent outdoors and he had a dirty but pleasant face with a surprisingly white set of teeth.

"Calex Maro," said the new arrival as he shook the captain's rough-skinned hand, aged beyond its years by the sea.

"You're in luck, Calex Maro," Yeknod said. "There will be a fine wind today."

The other sailor returned with the baby held to his chest and their bags over his back.

"So, young Crimson," the captain said, flashing his bright smile again. "There's room for you below deck. Our crew is smaller than usual. And no need to worry about food and water. There's plenty of that to go around. Especially as most of our cargo is dried fruit and nuts!" He laughed heartily and walked to the helm, Calex at his side. "So we're off to Eggon. We often do this route, plenty of custom. But we're happy to take you to wherever you like after that, if the price is right. We have trading partners all over the place really so there's no wrong answer. So, where can we take you?"

Calex took in the clean sea air and gazed at the view ahead. The early morning mist was clearing and he could see the clear line of the horizon stretching out as if for infinity. The sea was the deepest possible shade of blue and seemingly never-ending. The air was so fresh, the day young and Calex's heart was filled with liberty and joy. Hero had appeared on the deck and he wanted to kiss her and hold her and spend every day for the rest of his life with her. There was so much to look forward to and he was so happy to be here, so happy to be alive. The other sailor had climbed up the riggings and was unfurling the sails of the mighty ship.

Yeknod was still waiting for an answer. "Where can we take you? Where do you want to go?"

"I..." Calex began to speak but stopped himself.

He would answer this question soon enough but first he wanted to revel in this moment of almost unlimited choice. He closed his eyes, took a deep breath, and laughed softly to himself.